The Infinite Passion
of Expectation

Twenty-five Stories by
Gina Berriault

North Point Press
San Francisco
1982

Most of the stories in this selection were published
originally by Esquire, Paris Review, Harper's
Bazaar, Mademoiselle, Saturday Evening Post,
Ploughshares, Contact, Genesis West, Redbook, San
Francisco Review, Charles Scribner's Sons, E. P.
Dutton, San Francisco Review of Books and the
author gratefully acknowledges their permission to
reprint. All characters are from the author's
imagination.

Contents

Again for Julie Elena

The Infinite Passion
of Expectation

The Infinite Passion of Expectation

The girl and the elderly man descended the steep stairs to the channel's narrow beach and walked along by the water's edge. Several small fishing boats were moving out to sea, passing a freighter entering the bay, booms raised, a foreign name at her bow. His sturdy hiking boots came down flatly on the firm sand, the same way they came down on the trails of the mountain that he climbed, staff in hand, every Sunday. Up in his elegant neighborhood, on the cliff above the channel, he stamped along the sidewalks in the same way, his long, stiff legs attempting ease and flair. He appeared to feel no differences in terrain. The day was cold, and every time the little transparent fans of water swept in and drew back, the wet sand mirrored a clear sky and the sun on its way down. He wore an overcoat, a cap, and a thick muffler, and, with his head high, his large, arched nose set into the currents of air from off the ocean, he described for her his fantasy of their honeymoon in Mexico.

He was jovial, he laughed his English laugh that was like a bird's hooting, like a very sincere imitation of a laugh. If she married him, he said, she, so many years younger, could take a young lover and he would not protest. The psychologist was seventy-nine, but he allowed himself great expectations of love and other pleasures, and advised her to do the same. She always mocked herself for dreams, because to dream was to delude herself. She was a waitress and lived in a neighborhood of littered streets, where rusting cars stood unmoved for months. She brought him ten dollars each visit, sometimes more, sometimes less; he asked of her only a fee she could afford. Since she always looked downward in her own surroundings, avoiding the scene that might be all there was to her future, she could not look upward in his surroundings, resisting its dazzling diminishment of her. But out on these walks with him she tried looking up. It was what she had come to see him for—that he might reveal to her how to look up and around.

On their other walks and now, he told her about his life. She had only to ask, and he was off into memory, and memory took on a prophetic sound. His life seemed like a life expected and not yet lived, and it sounded that way because, within the overcoat, was a youth, someone always looking forward. The girl wondered if he were outstripping time, with his long stride and emphatic soles, and if his expectation of love and other pleasures served the same purpose. He was born in Pontefract, in England, a Roman name, meaning broken bridge. He had been a sick child, suffering from rheumatic fever. In his twenties he was a rector, and he and his first wife, emancipated from their time, each had a lover, and some very modern nights went on in the rectory. They traveled to Vienna to see what psychoanalysis was all about. Freud was ill and referred them to Rank, and as soon as introductions were over, his wife and Rank were lovers. "She divorced me," he said, "and had a child by that fellow. But since he wasn't the marrying kind, I gave his son my family name, and they came with me to America. She hallucinates her Otto," he told her. "Otto guides her to wise decisions."

The wife of his youth lived in a small town across the bay, and he often went over to work in her garden. Once, the girl passed her on the path, and the woman, going hastily to her car, stepped shyly aside like a country schoolteacher afraid of a student; and the girl, too, stepped sideways shyly, knowing, without ever having seen her, who she was, even though the woman—tall, broad-hipped, freckled, a gray braid fuzzed with amber wound around her head—failed to answer the description in the girl's imagination. Some days after, the girl encountered her again, in a dream, as she was years ago: a very slender young woman in a long white skirt, her amber hair to her waist, her eyes coal black with ardor.

On the way home through his neighborhood, he took her hand and tucked it into the crook of his arm, and this gesture, by drawing her up against him, hindered her step and his and slowed them down. His house was Spanish style, common to that vanward section of San Francisco. Inside, everything was heavily antique—carven furniture and cloisonné vases and thin and dusty Oriental carpets. With him lived the family that was to inherit his estate—friends who had moved in with him when his second wife died; but the atmosphere the family provided seemed, to the girl, a turnabout one, as if he were an adventurous uncle, long away and now come home to them at last, cheerily grateful, bearing a fortune. He had no children, he had no brother, and his only sister, older than he and unmarried, lived in a village in England and was in no need of an inheritance. For several months after the family moved in, the husband, who was an organist in the Episcopal Church, gave piano lessons at home, and the innocent banality of repeated notes sounded from a far room while the psychologist sat in the study with his clients. A month ago, the husband left, and everything grew quiet. Occasionally, the son was seen about the house—a high school track star, small and blond like his mother, impassive like his father, his legs usually bare.

The psychologist took off his overcoat and cap, left on his muffler, and went into his study. The girl was offered tea by the woman, and they sat down in tête-à-tête position at a corner of the table. Now that the girl was a companion on his walks, the woman expected a womanly intimacy with her. They were going away for a week, she and her son, and would the girl please stay with the old man and take care of him? He couldn't even boil an egg or make a pot of tea, and two months ago he'd had a spell, he had fainted as he was climbing the stairs to bed. They were going to visit her sister in Kansas. She had composed a song about the loss of her husband's love, and she was taking the song to her sister. Her sister, she said, had a beautiful voice.

The sun over the woman's shoulder was like an accomplice's face, striking down the girl's resistance. And she heard herself confiding—"He asked me to marry him"—knowing that she would not and knowing why she had told the woman. Because to speculate about the possibility was to accept his esteem of her. At times it was necessary to grant the name of love to something less than love.

On the day the woman and her son left, the girl came half an hour before their departure. The woman, already wearing a coat and hat, led the way upstairs and opened, first, the door to the psychologist's bedroom. It seemed a trespass, entering that very small room, its space taken up by a mirrorless bureau and a bed of bird's-eye maple that appeared higher than most and was covered by a faded red quilt. On the bureau was a doily, a tin box of watercolors, a nautilus shell, and a shallow drawer from a cabinet, in which lay, under glass, several tiny bird's-eggs of delicate tints. And pinned to the wallpaper were pages cut from magazines of another decade—the faces of young and wholesome beauties, girls with short, marcelled hair, cherry-red lips, plump cheeks, and little white collars. She had expected the faces of the mentors of his spirit, of Thoreau, of Gandhi, of the other great men whose words he quoted for her like pass-words into the realm of wisdom.

The woman led the way across the hall and into the master bedroom. It was the woman's room and would be the girl's. A large, almost empty room, with a double bed no longer shared by her husband, a spindly dresser, a fireplace never used. It was as if a servant, or someone awaiting a more prosperous time, had moved into a room whose call for elegance she could not yet answer. The woman stood with her back to the narrow glass doors that led onto a balcony, her eyes the same cold blue of the winter sky in the row of panes.

"This house is ours," the woman said. "What's his is ours."

There was a cringe in the woman's body, so slight a cringe it would have gone unnoticed by the girl, but the open coat seemed hung upon a sudden emptiness. The girl was being told that the old man's fantasies were shaking the foundation of the house, of the son's future, and of the woman's own fantasies of an affluent old age. It was an accusation, and she chose not to answer it and not to ease the woman's fears. If she were to assure the woman that her desires had no bearing on anyone living in that house, her denial would seem untrue and go unheard, because the woman saw her now as the man saw her—a figure fortified by her youth and by her appeal and by her future—a time when all that she would want of life might come about.

Alone, she set her suitcase on a chair, refusing the drawer the woman had emptied and left open. The woman and her son were gone, after a flurry of banging doors and goodbyes. Faintly, up through the floor, came the murmur of the two men in the study. A burst of emotion—the client's voice raised in anger or anguish and the psychologist's voice rising in order to calm. Silence again, the silence of the substantiality of the house and of the triumph of reason.

"We're both so thin," he said when he embraced her and they were alone, by the table set for supper. The remark was a jocular hint of intimacy to come. He poured a sweet blackberry wine, and was sipping the last of his second glass when she began to sip her first glass. "She offered herself to me," he said. "She came into my room not long after her husband left her. She had only her kimono on and it was open to her navel. She said she just wanted to say goodnight, but I knew what was on her mind. But she doesn't attract me. No." How lightly he told it. She felt shame, hearing about the woman's secret dismissal.

After supper he went into his study with a client, and she left a note on the table, telling him she had gone to pick up something she had forgotten to bring. Roaming out into the night to avoid as long as possible the confrontation with the unknown person within his familiar person, she rode a streetcar that went toward the ocean and, at the end of the line, remained in her seat while the motorman drank coffee from a thermos and read a newspaper. From over the sand dunes came the sound of heavy breakers. She gazed out into the dark, avoiding the reflection of her face in the glass, but after a time she turned toward it, because, half-dark and obscure, her face seemed to be enticing into itself a future of love and wisdom, like a future beauty.

By the time she returned to his neighborhood the lights were out in most of the houses. The leaves of the birch in his yard shone like gold in the light from his living room window; either he had left the lamps on for her and was upstairs, asleep, or he was in the living room, waiting for the turn of her key. He was lying on the sofa.

He sat up, very erect, curving his long, bony, graceful hands one upon the other on his crossed knees. "Now I know you," he said. "You are cold. You may never be able to love anyone and so you will never be loved."

In terror, trembling, she sat down in a chair distant from him. She believed that he had perceived a fatal flaw, at last. The present moment seemed a lifetime later, and all that she had wanted of herself, of life, had never come about, because of that fatal flaw.

"You can change, however," he said. "There's time enough to change. That's why I prefer to work with the young."

She went up the stairs and into her room, closing the door. She sat on the bed, unable to stop the trembling that became even more severe in the large, humble bedroom, unable to believe that he would resort to trickery, this man who had spent so many years revealing to others the trickery of their minds. She heard him in the hallway and in his room, fussing sounds, discordant with his familiar presence. He knocked, waited a moment, and opened the door.

He had removed his shirt, and the lamp shone on the smooth flesh of his long chest, on flesh made slack by the downward pull of age. He stood in the doorway, silent, awkward, as if preoccupied with more important matters than this muddled seduction.

"We ought at least to say goodnight," he said, and when she complied he remained where he was, and she knew that he wanted her to glance up again at his naked chest to see how young it appeared and how yearning. "My door remains open," he said, and left hers open.

She closed the door, undressed, and lay down, and in the dark the call within herself to respond to him flared up. She imagined herself leaving her bed and lying down beside him. But, lying alone, observing through the narrow panes the clusters of lights atop the dark mountains across the channel, she knew that the longing was not for him but for a life of love and wisdom. There was another way to prove that she was a loving woman, that there was no fatal flaw, that she was filled with love, and the other way was to give herself over to expectation, as to a passion.

Rising early, she found a note under her door. His handwriting was of many peaks, the aspiring style of a century ago. He likened her behavior to that of his first wife, way back before they were married, when she had tantalized him so frequently and always fled. It was a humorous, forgiving note, changing her into that other girl of sixty years ago. The weather was fair, he wrote, and he was off by early bus to his mountain across the bay, there to climb his trails, staff in hand and knapsack on his back. *And I still love you.*

That evening he was jovial again. He drank his blackberry wine at supper; sat with her on the sofa and read aloud from his collected essays, *Religion and Science in the Light of Psychoanalysis,* often closing the small, red leather book to repudiate the theories of his youth; gave her, as gifts, Kierkegaard's *Purity of Heart* and three novels of Conrad in leather bindings; and appeared again, briefly, at her door, his chest bare.

She went out again, a few nights later, to visit a friend, and he escorted her graciously to the door. "Come back any time you need to see me," he called after her. Puzzled, she turned on the path. The light from within the house shone around his dark figure in the rectangle of the open door. "But I live here for now," she called back, flapping her coat out on both sides to make herself more evident to him. "Of course! Of course! I forgot!" he laughed, stamping his foot, dismayed with himself. And she knew that her presence was not so intense a presence as they thought. It would not matter to him as the

days went by, as the years left to him went by, that she had not
come into his bed.

On the last night, before they went upstairs and after switch-
ing off the lamps, he stood at a distance from her, gazing
down. "I am senile now, I think," he said. "I see signs of it.
Landslides go on in there." The declaration in the dark, the
shifting feet, the gazing down, all were disclosures of his fear
that she might, on this last night, come to him at last.

The girl left the house early, before the woman and her son
appeared. She looked for him through the house and found
him at a window downstairs, almost obscured at first sight by
the swath of morning light in which he stood. With shaving
brush in hand and a white linen handtowel around his neck, he
was watching a flock of birds in branches close to the pane,
birds so tiny she mistook them for fluttering leaves. He told her
their name, speaking in a whisper toward the birds, his profile
entranced as if by his whole life.

The girl never entered the house again, and she did not see
him for a year. In that year she got along by remembering his
words of wisdom, lifting her head again and again above deep
waters to hear his voice. When she could not hear him anymore, she phoned him and they arranged to meet on the beach
below his house. The only difference she could see, watching
him from below, was that he descended the long stairs with
more care, as if time were now underfoot. Other than that, he
seemed the same. But as they talked, seated side by side on a
rock, she saw that he had drawn back unto himself his life's
expectations. They were way inside, and they required, now,
no other person for their fulfillment.

Nights in the Gardens of Spain

The boy beside him was full of gin and beer and wine and the pleasant memory of himself at the party, the great guitarist at seventeen, and he had no idea where he was until he was told to get out. His profile with that heavy chin that he liked to remind everybody was Hapsburg hung openmouthed against the blowing fog and the cold jet-black ocean of night.

Berger had no intention of forcing him out, but to command him to get out was the next best way of impressing his disgust on his passenger. "I asked you when you got in, friend, if you had twenty-five cents for the bridge toll and you haven't answered me yet. You want to get over this bridge tonight and into your little trundle bed you look for two bits because I'm sick of paying your way wherever we go and getting kicked in the face for a thank you. What the hell did I hear you say to Van Grundy? That you got bored by musicians because all they could talk about was music?" His breath smelled of cheese and garlic from all the mounds of crackers and spread he had eaten, not the kind of breath to accuse anybody with. "And that meant me, of course, because I'm what's known as your constant companion, that meant old ignoramus Berger. For a guy who's got all the famous relatives you're always bragging about—big dam builders, big mummy diggers, big marine commandants—you ought to be able to come up with a miserable nickel once in a while." He held out his hand for the coins that David was searching for and found.

"What the hell." David gripped his guitar between his knees again, settling back uncomfortably. "You sore because they wanted *me* to play?"

He shifted into low to start the car again. "You don't know

what anybody wants, you're too busy playing all night."

The boy waited a minute, then sprang the big psychological question with a rare timidity in his voice: "You sore because it's me that's going to play for Torres tomorrow?"

"Jaysus Christ, I'm sittin' next to Freud here!" he cried, disgusted.

They went on in silence over the long bridge. The deputy at the toll gate reached out his hand to take the coins that Berger pressed into it with his gray-gloved fingers, suede driving gloves to keep his hands warm so that he could commence to play soon after entering a room, but David wore no gloves, came with cold, thin hands into a room and played slickly, charmingly, his first number and afterward blew on his fingers to impress upon the audience how cold they were still and how much they had accomplished even so.

Along under the neons of the motels, assured by the rainbow lights and the traffic signals that the time had passed for his abandonment on the bridge, the boy spoke again, "Listen, nobody's destroying you but yourself," his voice empty of experience.

Berger gave a whooping laugh. "Listen yourself, I'm not the one who's destroying himself, you worry about yourself. Some day you're going to explode, a hundred different colors and a sonic boom. Big little David, folks will say for miles around, got too big for himself. God, you slaughtered that Purcell. If you play that for old Torres he'll ask for a change of rooms after you're gone." He unloaded now all the complaints accumulated against the boy—criticism of his teacher-companion that David made to friends: *"Berger could be the best, good as Tomas Torres, but he doesn't look the part, hasn't got the urbanity, short you know, big shoulders, like a wrestler's that don't fit him, big face, and the way he telegraphs his mistakes to you before he makes them, like 'this hurts me worse than you, dear audience.' But the best, really the best, could have been the best, but came to it too late, a jazz musician until he was thirty, still got the mannerisms of a jazzman in a nightclub, smiling at the audience, smiling at himself. You can't do that with a classic guitar. He's good all right but he should have come to it at eighteen, twenty, then he would have been great."* "Things come back to me!" Berger was shouting. "For a man of few friends, like you say I am, they come back to me!"

He drew the car to the curb, leaned across the boy to open the door. "Get out here, man. From here it's just a mile to your mother's place. I'd take you there but it's a mile out of my way."

Under the green-blue motel neon, David stepped out to the sidewalk, knocking his guitar case against door and curb and hydrant.

"You're doing it to yourself," said David again, warningly.

"You keep knocking that guitar around like a dumb bastard with a normal IQ!" he bellowed, slamming the door.

He went through the amber lights of intersections as if they were red and he was drunk. Somebody else on the verge of fame, somebody else awaiting the encircling arm of the already great, sent him, Berger, over the edge, down into the abyss of his own life. It was not fame he wanted for himself, he would never have it now, anyway, at thirty-seven, with all the faults that David had so meticulously listed for everybody. Not that, but what? The mastery, the mastery, play without telegraphing the errors, play without the errors, play with the mastery of the great yet indifferent to fame if it came. Palermo was nothing, that mecca of all the world's guitar students where Torres, old Torres of the worldly jowls, laid his arm across the jaggedy, humped young shoulders of the most promising. The photos of the students in the guitar magazines made him laugh. They came from everywhere to study under Torres at the *academia,* they stood around the silk-jacketed Tommy like fool disciples; a middle-aged woman with a Russian name; a young curly-locks guy from Brazil, making hot amorous eyes at the camera; a stiff-elbowed kid from England who looked as if he stuttered; and the girls with their big naive eyes and their skirts full to make it easier to part their legs for the correct position of the guitar. He saw them gathering in the hallways of some musty building in Palermo after school, saw them descend the street into the town with the stiff-swinging walk of youth attempting youth, and he had no desire to be among them, to be twenty again and among them. The older he got the less he wished for a new beginning and the more he wished for a happy ending. But sometimes, as in these last few weeks, the wish for that beginning laid him low again like a childhood disease.

Before his apartment house he let the car door swing heavily open and lifted his guitar case from the back seat. The slam of the door reminded him that there was something else in the car that ought to be brought in, but unable to recall what it was he concluded that it was nothing stealable and went up the stairs in his neat, black, Italian-style moccasins, wishing that he were lurching and banging against walls. Not since he fell down somebody's stairs six years ago, cracking a vertebra and breaking his guitar in its case, had he taken a drink, not even wine, and he had taken none tonight though everybody was awash around him, but he felt now that drunkenness again, that old exaltation of misery. Sick of black coffee after a dozen cups through the night, he found a cupful in a saucepan, heated it to boiling, poured it into a dime-store pale green mug and willfully drank, scalding the roof of his mouth. He opened his mouth over the sink and let the black coffee trickle from the corners, too shocked to expel it with force, bleating inside: *To hell with all the Great, the Near Great, the Would-be Great, to hell with all the Failures.*

From the windowsill he took his bottle of sleeping pills, put two on his tongue, drank down half a glass of water. He dropped his tie on the kitchen table, his jacket on the sofa, stepped out of his moccasins in the middle of the living room. He put on his tan silk pajamas (Who you fooling with this show of opulence?) and crawled into his unmade bed. At noon he was wakened by a street noise and drew the covers over his ear to sleep until evening, until the boy's interview with the Great Tommy was over.

At four, moving through the apartment in his bare feet, in his wrinkled pajamas, he tore up the memory of himself that early morning as he had once, alone again, torn up a snapshot of himself that someone had thrust upon him—a man with a heavy face in the sun, hair too long and slick, a short body and feet small as a dandy's. For with no reminders he was the person he fancied himself. But, dumping coffee grounds into the sink, he realized suddenly that the jawing he had given the boy had been given as a memento of himself, something for the boy to carry around with him in Palermo, something to make him feel closer to Berger than to anybody else, because Berger was the man who had told him off, a jawing to make him love and hate Berger and never forget him because it is impossible to forget a person who is wise to you. If the boy never got to first base as a guitarist then the jawing lost its significance, the triumph was denied to Berger. It was on David's fame that he, Berger, wanted to weigh himself. *Jaysus,* he wailed, *what kind of celebrity chasing is that?* He smelled of cheese and bed and failure, sitting at the table with his head in his hands. The interview was over an hour ago and now he would hear from friends the words of praise, the quotations from Torres, as if these friends of David had been there themselves to hear the words drop like jewels from his lips, all of them closer to God because they were friends of him who sat up there in God's hotel room, playing music to enchant God's ears.

So he stayed away from his friends, who were also David's friends; for almost two weeks he eluded any knowledge of that interview. He gave lessons to his students in his own apartment or in their homes and in this time it was as if he were seventeen again, living again that period of himself, and sometimes during the lessons his hands or his voice shook with shyness. He felt as if he were instructing them without having learned anything himself first, and he hated his students for exacting more of him than he was capable of giving. Once again he was in that age of terrible self-derision and of great expectations: Somebody great would recognize him and would prove, once and for all to himself and to everybody, his nobility. After every lesson his armpits were sticky and he would have trouble in civilly saying goodbye.

On the evening of the twelfth day he drove across the bridge to visit the Van Grundys. They were still at supper, Van and his wife and the two kids, eating a kind of crusty lemon dessert, and they made a place for him to pull up a chair. He had coffee and dessert with them and joked with the boy and the girl, finding a lift in the children's slapstick humor, the upside-down, inside-out humor, and in the midst of it he turned his face to Van Grundy at his left, the smile of his repartee with the children still on his lips, the hot coffee wet on his lips, his spoon, full of lemon dessert, waiting on the rim of his bowl—all these small things granting him the semblance of a man at ease with himself—and asked, "Well, did Torres flip over our Davy?"

"You don't know?" Van Grundy replied. "He told everybody as fast as if it were good news," raising his voice above his children's voices demanding the guest's attention again. "Torres kept interrupting. Every damn piece Davy played, Torres didn't like the way he played it. What's the matter you haven't heard? Something like that happens to a person he's got to spread it around, along with his excuses, as fast as he can."

The coffee he sipped had no taste, the dessert no taste. "Is he going to Palermo anyway?"

"Oh," said Van Grundy, stretching back, finding his cigarettes in his shirt pocket, offering one to his wife by reaching around behind the guest's chair, "he won't go to Palermo now. He can if he wants to, he's okayed as a pupil, but since Torres isn't throwing down the red carpet for him he won't go as less than a spectacular. You know David."

"Even if he doesn't like old Tommy anymore he can learn a thing or two from him, if he went," Berger said, sounding reasonable, sounding as if all his problems were solved by bringing reason to bear.

"He's already taken off for Mexico City. A week ago. He's going to study under Salinas down there if he can get that cat to stay sober long enough. Says he's always said that Salinas was better than Torres. He's stopping off in Los Angeles to ask a rich uncle to subsidize him. He was going to do it anyway to get to Palermo on, so now he'll need less and maybe get it easier. Hasn't seen his uncle since he was twelve. Got a lot of nerve, our Davy."

"What did you think of that Rivas woman?" Van Grundy's wife was asking, and he turned his face to hear, regretting, for a moment, that he heard her, usually, only with his ears and not his consciousness. He had known her for ten years now, she had been the vocalist with a combo he'd played string bass in and it was he who had introduced her to Van Grundy—a tiny woman with short, singed-blonde hair and an affectation of toughness. "Rivas?" he asked.

"Rivas, Maruja Rivas. The girl on the record we lent you. Last time you were here." The smoke hissed out from between her lips, aimed into her empty coffee cup. "Don't tell me she didn't mean anything to you."

"Did you play the record?" Van Grundy asked.

"I can't remember borrowing it," he said.

The last student was gone. He had come home from the Van Grundy's to find the first student waiting on the apartment steps and he had put aside the record on a pile of sheet music and there she had waited in the silence of the confident artist. He had noticed that proud patience of hers when, in the streetlight that shone into his car parked before the Van Grundys' gate, he had looked for the record and found it on the floor, under the seat, where David had slipped it so he could sit down. After she had waited for so many days she had waited again until the last student was gone, and when he picked up the record cover, the racy cover with orange letters on purple background and the woman in the simple black dress, there was that unsmiling serenity again.

He turned his back to the record going around, half-sitting on the cabinet, chin dipping into his fingers, elbow propped in his stomach. He cautioned himself to listen with his own ear, not Van Grundy's, but with the first emerging of the guitar from the orchestra, the first attack on the strings, he found himself deprived of caution. His head remained bowed through all the first movement, and at the start of the second he began to weep. The music was a gathering of all the nostalgia of his life for all the beautiful things of the earth, it was his desire to possess the fire, to play so well that all the doors of the world would spring open. Wiping his nose with his shirt sleeve, he sat down on the sofa.

With the cover in his hands he watched her as she played, though he knew that the photo was taken while her hands were still, the left-hand fingers spread in a chord. He watched her, the pale face and arms against some Spanish wall of huge blocks of stone and a gate of wrought-iron whorls. Her hair was olive-black, smoothed back from the brow, the face delicately angular, the black eyebrows painted on, the nose short, straight, high-bridged, and the lips thin and soft and attuned to the fingers that plucked the strings. He knew the sensation in the lips, the mouth wanting to move over the music as if it were palpable. *Concierto de Aranjuez,* and the fine print on the back of the cover told him that Aranjuez had been the ancient residence of the Spanish kings. *I believed myself in some enchanted palace. The morning was fresh, birds singing on all sides, the water murmuring sweetly, the espaliers loaded with delectable fruit.* Why did they quote some Frenchwoman back in 1679? He knew the place without any help. The memory of another Aranjuez came to him, the party he'd played for last summer down the Peninsula, the sun hot on the pears and the plums even at six in the evening, and the shade waiting along with everything else for the cooling night. He had played all night under the paper lanterns of the brick patio and tiny bells were tied to the trees and tinkled in the night's warm winds, and, early in the morning when all the guests were gone, that party-thrower, that divorcee with a dress the color of her tan, had told him her checkbook was in her purse and her purse in her bedroom, and he had awakened at noon in a sweat from the heat of the day and the fiery closeness of her little body. He had phoned her in the evening from the city, but she had spoken to him as to an entertainer who has already been paid and who says he hasn't. Years ago it would have been a pleasure and a joke. He had known a lot of women briefly like that, a pleasure and a joke, but for some reason—what reason?—that time had hurt him. Was it because it had shown him—graying, smiling, almost forty—the truth that he was no more than an entertainer, not artist but entertainer, one who drove up the hedge-lined driveway in his 1950 magazine solicitor's Chevy, one for whom the door was closed after the glasses and ashtrays were cleared away and the woman had bathed away his odor and his touch. The music from the fingers of that woman on the record cover caused the ache of his mediocrity to flare up and then die down. He needed nobody now to blame for that mediocrity, neither himself nor that middle-class woman who had withheld greatness from him by withholding everything owing to him, for that Madrid woman went in everywhere and took him along. The great went in doorways hung across with blankets and they went in the gates of palaces, and everywhere they were welcomed like one of the family.

The disc went around all night, except for the hours he himself played, and he had another two cups of coffee and, along about four o'clock, stale toast with stringy dark apricot jam which he did not taste as he ate and yet which tasted in his memory like a rare delight that he could, paradoxically, put together again easily. His shoes were off, he was more at home than he had ever been in his rented rooms anywhere, and the woman with him was like a woman he had met early in the evening and between himself and her everything had been understood at once. The disc went around until the room was lighted from outside and the globes drew back their light into themselves, and water began to run through the pipes of the house.

He heated the last of the coffee, sat down at the kitchen table and pushed up the window, and through the clogged screen the foggy breath of morning swept in. What was morning like in Madrid? What was her room like, what was she like with her hair unbound, in what kind of bed did she sleep and in what gown?—this woman he had spent the night with.

He tipped his chair back against the wall and the thought of David Hagemeister struck him like somebody's atonal music.

Now in the morning, whose silence was like the inner circle of
the record, there returned to him the presence of David, but
the discord was not a response anymore from his own being,
the discord was in David himself.

Davy's mother must be up by now, he thought. One morning he had brought the boy home at six, after a Friday night of
playing duets here and there, and she was already up in a cotton
housecoat, dyed yellow hair up in curlers, having tea for
breakfast and not a bit worried. She was the kind who would
have sent him to Europe at seven by himself because he was the
kind who could have done it fine. Carrying his cup to the phone
in the living room, he sat on the sofa's arm, and after he had
dialed the number he pulled off his socks, for his feet were
smothering from the nightlong confinement.

"Edith, this is Hal Berger. Did I wake you?" his voice as
thickly strange to himself as it must be to her.

"I was just putting my feet in slippers." Her voice sailed
forth as if all mornings were bright ones. She always spoke on
the phone as if her department manager at the Emporium
picked up his phone whenever hers rang, a third party on the
line listening for signs of age and apathy.

"Where's David? Somebody said he's zooming down to
Mexico," massaging the arch of his pale foot.

"He's in Nogales. It's on the border."

"What's he on the border for?"

"He's waiting for some money from me."

"What about the uncle in Los Angeles?"

"He gave him supper and twenty-five dollars to come back
north on and buy himself a new pair of cords. He went to
Nogales, instead, wearing the same pants and sent me a telegram from there."

"You sending him something?"

"Yes."

He began to subtract several dollars from the substance of
himself, and fear was left like a fissure where the amount was
taken away. But then why phone her at quarter-to-six in the
morning, rushing his voice at her with its big, benevolent

question? "Send him an extra fifty for me," he said, "and I'll drop you a check in the mail to cover it." Overcome by a great weariness, he hung up.

He lay down on the sofa. His shirt stung his nostrils with the night's nervous sweat and he tried not to breathe it. In the Nogales Western Union the boy would pick up the check, the total drawn from the days of his mother's captivity behind the counter, drawn from the hours of Berger's teaching, but since it had come to him, this money, then was it not his due because he was David Hagemeister? Poor Davy H! Maybe the boy would be always on borders, always on the border of acclaim waiting for something to come through and get him there. But once in a while as he grew older and envious of those who had got across the border, he would hear somebody great and lose all envy. It might be, he thought, that this Rivas woman wasn't as great as he thought she was, but he had needed, this night, to think that she was great.

His crossed arms weighting down his eyes, he fell asleep to the sound of someone running lightly down the carpeted interior stairs, some clean-shaven and showered clerk running down into the day.

Wilderness Fire

A wilderness fire was raging in the mountains east of Los Angeles, and a great brown cloud of smoke, tinged copper by the sunrise, lay over the desert and the small towns she passed through on her way to her mother. The first few miles she was alarmed under the cloud. Only in a nightmare could the sky be like this. Or was it this bad only because she wanted to turn back and the smoke gave her a good enough reason? If she wasn't going to be forced over to the side of the road by the highway patrol and interrogated as to why she was driving so fast in this smoke, she just might pull over on her own, under that long row of eucalyptus up ahead, under those towering, dry, lonely, gray trees, and bend her head to the steering wheel and sleep. Sleep, to put off the moment when she would embrace her mother, bringing her news from the world outside the pink stucco bungalow on the desert's edge.

She went past the eucalyptus row and past the acres of fields planted with something she'd never remember the name for even if she were told twelve times; past shacks far away at the end of dirt roads; past a huge, dusty fig tree branching out over the highway; past a black dog ambling along in a ditch. On the seat beside her—the novel, untouchable, ominous, like an object stolen from a tomb. It slipped closer when she took a curve, and she hit it away with the side of her hand.

The folded letter slipped out from the book and fell to the floor, and it, too, slipped sideways. It was slipping close to the pedals and in another minute she could put her foot on it and grind it down. *All those who practice this profession betray. No, not all. Not the great ones. But maybe they betrayed too. Just because everybody said 'See how far they can see into the human heart,' that didn't exonerate them in their own eyes. Maybe they, too, felt blind and deaf and dumb and cruel. I have betrayed you, your confidences, your soul, and I will regret it for the rest of my life.*

She went faster past the entrance to a trailer park. Above the hedge the trailer homes swept by with their green awnings of rippled plastic. Oh, thank God her mother didn't live in a trailer park. She almost wept, imagining it. The heat of this desert edge was enough, and to have to live in a trailer with all its dinky built-in things, with plastic flowers planted in tanbark by the doorstep—that was the end. She had always wanted to be rich, not just for herself but for her mother, too. And she had never got rich and never would, not the so-so actress that she was, and married, not now but not long ago, to a man just as poor, though he was going to be less so, now, because his novel might elevate him into all kinds of upper brackets.

The scorched air, the dark cloud were almost left behind. The tall, tall date palms, acres of them, she was passing had always seemed from some far reaches of the earth, brought to a desert from deep swamps, and grotesquely lonely, out of place. She had told only her mother about how they looked to her. Who else would see they wanted swamps? And her mother had agreed they did look like prehistoric swamp plants, out of their element, enduring.

On the outskirts of the town where her mother lived, she slowed down past clapboard houses and stucco bungalows, low to the ground, some in weeds, some in squares of very green grass, one with the same silver porpoise-shape trailer out in back, one with the lemon tree; past the small, stucco school. And now the pink stucco house, small, too, box-like, but showy in this place because it had two stories. Before it, a squat palm tree that never gave dates, just tiny, yellow, waxy droppings, and a midget fig tree; and, in the back, towering way above the house, one lone palm. All around the yard, a scalloped-wire fence, a foot high, protecting the house and the short dry grass and the three trees from nothing. *Oh, Mother, I had wanted an airy glass house for you by a blue, blue sea, say the Caribbean, lush plants all around with large, deep green leaves, always with drops of clear water on their surface. And birds, birds of miraculous plumage.* She parked in the gravel driveway, stuck the letter into the book and the book into her purse so fast her hands had no time to begin to shake, and, swinging along, very erect in high heels, purse slung over her shoulder, she went up the paved walk to the front door.

For the moments of their embrace and the moments after, her mother couldn't speak, and then she went on ahead, leading the way into the kitchen, tossing her head from side to side with delight, like a child. Her mother was bare-legged and clopping along artfully on backless wedge sandals. Her flowered cotton dress had once been her daughter's and worn in a fifth-of-a-second scene in an awful movie; but it had been expensive and was kept neater now than its original owner had ever kept it. Her mother's short hair was tinted a pink-blond, like a faint reflection indoors of the exterior of the house. In the four months since the daughter's last visit, the mother seemed to have got quite a bit older. Or maybe it was the heat of the desert summer that shrinks the thin ones and expands the fat ones. And, coming along behind her mother, she said, *Mother, Mother, Mother,* just to herself. *If there was anything I did that made you get old, forgive me for that.*

"Penny, dear shiny-bright Penny," her mother said, and here in the dim kitchen, the striped curtains closed against the heat swarming at the windows, here where her mother turned to clasp her again, the daughter felt again how much she was thought about in this house. Her mother's face in the shade of the room told her again how brief was the time of their knowing each other, only twenty-five years so far, and told her again of the unknowable limits of the time left.

"There's a fire in the mountains, if I smell of smoke," she said.

"You've brought me Chris' book," her mother said, hands palm to palm under her chin, like a child praying at bedtime—bless everybody, amen.

"Oh yes, that's right," the daughter said, tantalizingly, wagging her finger under her mother's nose. "Patience, patience."

"You left so early," her mother said. "Shall I make you some breakfast?"

"Never hungry 'til two," she said. "Same as always. Let's just drink a toast. Some mineral water will do fine."

"Is he happy?" her mother asked. She had been an actress and had even got her name up on the screen—in much smaller letters than the leads. She had always played innocents, girls from small towns, from farms, and now, when she was called upon to express happiness, it came across like that of a girl who didn't know yet that happiness wasn't that simple. Her mother was a smart woman, but seeing her smile like that, you couldn't guess how smart she really was.

"Oh, he's happy, of course," she said, smiling at her mother the same sort of smile from the backwoods. "A novel with his name on it, what else can he be but happy? He's living with a friend of his—I guess it's a woman, he just says *friend*—at her or his apartment in New York. He's happy."

"He says that?"

"He says what?"

"That he's happy?"

"If he says so it must be so," she said, coming out smiling from behind her hands, as if she had spread them over her face only to rub away the soot or the dust or whatever that cloud of smoke had left. "He says he's going to write to you. You and he always had such wonderful discussions. Just about everything from quasars to cucumbers. He says he's going to mail you an autographed copy with something like 'Love to Melanie, whom I thank for giving birth to Penelope.'"

"That's nice, but you're making it up."

The daughter was wandering around the kitchen, restlessly, as if she'd come to the wrong house and was going to have to leave at once. She came to the other end of the long kitchen, where there was a couch and a television and a sewing machine, and where, on a table, there were magazines and a row of African violets in little painted Mexican pots that had been hers when she was a little girl—a collection of sorts, and her mother brought over the misted glass to her, there.

"I made it up and it's not nice," she said. "He admires you for just being you and he loves you. It's easy, you know, to love you. He'll just write, 'To Melanie, dear friend, all my love.' Let's drink to that. If he gets to be famous your copy will be worth a small fortune." But how little love, none at all, he had shown in his novel for her mother; she wasn't mentioned, but what he had written about the daughter was to wound the mother beyond amends.

They raised their glasses, and her mother's brief laugh rang as crystal clear as the touch of glass on glass, one sound inseparable from the other.

"Chris has a good heart," her mother said.

"Chris has a great heart," she said. "Everybody's going to know that soon, not just you and me. They'll say, 'See how far he sees into the human heart. You have to have a great heart to go that far.' " But she couldn't drink, because the ice cubes were making such a racket she had to set her glass down.

"Sit down now," her mother said, sharply.

"Mother, it isn't me," she said. "The girl in his novel isn't me. He got it wrong. There's no resemblance whatsoever. I never gave him all that trouble and I was never loved like the girl in there was loved. Everybody will think it's me and it isn't me."

"Where is it?" her mother asked, afraid.

"Mother, he was always fascinated by women made of words. If you want to know their names I'll try to remember. Emma Bovary and Molly Bloom and Brett, and that girl who was mad over Heathcliff. Oh, and women in the flesh, too. Of course. But when he put me into words he got me wrong. It's not me, Mother."

"Sit down," her mother said, and the daughter sat down. "It's all made up," her mother said soothingly, sitting, facing her daughter. "Everybody knows that. That's what novels are all about."

"If I gave him trouble, mother," she said, "it was because he gave me trouble."

"That's usually the way it goes," her mother said, stroking her daughter's arms, down and down again along the long silk sleeves. "And nobody ever knows who started the trouble."

"Mother, nobody can ever know what life feels like in another person. You only think you know. I never could know him, his desires for his life, his life in here," taking her hands away from her mother's to spread them over her chest, "and he could never know me. It's unknown territory. It's unknown in here, Mother. I don't know myself. All I hear is the uproar."

"Give me your hands," her mother said, reaching for her daughter's hands again and holding them down.

The daughter had been avoiding the mother's face. She had been looking everywhere, sideways and down, anywhere but at her mother, and now she looked at the target, at her mother's face made smaller by age, the slack cheeks, the fear in the eyes. And the ears through the pink-blond curls seemed comically large, waiting.

"Once I tried to kill myself," she said, and began to sob. She pulled her hands away and held them up, palms toward her mother, and the long sleeves slipped away from the wrists, exposing on each wrist the thin, pale-pink line of an old scar.

They stood up at the same time and came together, clasping each other. She had betrayed this woman who had given her birth, betrayed this woman's hopes for her daughter to endure, endure against all the terrible puzzles life comes up with. She was taller than her mother—her mother, over the past few years, was getting smaller, and the daughter was wearing high heels—and her mother's face was pressed against her breasts, her tears wetting the blouse and the nipples under the cloth. Long ago, her mother had told her that when she was newborn and began to cry, the milk seeped out at once from her mother's breasts, wetting her dress. At once, though mother and child were rooms apart.

"Mama, I didn't die," she pleaded. "You see I didn't die. I'm alive. I'm alive." But her mother would not let go and would not raise her head.

With her arm about her mother, she walked her out into the yard, because the broad desert light might force them to calm down and to endure. Even the tall palm they stood beside might force them to be calm. Way far to the west, the smoke was like evening at the wrong time of day.

The Bystander

The room on Vernal Street in Los Angeles was the last room
my father rented for us. In that old green three-storied house
with pigeons and gables and fire escape, he went over the line
and his decline wasn't anymore a matter between father and
son. For he assaulted a woman in that house, the woman he had
liked the most and spent some nights with. It was a Saturday
twilight and I had been reading on the bed up in our room and
had thought the noise nothing unusual. Outbursts of voices
came at any hour from the rooms below us, and along the
hallways after two in the morning the homing tenants bungled
and cursed. But someone leaped up the stairs and threw open
the door and shouted at me to grab a blanket or a coat or
something for crissakes and wrap your old man up. He had run
out of the house with nothing on but the soap from the bath
he'd been taking in the woman's rooms.

Under a date palm in the yellow dirt and yellow grass of the
steep front yard of another roominghouse half a block away,
he stood shouting threats at the woman he'd left lying on the
floor; and roomers watched from porches and from windows,
and across the street men and women from the bar stood under
the red neon goblet, laughing. He was marble white in the
twilight, and the sour bar smell of his breath mingled with the
fragrance of the soap. When I tried to cover him, he struck me
away with his elbow, sharp in my ribs as a crowbar, but when
the police came, when he heard the siren, he allowed me to
throw the blanket around him.

The ward was located in the old hospital, as it was called, a
rambling place of red brick curtained by ivy, and a block west

of the new many-storied structure of concrete. I brought his suitcase, as the young man social worker had told me in some huge loft of hundreds of desks and social workers in an agency building somewhere else in the city. It contained his suit of navy blue worsted; his one white shirt and striped tie; his gray work shirt and white work socks, and his dry, bumpy, carpenter's work shoes. And over my arm I carried his raincoat and in my pocket his wallet, containing, under celluloid, a snapshot of my mother taken the year before she died—a dark-haired girl in a short, flowered dress—and a snapshot of myself at the age of five, standing high in the bowl of a drinking fountain.

The bald fellow in shirtsleeves in an office on the first floor told me, as he accepted the personal property across the counter, that my father had shown enough improvement in the past week to permit him among the more tractable patients on the second floor and that yesterday he had been moved up from the basement quarters. He told me, also, that my father had been examined by staff psychiatrists and the institution they'd chosen for him was Camarillo, in the coastal hills near Ventura. I was leaning my elbow on the counter, smoking a cigarette, demonstrating with that pose my reasonable nature. If the father was unreasonable it did not follow that the son was, also; the son, said the leaning elbow, said the cigarette in hand, might profit in wisdom by the father's breakdown in a six weeks' ordeal in hotel and housekeeping rooms. Though it did not matter to this clerk whether I approved or disapproved of their taking my father off my hands. In this old brick building of ramps and ivy and barred windows, the personal element was extraneous; it was a place run by public taxation and the public was protecting itself. The thousands of the city who had never heard of him and never would hear of him were afraid of him, and his confinement and classification was a matter between him and them. When the police rushed him up to our room for his clothes and down the stairs again, the tenants' fear and contempt had seemed to shove him out of the house forever—the dazed, quaking man in soiled trousers and unbuttoned shirt.

Climbing the rubber-carpeted ramp to the second floor and crossing the hallway, I pressed the bell to the side of double doors.

"Lewis Lisle," I said to the orderly unlocking the doors. "He's my father," and jarringly discovered that the name I was saying was that of a mentally incompetent person confined in these quarters that the orderly guarded. Before, I had thought that a name was like a mentor, even determining the person's physical peculiarities; now, I found that a name followed after, an echoing of a person.

The room I entered was long and furnished as a living room with many wicker chairs and three wicker sofas with flat and faded cretonne cushions. The patients here were males, dressed in pajama-like, gray, cotton-flannel trousers and shirts, and on their feet were gray canvas slippers. Some sat with relatives and some sat by themselves, and one lay upon a sofa with his back outward. A group of them were conversing at the wide door to the sleeping room, and he was among them, his hands clasped behind him, his head tilted by a smug, lonely amusement with the peculiar reasoning of the others. The impact of his presence in this alien place made my throat swell, and I went up to him quickly and laid my hand upon his back but could not say the word, could not recall the name of what he was to me.

At first I thought my hand was unfelt, he responded so slowly to it, but then I saw in the slow, annoyed turn of his eyes that he mistook me for a fellow inmate, bothering him with some crazy kind of confidence. He said my name "Arty," and the smell of oranges was on his breath. That was good, I thought; if he had eaten an orange then he was comparatively content.

"Did you have an orange?" I asked him.

"A visitor brought them to one of the boys," he said, and these were the first words exchanged between us in five days, the calmness of our voices recalling the shouting.

We sat down together on a wicker sofa, and the stun of exile was in his eyes and in his joints. He had lost more weight and his hair had grown longer and seemed grayer, an iron gray that was the heavy color of an ending; in spite of the orange, his lips were dry, rimmed by a white dust in the cracks. He sat with legs crossed, his troubled hands clasped on the upper knee.

"What you been doing with yourself, Arty?" he asked.

"Oh, I had a cold for a couple of days," I said.

"What did you do for it?"

"I did what you always said, I sweated it out."

But he was embarrassed by the absence of one front tooth, lost a few weeks before, one night he got in a brawl in a cafe. His tongue hissed a little in the gap.

Beyond the door to the sleeping room were two rows of cots, several of them occupied. The men lay fully clothed atop the blankets, each enwrapped in his delusions as in a mummy winding, and one turned over with a great lethargic wrench, pushing with his elbows. At a table by a window in the sleeping room two patients were playing cards, one of the players a Negro, and his wife sat by him, feeding him pink ice cream from a pint carton with a little wooden spoon. In the room with us a young patient was playing the upright piano with meticulous discordancy, and among the relatives and patients and piano notes wandered an elderly man who recalled Caesar, anciently Roman, and yet would not have come to his prototype's shoulder. With warning flashes of his small black eyes he struck into being everyone he glanced at. A woman's bathrobe was tied smartly about his stocky body, a dark robe patterned with flowers.

"I want you to stay and meet my son," he said to me, laying his hand on my shoulder.

"Go on, beat it, go on," my father said to him, the jerking of his elbow establishing his brotherhood with the rest.

"He's a bastard, my son," the Caesar said.

The orderly, lounging in a wicker chair at the far end of the piano, lay his *Argosy* down upon his thigh and watched, and the old man, seeing my eyes darting to the place behind him where he knew the orderly sat, lifted his hand from me and went into the sleeping room where he stood with his back to us, watching the card players.

"A son of a bitch himself," my father said, shifting position sprawlingly. "The loony tried to murder his own son. This guy is always talking about how his son and his son's wife were figuring to dig up some three thousand bucks he's got buried somewhere. What the hell he thinks three thousand bucks is? I made that much in overtime the couple years I worked at Douglas Aircraft during the war. That's what it amounts to—nothing. A down payment on a Ford, a funeral, a loan to your uncle, a week for you and me at Catalina, and it was gone. And this guy thinks it's enough to kill his son about. A loony."

The long living room was like Sunday—the inmate curled on the sofa, the visitors, the scent of oranges; the only thing missing was the comic papers. Over by a closed door to somewhere, a middle-aged woman in a black dress and a black straw hat with red cherries that had ripened before I was born sat on one side of a gray clad patient and her middle-aged sister sat on the other side of him—a middle-aged brother whom sunlight hadn't touched in a long while—a man who had sat all day on an army cot in a screened porch. Now, out in the world, he sat as stooped and as deaf, watching me with fear in his pale eyes. I saw him rise and stroll away, feeling more cornered by my glance than by the women who pressed him in between them. They continued to talk across him, not missing him, but I was interested in my effect upon him and sought him out wherever he had wandered, glancing into the sleeping room and finding him standing sideways, ten feet away, still as a stone, waiting for me to meet his eyes.

"What do you think they'll do to me, Arty?" my father was asking petulantly. He slid down, resting his elbow on the arm of the sofa and with his hands forming an arch to hide his face from the orderly, and his dominance over me and his dependency sprang across the week of our separation and we were as before. "I'd like to get rid of this cough," he said. "My chest has been bothering me from the coughing. They had me in the basement for a while, and the cold came up from the floor. Ah,

Jesus, it was miserable down there, like a menagerie in the hold of a ship. The croakings and cryings."

"They do anything for your cough?"

"Nothing. The hell with them. Maybe they like you to come in with lung cancer or TB or whatever it is I got. Maybe they want you to die as soon as you can, conditions in bug-houses being as crowded as they are."

"They got these places to cure people," I said.

He laughed explosively, folding up with the coughing laugh and then unfolding so far that his legs stretched straight out and his back arched out from the sofa's back. The patient on the next sofa turned over and, his head hanging over the edge, watched my father with the unblinking eyes of a mild and curious animal.

"They give us hot chocolate before we go to bed," my father said, "and a little cookie, star-shaped. You see how far man has progressed? They never did that in Bedlam, Arty, you tell that to any cynic you meet. You tell them in the psycho ward they give your father hot chocolate and a little cookie."

We were sitting facing the double doors to the hallway, and through the screen saw an orderly come up the ramp pushing a food conveyance and wait in the hallway, ringing for admittance. He pushed the metal cart through the living room and to the closed door, and the door was left open after he had passed through and I saw that the room beyond was a dining room. Two women attendants were setting the long, dark table, and beyond that room was a kitchen with cabinets and a sink; and the sound of plate on plate from those rooms was a reassuring sound, and it seemed, though I knew it was impossible, that a wood fire had been lighted behind a screen somewhere in that room where the women set the table. The noises of the plates and silver prophesied for me the meals that I would spend in company of persons whose existence I did not know of, in houses I did not know of, as I had not known of this locked living room with the gray inmates and the wicker chairs.

Over on the sofa by the dining room door the sisters wound the straps of their purses around their right wrists, set their black oxfords heavily on the floor, and went to the sleeping room to find their brother and say goodbye. The Negro woman, tall and with the composure of a civil service clerk, drew on her coat over her high shoulders.

"They make everybody leave at suppertime, I guess," I said.

"Where you going to eat?" my father asked.

"I don't know," I said, not wanting to eat anywhere.

"There's a Chinese dump around the corner from Vernal," he said. "You seen it. They got chicken giblet chop suey and they don't leave the liver out—most gyp joints save the liver for something fancy—and they got those peas cooked in the pod, you know how they do." And disgusted by his detailing of trivia, he set his palms over his eyes. Under his blindfold, his mouth asked me, "You still at that place on Vernal?"

"Yes," I said.

"You going back to your Aunt Glorie's?"

"I guess I won't," I said.

"You going back to San Diego at all?"

"No, I guess I won't." We were talking lower for the other visitors were moving past us to the door, and the inmate lying on the next couch was awake on his back, his arms under his head.

"What you going to write to her then?"

"What you want me to write to her?"

He thought about it a minute as if he had not thought about it every day of his confinement. "Well, I'd like her to keep my tools intact," he said. "I got the key to my toolbox with me, or maybe you got it now, but that don't mean anything if she wants to sell them. I got some London spring steel saws in there I'd hate to lose. I'm afraid if you tell her where they got me, she'll sell my tools, she'll think I'm never coming back to live there anymore and hoping I won't. So you tell her not to sell my tools and that's all. Just write it in a letter and don't say anything else." He removed his hands to see if I were nodding.

"All right." I nodded.

"You could get a job in this lousy town. I was working in a laundry when I was eighteen."

We stood up, then, to be with the rest of the visitors gathering by the double doors, waiting for the orderly. The card-
player, a heavyset fellow with a shaven head, came out to his
wife, but the army cot patient did not come out with his sisters.
Caesar in his flowered robe stood by the sofa we had vacated,
muttering his chagrin with his son's failure to show up even at
the last moment. The orderly in his white uniform strode from
the dining room, jangling his keys playfully under the visitors'
noses, and the visitors, stuporous from the afternoon's confinement, smiled servilely.

My father shook hands with me, it was the thing to do in
public. In the corners of his eyes were white dots of weariness,
and there was a sickly smell of anxiety upon him; I felt the
sweat of it in the palm of his hand.

"The clerk says I can take the Greyhound bus, it'll get me
there, or almost. Then I take a jitney that runs from the town to
the hospital," I told him.

"They got a private bus for us patients," my father said,
loudly so the orderly could hear his joking. "I hear it's a nice
ride, see the ocean, see the hills, go past them mansions of the
movie stars in Malibu."

The orderly, his *Argosy* folded in his hind pocket, smiled as
he turned the key. There was no hanging back after that, the
atmosphere of the ward became unbreathable at the final moment when the door was opened to the outer air, and I followed
the three women down the ramp, out through the swinging
glass doors, and down the concrete steps with the metal rail
that the sisters held onto.

As I went along by the high wire fence, ivy-woven, I glanced
up to the second floor, not expecting at all to locate that particular ward and was surprised to find myself looking into the
windows of the sleeping room. I saw the bent heads of the
cardplayers and the back of the chair that the wife had sat in. By
another window in that room the army cot inmate was standing in his gray garments, watching me go. For a second I thought
he was my father, and I knew then, meeting eyes with the man,
that I was guilty of something and he was accusing me of it, and

it was the guilt of sight. For the man *was* my father and was also the father in the flowered robe who was probably still facing the locked doors. He was the parent who breaks down under the eyes of his child, the parent in the last years when all the circumstances of his life have got him trussed and dying, while the child stands and watches the end of the struggle and then walks away to catch a streetcar.

Death of a Lesser Man

In the midst of several friends drinking Danish beer from tall Mexican glasses, in an apartment of red naugahyde furniture and black shag rugs, right at the moment when the hostess, who had been a Las Vegas showgirl, was leaning over to laugh something in his ear, right at that moment he threw himself off the couch and onto the rug. The others, his wife among them, thought that he was faking a fit to comically demonstrate the effect of the hostess' bosomy proximity or her words in his ear, although that sort of fakery was utterly foreign to his shy, gracious, reflective person. Then, because it *was* foreign, they realized it was a true fit, an act beyond his control. Those who were sitting near him got out of his way and stood back with the others, who had also risen, and his wife fell to her knees at his side.

For several seconds he lay rigid, eyes up, a pink-tinged froth along the lower edge of his neat, blond moustache, while his wife stroked his face and fondled his hands. The others walked around in a state of shock, conversing with mourners' voices. Someone asked her if he had ever done that before, and she said, "No, never" and repeated it to the first question asked by the young doctor who, summoned by the hostess from an apartment upstairs, knelt down at the other side of the now limp man.

Claudia, the wife, stood away while the doctor with encouraging hands and *Ah ups* assisted her husband to the couch and laid him out, long and weak. She refused a chair, feeling called upon to stand in deference to unpredictable blows. The hostess embraced her waist, but she offered no yielding to this comfort and was left alone. She watched the shocked face of her husband watching abjectly the doctor's face above his, and watched the stethoscope move over the exposed broad chest. The young doctor glanced up to ask her which arm had jerked, which leg, and replying that she had been too alarmed to notice, she saw his fleeting response to her person, the same response in the eyes of men and women seeing her for the first time—a struggle to conceal from her the emotion that a woman's beauty aroused, whatever that emotion was, whether fear or envy or desire or covetousness. The struggle in the doctor's eyes stirred an anxiety over herself—was she to be alone now?—and, at the same time, assured her that she would not be alone for long. It lasted half a second, this fear and assuaging of fear, and was followed by shame and by love for her husband, by a devotion that came over her with such force she was, again, the girl she had been for him at the beginning of their nine years together.

When he stood up, shakily, joking weakly with dry lips, someone said the pickled mushrooms were hallucinatory and someone else laughed loudly and caved in. The hostess helped him on with his overcoat, and Claudia, her arm across his back, with the host on his other side, took him down the five slow flights in the elevator and along the street.

As she drove homeward she remembered with remorse their quarrel early in the evening. She hadn't wanted to go to the party. "So they don't know who the hell Camus is," he had said, tugging the words up from his throat as he tugged unnecessarily at his socks. "Why don't you get down to the human level?" They both had got down to the human level tonight, and now he was deeply asleep, his chin sunk into his muffler, his long legs falling away from each other, his hands in his overcoat pockets where, in one, he had slipped the doctor's note with the name of a neurosurgeon. The doctor had given him no sedative, but his sleep was as heavy as doped sleep.

On the bridge they were almost alone, behind them the headlights of two cars and far ahead of them, with the distance widening, the red taillights of one, and her fear of his sleep as a prelude to death changed the familiar scene of the dark bay and

the jeweled, misty cities ringing the bay, changed the scene
into the very strange, as if, were he to open his eyes, that would
be his last sight of it. She felt, then, almost shamefully, that
close affinity with Camus again, and although Camus was
dead, the adoration that had taken her to Paris seven years ago
was revived from her memory. She had gone there alone and
lived there for three months, the sojourn made possible by a
small inheritance from an aunt, but the money had run out
before the destined meeting could take place. It was true she
hadn't made much of an effort to meet people who knew him.
How was she to do that? She had hoped that just by wandering
the street where he might wander a chance meeting would
come about and he would see at first glance how far she had
come to be with him. Yet in that time she had felt humiliated by
her pursuit, no matter how inconspicuous it was to everyone
else; she had felt her pursuit was as obvious as that of a friend of
hers who, enamored of Koestler, had managed a front seat at
his lecture at a university and with her transfixed gaze had
caused him to stumble a time or two over his words, and, later,
had accosted him in the hall and proved how deep into his
work she was by criticising some points of his lecture in which
he had seemed untrue to his own self. Nothing had come of her
own obsessive time in Paris, and in despair—what was her life
to be?—she had returned to New York. But she had refused to
board the plane to San Francisco. In the waiting lounge a terrible prophetic sense had come over her: all the persons waiting
to board that plane—the chic, elderly woman in black, the
young mother with her small son in his navy coat and cap, the
rest, all were to die that day. She had not yet left the lounge, she
was still on the bench, unable to rise, unable to return to Camus
and unable to return to her husband, when the plane crashed as
it was taking off. She had gone back to the hotel and cried all
day in her room, shaking with fear of her prophetic sense that,
if she were to heed it again, would show her in old age, all
beauty gone, all curiosity for life gone, all hope for a great
passion gone.

On the long curving road down through the hills and into

the town, only the low white fence between the car and the dropoff into space, her sleeping husband beside her, she felt again on the verge of something more. If she had found another existence, those seven years ago, her husband would have found another wife and gone on living; now, another existence for her would be the result of his dying. The sense of crisis was followed by guilt that came on as an awful weariness, and when she waked him and was helping him from the car, she felt in her body the same weight that was in his.

She pulled off his shoes and his socks while he sat on the bed, and he was asleep on his back a moment after she had covered him to his chin. His sleep dragged on her body as she undressed and slipped her nightgown on. It forced her down beside him punitively, and she lay towards him, her hand on his bare chest, persuading him with her hand, with her heart, to stay alive. Dear Gerald, Sweet Gerald, stay alive.

All Sunday Gerald slept, wakened every few hours by Claudia, who was afraid he had lapsed into a coma, and she brought him milk and toast and fruit as an excuse for waking him. After poking around a bit that Sunday evening, trying to recall the sensations, the thoughts preceding the seizure, reading the papers, showering, he returned to bed at ten o'clock and slept until noon of the next day, when she wakened him by stroking the smooth, veined underside of his arm that was bent on the pillow, a half-frame for his pale, unshaven face. She told him that the neurosurgeon could give him an appointment no sooner than Friday of that week, and this information liberated his eyes from the startled frown. If the specialist was in no hurry to see him, then nothing much could be wrong. He flung off the covers, his legs kicking and pushing out into air, and sat up. "I'll get up, I'll get up," he said.

Always he was already up and about at this hour, carving his fine wood sculptures or roaming the forest trails or the beaches, doing what he liked to do before he walked down the hill and caught the bus to the city and worked at his desk until midnight on the next day's paper. Up he got, and the moment he was on his feet again she felt again the inertia that came of her accep-

tance of the way her life was. The fact that he was up again,
ready to return to work without having missed a day, deprived
her of this crisis in her life, this crucial point of change, and
alarmed by her reaction she embraced him from behind, pressing her face against his back, kissing him so many times over
his back that he had to bend forward with the pleasure of
conforming to her love.

Claudia was in the tub when he left, and she imagined how
he looked going down the hill, under the arcade of trees, a
bareheaded, strong-bodied man of thirty-six, going to work
at the hour when most men were about to return home. At that
moment, imagining him disappearing, she felt the emptiness
of the house, and in that empty house felt her own potential for
life. She was aware of herself as another person might become
aware of her as so much more than was supposed. And, the
next moment, afraid that a prowler was in the house, she
climbed from the tub, shot the bolt on the bathroom door, and
toweled herself in a fumbling hurry. After listening for a long
minute for footsteps in the empty house, she unlocked the
door and, holding her kimono closed, went barefoot through
the rooms, knowing as she searched that there was no one in
the house but herself.

Some nights she ate supper at home, alone, reading at the
table, and some nights she went down into the town to one of
the restaurants along the water's edge, went down with the
ease of a resident in a tourists' mecca and was gazed at with
curiosity—an attractive young woman dining alone. And
some nights she went out later in the evening, tired of reading,
restless, to the bookstore that stayed open until midnight, to sit
at a little round table and drink coffee and read some more, the
literary periodicals from England and France. The years her
husband had worked days, she had held a few jobs. She had
been a receptionist in a theatrical agency, a salesgirl in the high
fashion section of a department store. But the artificiality, the
anxiety of everyone, along with the obviousness of her own
person when she was by nature seclusive, brought on desperate
nights, and she had quit; yet she had chosen not to work in

lackluster places. She wanted only to read. The only persons beside Gerald whom she could converse with were the celebrated writers and some obscure ones whose work she came upon unguided. It was always like a marvelous telepathy going on, both ways. While she read *their* thoughts, they seemed to be reading *hers*.

This night she took less care than usual with her clothes. Wherever she went she always took extreme care with her appearance, afraid of critical eyes. And always her head was bare, because the blondness of her hair was a loving gift from Scandinavian ancestors. The mauve silk blouse she put on was stained from wine and near the hem of the gray wool skirt was a small spot. To wear these clothes without embarrassment was, she felt, an acceptance of the stain on the soul of the woman who allowed herself to dream of another existence.

She left the old, raffish convertible by the small, dim park and walked along the sidewalk bordering the water that, a yard or so below, lapped the stone wall, and the reflection on the dark water of an island of low-lying fog out near the channel, and the clear, faintly starred sky, and the cluster of sea gulls floating where the waters were lit by the restaurant globes, all evoked the promise she had experienced in Paris. Just before she reached the restaurant on pilings over the water, she heard a low whistle at her back, suggestive of a hand shocked by the delight it found, and someone fell into step behind her. She felt his close gaze, she felt his bumbling, beastly obstinance, and she wanted to turn and shout at him to get away, a woman had the right to go out into the night alone, and, at the same time, she wanted to run away and escape her accusation that she had enticed him with her long, rippling, moonlit hair, her legs in black nylons, her white silk scarf with its fringed ends. On the restaurant step he spoke to her, some word to halt her or caution her about the step, and she pushed the door wildly open, banging it into a young man leaving. She chose the farthest table from the door, up close to the window over the water. The encounter with the man whose face she was afraid to see marred this night in which she had meant to be released, harmlessly, into an old dreaming of another future. She saw her hands trembling, they couldn't lift the fork without dropping food back to the plate. Able to manage only a few morsels, she waited to leave, waiting until the man must have wandered away, waiting for her heart to calm down.

But after she had gone several steps along the sidewalk, she heard his heels again. This time he did not speak, he followed as if *she* had spoken, as if they had become invitation and answer. Her heart knocking crazily, she climbed into her car, slamming the door. Her heavy skirt and coat lumped under her legs but she was afraid to take a moment to jerk them free. She swung the car around and, long before the time she intended to return, she was returning up the hill. Just before she took the first curve, her rear view mirror flashed headlights, and she took the curve too fast, almost crashing into somebody's quaint iron gate.

She stood in the unlit house, gripping the curtains, her shaking hands causing the brass rings to jangle against the rod. If Gerald had experienced a foreboding before his seizure, this sensation must be the same. The man was standing out under the gate lamp, an obscene clod out of doorways, following a woman whom he could not believe would turn him away, a woman waiting in the dark house to open the door to him and draw him down upon her. Raising his arm to fend off the branches, he came up the path. Why should he have come so far if he was not already in the arms of the woman who went out with her fringed scarf to bring a strange man back to her bed? She heard his step on the stone doorstep and heard his two raps, and heard her voice, thick with fear, shouting, "Get away! Get away!" She clung to the curtains until she heard a car's motor start up and saw the red taillights reflected on the foliage in the yard and heard the car go down the hill.

A desolation came over her, then, as she moved through the dark house. The obscene dolt must have stolen away her dream of herself in the future, the dream that was only a memory of herself in the past, that brief time in Paris, alone, desirous of a destiny, desirous of the one with a destiny, the man who would break the hull of her guilt, guide her into the intricacies of his intellect, anoint her with the moisture of his kisses. The intruder must have stolen away the past and the future, and she was nowhere else but in this dark house where she might be forever. In the dark her slender heel was caught by the grille of the floor heater in the hallway, and she left both shoes on the cold, trapping metal.

By the time Gerald came home all the lamps were lit and his late supper was on the stove, plates were set out on the table, and wine was cooling; and facing him across the small table she complained about the number of days they must wait before his appointment.

"Must be lots of people throwing fits," he said. And later, tossing the covers over himself, "Anyway, the serious things are nothing to worry about. By the time you've got a symptom you're usually too far gone to do much about." For a minute he lay gazing up, then he switched off the lamp to conceal from her the fear in his face. She heard him mutter half a word and then he was quiet. With his few words tonight he had expressed more pessimism than in all the years of their marriage. To indulge in pessimism, as to give way to anger or criticism, was to weaken the marriage, and he did not care to weaken it. He had never appeared to be dissatisfied with his life. He had not mapped out his life for a grand endeavor and been diverted. Everything about him gave evidence of his stolidity—his deliberation over small things, his way of absorbing circumstance rather than attacking it, the almost perverse unnecessity to change his existence, to strike, to wrestle, and she had clung to him for that enduring nature. But now, lying beside him, she felt in his being the invasion of futility, she felt his resentment of the specialist for his inaccessibility, and of her, his wife, for belittling him with her other life without him. The seizure and the suspense, the possibility that he might be at the mercy of physicians and of some malady and even of the end itself, all was enough of a belittlement. The husband who had always slept with a trusting face turned up toward the coming morning lay fearfully asleep, and she was afraid to touch him. She fell asleep with her hands tucked in under her heart.

Oh God, what was going on? The obscene dolt, the faceless presence, the stranger in the night, the follower had lifted aside the hanging branches and was there, and he was cutting off her hair, crudely, with large, cold scissors. It fell in rippling, palely shining strands, moonlit, alive. It fell to the floor and the bedcovers, and her rage against that faceless presence gave way to an awful weakness as her hair was shorn. But was this really herself in a bed alone, a narrower bed? Was she really the young woman with the cropped hair, with the suffering face, the face gone beyond suffering? Was this herself? Oh God, dear God, it was herself and she was dying years before Gerald. And how young she was, this woman, herself, who was never to know that old age she had so senselessly feared. Wailing, she struck weakly at the faceless presence cutting off her hair, but he went on cutting. In the empty bed someone suddenly moved, someone beside her rose up and bent over her. It was Gerald, and her terror, her sorrow over herself was over him, instead, and into his hand that was taking her hands away from her face she wailed her anguish of love for him and his life. With both hands she gripped his wrist, wailing his name into his large, gentle hand that was soothing and calming her into waking.

The Stone Boy

Arnold drew his overalls and raveling gray sweater over his naked body. In the other narrow bed his brother Eugene went on sleeping, undisturbed by the alarm clock's rusty ring. Arnold, watching his brother sleeping, felt a peculiar dismay; he was nine, six years younger than Eugie, and in their waking hours it was he who was subordinate. To dispel emphatically his uneasy advantage over his sleeping brother, he threw himself on the hump of Eugie's body.

"Get up! Get up!" he cried.

Arnold felt his brother twist away and saw the blankets lifted in a great wing, and, all in an instant, he was lying on his back under the covers with only his face showing, like a baby, and Eugie was sprawled on top of him.

"Whasa matter with you?" asked Eugie in sleepy anger, his face hanging close.

"Get up," Arnold repeated. "You said you'd pick peas with me."

Stupidly, Eugie gazed around the room to see if morning had come into it yet. Arnold began to laugh derisively, making soft, snorting noises, and was thrown off the bed. He got up from the floor and went down the stairs, the laughter continuing, like hiccups, against his will. But when he opened the staircase door and entered the parlor, he hunched up his shoulders and was quiet because his parents slept in the bedroom downstairs.

Arnold lifted his .22-caliber rifle from the rack on the kitchen wall. It was an old lever-action that his father had given him because nobody else used it anymore. On their way down to the garden he and Eugie would go by the lake, and if there

were any ducks on it he'd take a shot at them. Standing on the
stool before the cupboard, he searched on the top shelf in the
confusion of medicines and ointments for man and beast and
found a small yellow box of .22 cartridges. Then he sat down
on the stool and began to load his gun.

It was cold in the kitchen so early, but later in the day, when
his mother canned the peas, the heat from the wood stove
would be almost unbearable. Yesterday she had finished pre-
serving the huckleberries that the family had picked along the
mountain, and before that she had canned all the cherries his
father had brought from the warehouse in Corinth. Sometimes, on these summer days, Arnold would deliberately come
out from the shade where he was playing and make himself as
uncomfortable as his mother was in the kitchen by standing in
the sun until the sweat ran down his body.

Eugie came clomping down the stairs and into the kitchen,
his head drooping with sleepiness. From his perch on the stool
Arnold watched Eugie slip on his green knit cap. Eugie didn't
really need a cap; he hadn't had a haircut in a long time and his
brown curls grew thick and matted, close around his ears and
down his neck, tapering there to a small whorl. Eugie passed
his left hand through his hair before he set his cap down with
his right. The very way he slipped his cap on was an announcement of his status; almost everything he did was a reminder
that he was eldest—first he, then Nora, then Arnold—and
called attention to how tall he was, almost as tall as his father,
how long his legs were, how small he was in the hips, and what
a neat dip above his buttocks his thick-soled logger's boots
gave him. Arnold never tired of watching Eugie offer silent
praise unto himself. He wondered, as he sat enthralled, if when
he got to be Eugie's age he would still be undersized and his hair
still straight.

Eugie eyed the gun. "Don't you know this ain't duck season?" he asked gruffly, as if he were the sheriff.

"No, I don't know," Arnold sniggered.

Eugie picked up the tin washtub for the peas, unbolted the
door with his free hand and kicked it open. Then, lifting the tub

to his head, he went clomping down the back steps. Arnold followed, closing the door behind him.

The sky was faintly gray, almost white. The mountains behind the farm made the sun climb a long way to show itself. Several miles to the south, where the range opened up, hung an orange mist, but the valley in which the farm lay was still cold and colorless.

Eugie opened the gate to the yard and the boys passed between the barn and the row of chicken houses, their feet stirring up the carpet of brown feathers dropped by the molting chickens. They paused before going down the slope to the lake. A fluky morning wind ran among the shocks of wheat that covered the slope. It sent a shimmer northward across the lake, gently moving the rushes that formed an island in the center. Killdeer, their white markings flashing, skimmed the water, crying their shrill, sweet cry. And there at the south end of the lake were four wild ducks, swimming out from the willows into open water.

Arnold followed Eugie down the slope, stealing, as his brother did, from one shock of wheat to another. Eugie paused before climbing through the wire fence that divided the wheat field from the marshy pasture around the lake. They were screened from the ducks by the willows along the lake's edge.

"If you hit your duck, you want me to go in after it?" Eugie said.

"If you want," Arnold said.

Eugie lowered his eyelids, leaving slits of mocking blue. "You'd drown 'fore you got to it, them legs of yours are so puny," he said.

He shoved the tub under the fence and, pressing down the center wire, climbed through into the pasture.

Arnold pressed down the bottom wire, thrust a leg through and leaned forward to bring the other leg after. His rifle caught on the wire and he jerked at it. The air was rocked by the sound of the shot. Feeling foolish, he lifted his face, baring it to an expected shower of derision from his brother. But Eugie did not turn around. Instead, from his crouching position, he fell to his knees and then pitched forward onto his face. The ducks rose up crying from the lake, cleared the mountain background and beat away northward across the pale sky.

Arnold squatted beside his brother. Eugie seemed to be climbing the earth, as if the earth ran up and down, and when he found he couldn't scale it he lay still.

"Eugie?"

Then Arnold saw it, under the tendril of hair at the nape of the neck—a slow rising of bright blood. It had an obnoxious movement, like that of a parasite.

"Hey, Eugie," he said again. He was feeling the same discomfort he had felt when he had watched Eugie sleeping; his brother didn't know that he was lying face down in the pasture.

Again he said, "Hey, Eugie," an anxious nudge in his voice. But Eugie was as still as the morning around them.

Arnold set his rifle down on the ground and stood up. He picked up the tub and, dragging it behind him, walked along by the willows to the garden fence and climbed through. He went down on his knees among the tangled vines. The pods were cold with the night, but his hands were strange to him, and not until some time had passed did he realize that the pods were numbing his fingers. He picked from the top of the vine first, then lifted the vine to look underneath for pods, and moved on to the next.

It was a warmth on his back, like a large hand laid firmly there, that made him raise his head. Way up the slope the gray farmhouse was struck by the sun. While his head had been bent the land had grown bright around him.

When he got up his legs were so stiff that he had to go down on his knees again to ease the pain. Then, walking sideways, he dragged the tub, half full of peas, up the slope.

The kitchen was warm now; a fire was roaring in the stove with a closed-up, rushing sound. His mother was spooning eggs from a pot of boiling water and putting them into a bowl. Her short brown hair was uncombed and fell forward across her eyes as she bent her head. Nora was lifting a frying pan full of trout from the stove, holding the handle with a dish towel. His father had just come in from bringing the cows from the north pasture to the barn, and was sitting on the stool, unbuttoning his red plaid Mackinaw.

"Did you boys fill the tub?" his mother asked.

"They ought of by now," his father said. "They went out of the house an hour ago. Eugie woke me up comin' downstairs. I heard you shootin'—did you get a duck?"

"No," Arnold said. They would want to know why Eugie wasn't coming in for breakfast, he thought. "Eugie's dead," he told them.

They stared at him. The pitch crackled in the stove.

"You kids playin' a joke?" his father asked.

"Where's Eugene?" his mother asked scoldingly. She wanted, Arnold knew, to see his eyes, and when he had glanced at her she put the bowl and spoon down on the stove and walked past him. His father stood up and went out the door after her. Nora followed them with little skipping steps, as if afraid to be left behind.

Arnold went into the barn, down along the foddering passage past the cows waiting to be milked, and climbed into the loft. After a few minutes he heard a terrifying sound coming toward the house. His parents and Nora were returning from the willows, and sounds sharp as knives were rising from his mother's breast and carrying over the sloping fields. In a short while he heard his father go down the back steps, slam the car door and drive away.

Arnold lay still as a fugitive, listening to the cows eating close by. If his parents never called him, he thought, he would stay up in the loft forever, out of the way. In the night he would sneak down for a drink of water from the faucet over the trough and for whatever food they left for him by the barn.

The rattle of his father's car as it turned down the lane recalled him to the present. He heard the voices of his Uncle Andy and Aunt Alice as they and his father went past the barn to the lake. He could feel the morning growing heavier with sun. Someone, probably Nora, had let the chickens out of their coops and they were cackling in the yard.

After a while, a car, followed by another car, turned down the road off the highway. The cars drew to a stop and he heard the voices of strange men. The men also went past the barn and down to the lake. The sheriff's men and the undertakers, whom his father must have phoned from Uncle Andy's house, had arrived from Corinth. Then he heard everybody come back and heard the cars turn around and leave.

"Arnold!" It was his father calling from the yard.

He climbed down the ladder and went out into the sun, picking wisps of hay from his overalls.

Corinth, nine miles away, was the county seat. Arnold sat in the front seat of the old Ford between his father, who was driving, and Uncle Andy; no one spoke. Uncle Andy was his mother's brother, and he had been fond of Eugie because Eugie had resembled him. Andy had taken Eugie hunting and had given him a knife and a lot of things, and now Andy, his eyes narrowed, sat tall and stiff beside Arnold.

Arnold's father parked the car before the courthouse. It was a two-story brick building with a lamp on each side of the bottom step. They went up the wide stone steps, Arnold and his father going first, and entered the darkly paneled hallway. The shirt-sleeved man in the sheriff's office said that the sheriff was at Carlson's Parlor examining the boy who was shot.

Andy went off to get the sheriff while Arnold and his father waited on a bench in the corridor. Arnold felt his father watching him, and he lifted his eyes with painful casualness to the announcement, on the opposite wall, of the Corinth County Annual Rodeo, and then to the clock with its loudly clucking pendulum. After he had come down from the loft his father and Uncle Andy had stood in the yard with him and asked him to tell them everything, and he had explained to them how the gun had caught on the wire. But when they had asked him why he hadn't run back to the house to tell his parents, he had had no answer—all he could say was that he had gone down into the garden to pick the peas. His father had stared at him in a pale, puzzled way, and it was then that he had felt his father and the others set their cold, turbulent silence against him. Arnold shifted on the bench, his only feeling a small one of compunction imposed by his father's eyes.

At a quarter past nine, Andy and the sheriff came in. They all went into the sheriff's private office, and Arnold was sent forward to sit in the chair by the sheriff's desk; his father and Andy sat down on the bench against the wall.

The sheriff lumped down into his swivel chair and swung toward Arnold. He was an old man with white hair like wheat stubble. His restless green eyes made him seem not to be in his office but to be hurrying and bobbing around somewhere else.

"What did you say your name was?" the sheriff asked.

"Arnold," he replied, but he could not remember telling the sheriff his name before.

"What were you doing with a .22, Arnold?"

"It's mine," he said.

"Okay. What were you going to shoot?"

"Some ducks," he replied.

"Out of season?"

He nodded.

"That's bad," said the sheriff. "Were you and your brother good friends?"

What did he mean—good friends? Eugie was his brother. That was different from a friend, Arnold thought. A best friend was your own age, but Eugie was almost a man. Eugie had had a way of looking at him, slyly and mockingly and yet confidentially, that had summed up how they both felt about being brothers. Arnold had wanted to be with Eugie more than with anybody else, but he couldn't say they had been good friends.

"Did they ever quarrel?" the sheriff asked his father.

"Not that I know," his father replied. "It seemed to me that Arnold cared a lot for Eugie."

"Did you?" the sheriff asked Arnold.

If it seemed so to his father, then it was so. Arnold nodded.

"Were you mad at him this morning?"

"No."

"How did you happen to shoot him?"

"We was crawlin' through the fence."

"Yes?"

"An' the gun got caught on the wire."

"Seems the hammer must of caught," his father put in.

"All right, that's what happened," said the sheriff. "But what I want you to tell me is this. Why didn't you go back to the house and tell your father right away? Why did you go and pick peas for an hour?"

Arnold gazed over his shoulder at his father, expecting his father to have an answer for this also. But his father's eyes, larger and even lighter blue than usual, were fixed upon him curiously. Arnold picked at a callus in his right palm. It seemed odd now that he had not run back to the house and wakened his father, but he could not remember why he had not. They were all waiting for him to answer.

"I come down to pick peas," he said.

"Didn't you think," asked the sheriff, stepping carefully from word to word, "that it was more important for you to go tell your parents what happened?"

"The sun was gonna come up," Arnold said.

"What's that got to do with it?"

"It's better to pick peas while they're cool."

The sheriff swung away from him, laid both hands flat on his desk. "Well, all I can say is," he said across to Arnold's father and Uncle Andy, "he's either a moron or he's so reasonable that he's way ahead of us." He gave a challenging snort. "It's come to my notice that the most reasonable guys are mean ones. They don't feel nothing."

For a moment the three men sat still. Then the sheriff lifted his hand like a man taking an oath. "Take him home," he said.

"You don't want him?" Andy asked.

"Not now," replied the sheriff. "Maybe in a few years."

Arnold's father stood up. He held his hat against his chest. "The gun ain't his no more," he said wanly.

Arnold went first through the hallway, hearing behind him the heels of his father and Uncle Andy striking the floorboards. He went down the steps ahead of them and climbed into the back seat of the car. Andy paused as he was getting into the front seat and gazed back at Arnold, and Arnold saw that his uncle's eyes had absorbed the knowingness from the sheriff's eyes. Andy and his father and the sheriff had discovered what made him go down into the garden. It was because he was cruel, the sheriff had said, and didn't care about his brother. Arnold lowered his eyelids meekly against his uncle's stare.

The rest of the day he did his tasks around the farm, keeping apart from the family. At evening, when he saw his father stomp tiredly into the house, Arnold did not put down his hammer and leave the chicken coop he was repairing. He was afraid that they did not want him to eat supper with them. But in a few minutes another fear that they would go to the trouble of calling him and that he would be made conspicuous by his tardiness made him follow his father into the house. As he went through the kitchen he saw the jars of peas standing in rows on the workbench, a reproach to him.

No one spoke at supper, and his mother, who sat next to him, leaned her head in her hand all through the meal, curving her fingers over her eyes so as not to see him. They were finishing their small, silent supper when the visitors began to arrive, knocking hard on the back door. The men were coming from their farms now that it was growing dark and they could not work anymore.

Old Man Matthews, gray and stocky, came first, with his two sons, Orion, the elder, and Clint, who was Eugie's age. As the callers entered the parlor where the family ate, Arnold sat down in a rocking chair. Even as he had been undecided before supper whether to remain outside or take his place at the table, he now thought that he should go upstairs, and yet he stayed to avoid being conspicuous by his absence. If he stayed, he thought, as he always stayed and listened when visitors came, they would see that he was only Arnold and not the person the sheriff thought he was. He sat with his arms crossed and his hands tucked into his armpits and did not lift his eyes.

The Matthews men had hardly settled down around the table, after Arnold's mother and Nora cleared away the dishes, when another car rattled down the road and someone else rapped on the back door. This time it was Sullivan, a spare and sandy man, so nimble of gesture and expression that Arnold had never been able to catch more than a few of his meanings. Sullivan, in dusty jeans, sat down in another rocker, shot out his skinny legs and began to talk in his fast way, recalling everything that Eugene had ever said to him. The other men interrupted to tell of occasions they remembered, and after a time Clint's young voice, hoarse like Eugene's had been, broke in to tell about the time Eugene had beat him in a wrestling match.

Out in the kitchen the voices of Orion's wife and of Mrs. Sullivan mingled with Nora's voice but not, Arnold noticed, his mother's. Then dry little Mr. Cram came, leaving large Mrs. Cram in the kitchen, and there was no chair left for Mr. Cram to sit in. No one asked Arnold to get up and he was unable to rise. He knew that the story had got around to them during the day about how he had gone and picked peas after he had shot his brother, and he knew that although they were talking only about Eugie they were thinking about him, and if he got up, if he moved even his foot, they would all be alerted. Then Uncle Andy arrived and leaned his tall, lanky body against the doorjamb, and there were two men standing.

Presently Arnold was aware that the talk had stopped. He knew without looking up that the men were watching him.

"Not a tear in his eye," said Andy, and Arnold knew that his uncle had gestured the men to attention.

"He don't give a hoot, is that how it goes?" asked Sullivan.

"He's a reasonable fellow," Andy explained. "That's what the sheriff said. It's us who ain't reasonable. If we'd of shot our brother, we'd of come runnin' back to the house, cryin' like a baby. Well, we'd of been unreasonable. What would of been the use of actin' like that? If your brother is shot dead, he's shot dead. What's the use of gettin' emotional about it? The thing to do is go down to the garden and pick peas. Am I right?"

The men around the room shifted their heavy, satisfying weight of unreasonableness.

Matthews' son Orion said, "If I'd of done what he done, Pa would've hung my pelt by the side of that big coyote's in the barn."

Arnold sat in the rocker until the last man filed out. While his family was out in the kitchen bidding the callers good night and the cars were driving away down the dirt lane to the highway, he picked up one of the kerosene lamps and slipped quickly up the stairs. In his room he undressed by lamplight, although he and Eugie had always undressed in the dark, and not until he was lying in his bed did he blow out the flame. He felt nothing, not any grief. There was only the same immense silence and crawling inside of him; it was the way the house and fields felt under a merciless sun.

He awoke suddenly. He knew that his father was out in the yard, closing the doors of the chicken houses. The sound that had awakened him was the step of his father as he got up from the rocker and went down the back steps. And he knew that his mother was awake in her bed.

Throwing off the covers, he rose swiftly, went down the stairs and across the dark parlor to his parents' room. He rapped on the door.

"Mother?"

From the closed room her voice rose to him, a seeking and retreating voice. "Yes?"

"Mother?" he asked insistently. He had expected her to realize that he wanted to go down on his knees by her bed and tell her that Eugie was dead. She did not know it yet, nobody knew it, and yet she was sitting up in bed, waiting to be told, waiting for him to confirm her dread. He had expected her to tell him to come in, to allow him to dig his head into her blankets and tell her about the terror he had felt when he had knelt beside Eugie. He had come to clasp her in his arms and, in

his terror, to pommel her breasts with his head. He put his
hand upon the knob.

"Go back to bed, Arnold," she called sharply.

But he waited.

"Go back! Is night when you get afraid?"

At first he did not understand. Then, silently, he left the door
and for a stricken moment stood by the rocker. Outside everything was still. The fences, the shocks of wheat seen through
the window before him were so still it was as if they moved and
breathed in the daytime and had fallen silent with the lateness
of the hour. It was a silence that seemed to observe his father, a
figure moving alone around the yard, his lantern casting a
circle of light by his feet. In a few minutes his father would
enter the dark house, the lantern still lighting his way.

Arnold was suddenly aware that he was naked. He had
thrown off his blankets and come down the stairs to tell his
mother how he felt about Eugie, but she had refused to listen to
him and his nakedness had become unpardonable. At once he
went back up the stairs, fleeing from his father's lantern.

At breakfast he kept his eyelids lowered as if to deny the night.
Nora, sitting at his left, did not pass the pitcher of milk to him
and he did not ask for it. He would never again, he vowed, ask
them for anything, and he ate his fried eggs and potatoes only
because everybody ate meals—the cattle ate, and the cats; it
was customary for everybody to eat.

"Nora, you gonna keep that pitcher for yourself?" his father
asked.

Nora lowered her head unsurely.

"Pass it on to Arnold," his father said.

Nora put her hands in her lap.

His father picked up the metal pitcher and set it down at
Arnold's plate.

Arnold, pretending to be deaf to the discord, did not glance
up, but relief rained over his shoulders at the thought that his
parents recognized him again. They must have lain awake
after his father had come in from the yard: had they realized

together why he had come down the stairs and knocked at their door?

"Bessie's missin' this morning," his father called out to his mother, who had gone into the kitchen. "She went up the mountain last night and had her calf, most likely. Somebody's got to go up and find her 'fore the coyotes get the calf."

That had been Eugie's job, Arnold thought. Eugie would climb the cattle trails in search of a newborn calf and come down the mountain carrying the calf across his back, with the cow running behind him, mooing in alarm.

Arnold ate the few more forkfuls of his breakfast, put his hands on the edge of the table and pushed back his chair. If he went for the calf he'd be away from the farm all morning. He could switch the cow down the mountain slowly, and the calf would run along at its mother's side.

When he passed through the kitchen, his mother was setting a kettle of water on the stove. "Where you going?" she asked awkwardly.

"Up to get the calf," he replied, averting his face.

"Arnold?"

At the door he paused reluctantly, his back to her, knowing that she was seeking him out, as his father was doing.

"Was you knocking at my door last night?"

He looked over his shoulder at her, his eyes narrow.

"What'd you want?" she asked humbly.

"I didn't want nothing," he said flatly.

Then he went out the door and down the back steps, his legs trembling from the fright his answer gave him.

Bastille Day

Just after one o'clock Teresa came to the San Gotardo, the last bar on her round of bars this night of her fortieth birthday, July 14, 1970. The predictions overheard when she was young, about how you were going to feel when you got to be forty, had seemed false, like laughing fools' talk, and even in the last few years when that age appeared on the horizon like a sinking ship, a sailor signaling with those little flags, precisely, futilely, even then she had refused to conform to the tyranny of numbers, just as, all her life, she'd refused to conform to popular delusions. With her, the sense of mortality hadn't waited to take her by surprise at forty. It had been with her always, a seventh sense, along with the absolute preciousness of life, hers and everybody's. But who, she wondered, could possibly guess that about her, a drab woman pushing open the door to this last bar for the night, her face puffy, her no-color hair tied back with a narrow, dangling ribbon, the tail of hair hanging out over her dark, styleless coat.

The ones usually here were here now, along with a few unfamiliar ones, the dingy place as brightly lit as a cafe, making no attempt to hide itself in shadows, the jukebox wearily scratching up an Hawaiian song to which an old woman was dancing an impromptu hula. Teresa sat on a stool at the end of the bar. She had heard that this place and the hotel above it were in their last days, and she asked who had bought the property. The question, put to the man next to her, was like a match that set the fuse to a string of firecrackers.

"Some Chinaman!" At the top of his lungs.

"Koreans are not Chinamen!" A woman at the middle of the bar, neatly dressed in a gray suit and hat, her pumps dangling from her toes. "A filthy rich Korean bought it."

"Ho Chi Minh bought it." Away at the other end of the bar, a portly black man in a shabby suit and hat, standing. "Ho Chi Minh is taking over soon as he wins the war."

"Ho Chi Minh is dead." The caustic woman in gray, instructive again. A seat each side of her was empty.

"Japs!" The old woman, sprawled by her table after her dance. "They were snooping around upstairs. The way you tell a Jap is they all got a camera 'round their neck. That's how they tell themselves from Chinamen."

When Teresa had entered here for the first time, just twenty-one, the other patrons had been merchant seamen and cooks and stewards from the passenger vessels and old Italians always with their hats on. Only a few of the old bars were left in this Italian neighborhood that was taken over now by the manic facades of nightclubs where nude girls danced, and whenever she came in here now she wondered if anyone present had been among the customers years ago and grown unrecognizable. On the high ceiling the paint was the same antique ivory, and behind the bar the lineup of Fun Land prizes seemed the same. The Kewpie doll, the blue plush dog, the plaster Popeye. The flowerpot, wrapped in foil, held wax flowers in an era of plastic ones, and the two little girls in the photo garlanded with a faded paper lei were women now. Over in the dark dining section, separated from the bar by a low, flimsy partition and by a flowered curtain across the doorway, the same mural of Sicilian farm country graced the dim far wall.

Half a century ago the bartender must have been a pretty young man. His dyed black hair and large baby-blue eyes evoked a movie idol of her teens whose name she couldn't recall. He might *be* that one, come at last, or too soon, into his obscurity, a tinge of green on the teeth of his winning smile. Except for two young mailmen with beards, and a tall, bare-headed young black man in a long black overcoat, by himself at a table, no one was younger than herself. That was comforting, if only for the moment.

At the far end of the curved bar, a man sat facing Teresa. A long, bald, dead-eyed man in shirtsleeves, winking at her a

lewd command. "Joe Curran," he said, to nobody in particular, "got me into the Great Lakes."

"Man, don't talk to me about Joe Curran." The woman in
gray spoke into her drink, contemptuously. "You want to
know who was all right? I'll tell you. William Randolph Hearst
was a fantastic man. You better believe it. He called me in and
said I was a fantastic writer. Are you a Communist? Yes, I said.
I was always cocky honest. Nothing fuzzy. Well, he said, we
just won't send you out on any labor stories. A fantastic man!
But his son!"

Teresa had never seen the woman before, never in the past at
demonstrations nor at any of the big parties in rented halls,
benefits for this and that radical cause.

"Got to New York," the woman went on. "No job. Called
Hearst in San Simeon. He put me to work on his magazine in
New York. Fashion. Imagine. I retired from the Newspaper
Guild because I didn't want to go through the FBI. You know
who my son is? My little tiny baby boy is a big rock star. Far
out. I was far out in my time. If you were far out in my time you
could have got the electric chair."

"Don't die that way." The man on the woman's left, a stool
between them, sat in a crouch, an uneasy man in a black suit.
"You don't look so good after."

"You undertakers are 86 around here," the woman said to
him. And to the bartender, "You ought to prohibit him from
spreading gloom."

The man in the black suit got off his stool and moved toward
the jukebox, a somber stepper, smoothing back his slick hair
with slow palms.

"Play Duke Ellington!" the woman called after him without
turning. "If you put anything else on I'll kill you. Your boss
will be surprised when you turn up dead."

The Indian Love Call rose up faintly from an old record, and
the two mailmen got up from their table and danced a parody,
cupping their ears to hear the call through dense forest.

A younger woman, Teresa's age, came out of the door of the
staircase that connected the bar to the hotel rooms above and

sat down at the hula dancer's table. A girl out of a fairy tale after she had come alive and become a woman and lost some teeth but not yet all her beauty. Her long black hair was parted in the center and drawn back into a bun, and her downslanting emerald eyes were made to seem even larger by the compression of the almost toothless jaws. And Teresa was drawn to her. The woman was, sweetly, keenly, someone she would have wished to be a confidante for, back in the time of her young beauty when the future promised wonders.

Teresa carried her beer to that table and sat down with the two women. The old one in her house dress and shabby shoes, her pink barrette slipping from her short gray hair, was still undulating to the Hawaiian music that had been left behind, long before, by other songs. And at this table Teresa felt herself warming up to embrace all the benighted persons in this bar, embrace them as if she had never expected more of them, no change for the better.

"You live here?" she asked the fairy tale woman.

The fairy tale woman clasped her bare arms across her breasts. "I used to but I can't now. I always kept my room clean and I never made any noise except when I lost my mind. The owners, they'd be happy to have me back. I'm speaking of the social workers, they say I've got to live with a guarantor. He guaranteed them he'd take care of me, so they let me out of the asylum. If you look at him and then look at me you'll see he's old enough to be my father. Over and above that, he has an apartment and money in the bank and four suits and a pension. But he's filthy. They don't know that. I'll tell you what he's like."

The woman went silent. Teresa waited.

"If you come home with me," the woman said, "and poke your head in the door, he'll see you're a woman. It's only a few blocks from here. Otherwise he'll say I've been out with a man. If I come back without my coat he'll say I left it at my lover's. I left it at home because the sun was out and I was coming right back."

"I'll do that," Teresa promised.

"My lover hung himself. He's up there moaning." She smiled a young, knowing, almost toothless smile. "He's German. They're romantics. They kill everybody and they kill themselves. He says he's going to do it over again as soon as he gets his strength back."

A commotion at the far end of the bar. The portly black man slapped the lewd winker from the Great Lakes, who lost his balance and fell to the floor, along with his stool. The black man stepped up onto the fallen man's back and, hesitantly, as if he were only considering that which he was already doing, he jumped around up there. Then he stepped down and kicked the man in the face. No one shouted to him to stop, no one came to restrain him. But when he lifted a stool, straining to raise it above his head, a man left his table and with charitable ease gripped the upraised arms.

"Well that's enough," he said humoringly. "You kicked the shit out of him and that's enough."

"He was asking for it."

"He sure was asking for it," the man agreed, taking the stool away. "You better get the hell out before somebody calls the cops."

Slowly, only wandering out to another bar, the black man left, his hat unmoved, his face unmoved, his eyes pleased. The lewd winker got up from the floor and fell backward against the dining room partition, causing it to shake. He set up his stool and sat down. His nose was bleeding.

"I'll drop you," he said to his assailant no longer there.

The man who had intervened moved toward the street door, and Teresa saw he was someone she had known. Someone on the periphery of those familiar faces always anticipating great changes for the world. The old woman got up and almost fell against him, and he set her right by his hand at her elbow. Teresa recognized him, then. A steward aboard the passenger ships, he had brought them news for the union paper, he had sat with her and the staff at their favorite bars and cheap restaurants. He was not of the periphery, he was in the midst. Mayer. She spoke his name.

When he sat down, the fairy tale woman started to get up. "I'm in the way."

"No, no, you're not," he said, quickly, gently, and the woman leaned back in a submissive arc.

"I'm out on the town," Teresa told him. "I told Ralph I wasn't coming home till late. No, I didn't tell him. I'll tell him when I get back."

Mayer's eyes, striving to concern themselves with this woman he probably barely remembered, were no longer pure of shape and color. The flesh around them made them less revealing, made them flat and noncommittal. She wondered if she had looked at him with desire, in the past. She had felt desire toward a number of men in that time when they had all conferred over how to right the world. Once in that time she might have made love with him in a dream.

The bartender swung up the empty stools and slid them upside down onto the bar. The fairy tale woman, her arms against her breasts, stood up, Teresa and Mayer stood up, and the three went out into the night, followed by the young black man in the long overcoat, who towered over them.

"You want to drink some more?" the follower asked them. "I know where we can get some whiskey. You just knock on the window. It's a liquor store. He's closed but you knock on the window and he sells it to you. He says I owe him fourteen dollars but I only owe him six. He won't sell me no more til I pay up."

The fairy tale woman was hurrying on, soberly forward into the cold mist. Teresa caught up with her, and Mayer and the other man caught up. "I don't want to be nothing but drunk," the young man was saying, behind Teresa. "I got shot three times in Vietnam. They ain't supposed to shoot at you coming down. You see that red light over there? That's how a bullet feels when it hits you. Red hot. My buddy's parachute didn't open. When we found him he was flatter than this sidewalk. You know what they do with your dog tag when you're dead? They kick it into your teeth."

Teresa's lungs began to clamor with the pain of the cold fog of summer they had to take in, so fast. The fairy tale woman had got ahead again, but at the corner she turned and stood waiting, shivering. And Teresa wondered if she, herself, was an asylum inmate, on a night out just because it was her birthday and they allowed it to her. Not somebody as sane as anybody else, a woman with a good job and a scholar-husband reading into the night with the gas heater on or lying warmly asleep in his separate bed, books fallen to the floor.

The four of them stood in a huddle on the windy corner, the fairy tale woman afraid to urge them on. Teresa saw the fear of desertion in her pinched face that, under the harsh street light, was the face of a woman twice-as-old.

The young man was reluctant to part from them. "You got some crazy city," he said. "I was working the other night where my friend works. Up the street. I was washing dishes over at Mike's when this girl walks in. I looked so hard my eyes watered. Nothing on." His shoulders raised against the cold, his hands in his overcoat pockets, he walked backward a few steps. "It's been nice talking to you."

Three abreast, Teresa and the fairy tale woman and Mayer went on, Teresa on the inside, bumping against walls, and Mayer on the outside, nimbly stepping off the curb and around hydrants.

"You want my coat?" he asked the woman.

"It smells like a man," she said. "He'd smell it on me even after it was off."

After several blocks, the woman took Teresa's hand and drew her into the marble entrance of an old apartment building. Four doors in a row faced the street. The woman pressed a button, the buzzer sounded, and she opened the door.

"My friend walked me home," she called up.

Drawn in by the woman's hand, Teresa also raised her face. Almost imperial, strong, an old man was leaning on the banister at the top of the carpeted stairs, and his very white, smooth hair and his very white shirt shone under the light. The fairy tale woman started up the stairs. Teresa closed the door.

They walked back the way they had come, unspeaking,

Teresa stumbling only once, so far. She had no direction now. "I can't make it home," she said. "Over the bridge to Berkeley and another bus stop in the heart of darkness. Nothing's running this time of night. Or far between. I think I'm scared."

"You can sleep at my place," he said.

"You sleep on the bed, I'll sleep on the sofa."

"What makes you think I've got a sofa?" He told her he had a couple of rooms, a few blocks away, that he and his wife had separated a month ago, and that he was a ship's clerk now; then he was silent again.

Up three flights of stairs in an apartment building, the climbing, the key in the lock, quietly done. The bed was covered neatly with an Indian cotton spread. A clean place, a scent of toilet soap, even of apples, a Gauguin print on the wall of warm-fleshed Polynesian women. Teresa sat down in a chair and felt for cigarettes in her purse. His silence was telling her that she was a burden, unexpectedly added to some he already had, that this was a bad night for him because of her.

Mayer lit a hissing gas heater. "You can lie down."

She lay on the bed in her coat, flat on her back, shoes pointing ceilingward. And out of the blue, just like the winking man at the bar who rose up out of the Great Lakes, just like the rest with their memories that were like non sequiturs to everyone else, she said, "Some people we used to know got prosperous. Briggs is in real estate, I see his name in the papers. He wanted to change the world so he built half-a-million tract houses. Rupert is a restauranteur, he doesn't even have to cook anymore, he just shakes hands. Look at me, I'm a computer. Not rich yet, just upward mobility."

"How's Ralph?"

She gazed at the Gauguin print, her eyes evading the question. "Ralph's got himself a Ph.D. He's an associate professor."

"Of what?"

The long way around, tell it that way, the only way. "Well, first it was going to be Philosophy. He switched over to Economics and then he switched over to Modern European History. We felt it was all right for him to take so long. I had jobs.

Anyway, I always felt he was like the favorite child of Time, if you know what I mean. I think those others, the ones who got prosperous, they're like favorites of Time, too. They just had to wait to get over their bleeding heart phase, if you know what I mean."

When it was spoken aloud it had a maudlin, abusive sound, just what was to be expected of her at the end of her night's roaming. Some other nights, too, had their maudlin endings. Not long ago, coming home late after having found no one in the bars whom she had known, she had thrown herself down by Ralph, asleep. She had knelt on the floor, weeping up an awful storm, and her life, like a small boat on faulty mooring lines, was almost swept away.

"Mayer," she said brightly, "I bet you didn't know today was Bastille Day." She slid upward to lean against the head-board, nudged her shoes off and over the side, and shook her head to clear away the complaints. Her hair came loose from the ribbon and hung in strands to her shoulders, and, possibly, she looked young again.

"Never gave it a thought," he said.

"I know because it's my birthday. Same day. When Ralph told me a long time ago that my birthday was Bastille Day I said—listen to what I said, you won't believe it—I said, So *that's* why I've got this urge to release everybody from bond-age. I said, Isn't that the day the French peasants let loose the political prisoners? And he said, They released seven and they weren't politicals. They were after ammunition. And I said, Well, they made it a holiday, it must have meant a lot for the Revolution, you know, storming the Bastille. And he said, If you want that day for your very own, it's yours."

The room went dark. He had switched off the lamp. She saw him sit down in a chair and take off his shoes. "A great day for a birthday," he said. "I wish it was mine."

"You take the bed," she said. He must be angry with himself for bringing her home. "I can sleep in the chair."

"Get under the covers," he said, wearily.

She got in under the blankets, her coat on, and he lay down

on the outer edge of the bed, under the covers. She lay as close to the wall as she could get without touching it. Though she kept her face a few inches away from the wall, the cold came out of it like a ceaseless exhalation. Some nights she could scarcely breathe, and the doctor had told her that if she failed to stop drinking and failed to stop smoking, if she didn't begin to take care of herself, wear warm clothes in cold weather, then Oh! Beware! If she ever came down with pneumonia, she was a goner. And she knew she would die in her bed while Ralph read on and on in his room about great upheavals, debacles, revolutions, carnage. And when she was gone, he would simply go on as before, a slouchy, boyish, finical professor, and if his eyes were seen to be red-rimmed the cause would not be sorrow; he had always a problem with sties. She wanted to tell this to Mayer, to believe that he was the one she had been longing to find, the one who would care about whom she had become and what was to become of her, but her talk would seem only the ragtag end of her night's roaming. She listened to his breath change as he fell asleep. She heard his breath take over for him and, in that secretive way the sleeper knows nothing about, carry on his life.

The Mistress

It was almost an hour after his arrival before he was introduced to her, and in that time she watched him from her vantage point in the bow of the window that gave her a view of the garden and of the long room filled with people. She watched him because she knew at once, gazing down through the diamond panes to see how a boy came up through a garden to a house filled with party—this one coming up briskly to outdistance his shyness—that he was the son of the man who had been her lover ten years ago, the son who had been six then. She knew, because the similarity was so striking she felt that she was gazing down upon the lover as he must have been at sixteen and at a moment when he had lifted his face to attempt an impassive scanning of the windows and found, in one, the face of a strange woman transfixed by him. She watched him enter the room, be kissed by the hostess, and thread his way between groups and couples, his head bent with apology and with a determination that was affected, since he was, she suspected, looking for no one in particular but only yearning to be halted, to be embraced, to be enclosed by some group and by the entire party. For several minutes he stood only a yard away from her, half-in and half-out of a group, holding his goblet of sherry and gazing down as if waiting for the wine to be joggled from his glass to the rug. He was tall, he was almost a man, he was on the verge of composure—she saw it alternate with discomfort, and his presence among adults, most of whom were strangers to him, reminded her of the legend of Theseus entering as a stranger the kingdom he was to rule some day.

She watched him because he was completely absorbing to her, combining as he did the familiar figure of the father with the enticing strangeness of the boy himself. She was thirty-six, the number of her husbands was three—the present one had been unable to attend the afternoon party—and the number of her lovers who had meant something to her was firmly fixed in her memory at one and that one was the father of the boy whom she was now spying on. The elderly man beside her on the bench was so enamored of her, his old black eyes glancing out untiringly from far inside the folds of eyelids at her crossed legs and bare, braceleted arms, that he was unaware of and therefore unhurt by her own glancing and gazing at someone else.

The boy was following the hostess as she went her rounds. Every joke, every anecdote being more amusing to her than to anybody else, she was constantly bending her knees to laugh, bending her body in the tight green dress, and for a time she used the boy as a partner in this dance of hers, grasping his arm and bending toward him until her forehead touched the pit of his stomach. But she was almost as small as an elf and whatever postures she adopted were not exaggerated, as they would be with a larger person, but simply made her presence known. Although he chatted eagerly enough with those she introduced him to, he always left them after a time to find the hostess again, as if nobody but she could give him a reason for being there, and when, at last, the hostess brought him over to her in her window, she knew as they approached that the hostess regarded her as perhaps the only person who could restrain the boy from his trailing.

So here was the boy, at last, the resemblance to his father defined less by closeness than by distance; now he was himself altogether, there was nothing that was a replica of his father, there were only sharp clues, a continual reminding. The elderly man to her right, rather than appear to be pushed off into oblivion by the two younger persons, rose with a sprightly tugging at tie and coat and offered to bring her another gin and tonic. She refused the offer charmingly, relieved and also reluctant to see him go, for any man's attentiveness was appreciated. It was not an appreciation she had come to lately; she had always, even in her youth, felt the need to thank the admirer for admiring.

"She's a good friend of my mother," he said, when they spoke of the hostess and her vivacity.

"Is your mother here?" she asked brightly, implying that if the son was so delightful a person to meet then the mother must also be met and delighted in before the party was over.

He said that his mother was staying with her sister in another city, and she wondered if the woman was being cared for by the sister, remembering that at one time during her affair with the boy's father, the wife had left, after a wild scene with him, and gone to her sister's, taking the child, and had been ill there for several weeks.

"Your father? Is he here?" she asked, knowing that he was in London and that he had transferred himself there four years ago, right after the divorce.

"He lives in London." The boy fumbled out a packet of matches from his coat pocket and lit her cigarette with a steady flame that compensated for his awkwardness. "I spent last summer over there."

"How is he?" she asked. "He was once a friend of mine." That innocuous information, when told to the son, was like a revelation of the truth. When recalled to the son, the memory of the father was as fresh and pervasive to her as if the affair had begun or ended only the day before.

"Great, great," the son said. "He's married again, and they've got a baby now, a little girl." She felt, listening, that the son and herself were both attached to him by love, by resentment, by all the responses of the ones left in the past of somebody of prominence and promise and a life of his own and who had no time or inclination for memories of past loves. "I wouldn't like living there all the time," he said. "London, that is," laughing in case she might think he meant living in his father's house.

"How does he look now?" she asked.

"Look?"

"Fatter, skinnier, gray or bald?"

"Oh, thinner, I'd say."

"Oh, yes, thinner," she cried, laughing. "He's the fibrous kind. They get tough like dried fruit." They let themselves go with laughing. Other guests glanced over at them, surprised by and disapproving of this sudden intrusion of laughter into the several conversations. "Gray yet?" she asked, arching her brows.

"No, no, not at all," he said. "Got fewer gray hairs than I do." A splash of sherry on her leg as he, clumsy with clowning, transferred the glass to riffle his hair with his right hand.

"Nothing," she assured him. "It's nothing." But the clumsiness reminded them of that insufficiency in the self, the *manqué* element that is felt by the persons left in somebody else's past, the persons who were not in step and who were shocked by their own lagging. They stopped their laughing, and she saw that he was wondering about her—why she should laugh so eagerly over the present description of an old friend and why she could so easily compel him to join with her.

She rose, reaching down for his hand, all done in a moment as if he were doing the convincing and she was spontaneously amenable. "Come on, let's walk in the garden," she said over her shoulder as he followed her through the crowd, their hands linked. She turned her profile to him as they stood delayed by a congestion of guests near the door and spoke into his ear as he complyingly bent his head down. "When the air gets thick with smoke and gossip, I can't breathe," she whispered hoarsely, and, seeing him frown solicitously, baffled, as if she had named a rare disease, she patted his cheek to convey to him that her complaint wasn't serious. They each enjoyed the other's concern and, laughing about it, pushed out onto the wide arc of the brick steps.

She released his hand the moment they were in the open and took his elbow, instead, and swung along beside him with a movement in her hips more pronounced than she had tried for in a long time, yet wondering why her responses to the boy must be so extravagant. They crossed the bricks she had watched him cross and stepped out into the garden where other guests were walking the brick paths or sitting around the white, fancy ironwork tables. The flowers were so large and perfect that the garden seemed a greenhouse and this illusion was intensified by the humid air.

"It reminds me of Mazatlán, this weather," she said. "The weeks before the rains came. Hot, hot, everybody out along the beaches, the esplanade, till way past midnight, children and everybody. I remember the night the storm came, the first storm. The little trees by the window were bent over horizontal and the lightning continuous, sheets of lightning, and the rain and the wind, and the coolness coming into the windows, but the air still warm. I remember I went out into it, wrapped my raincoat over me and went out, but someone looking out a window told me to get back in, it was dangerous—the lightning, and the rain all over the ground in a flood." She glanced away. "The sand there is pink and gold, and weird birds—I guess they're vultures of some sort—hover over the beach. At night you can see the lights of La Paz across the water, or think you can. Your father was there at the time. He was there, too. In Mazatlán."

"Did you meet him there?" he asked.

"We knew each other before," she said, and was impatient to reveal to him a woman from out of his father's life, a woman he had not known existed, impatient to compel him to see her as he would imagine his father had seen her and to experience for a time, for the rest of the day, what she had meant to his father, impatient to re-create the father and herself, the lovers. With her head bowed over a yellow leaf she had picked up, she strolled down the path a step ahead of him to contend with her urge to reveal to him that which ought to be left in the father's past and in her own.

"I remember he went to Mexico when I was six," he said. "He wrote me a letter. I was just learning to write and I answered him. He kept my letter. My mother has it. God, the spelling!"

"He went there with me," she said. "Or I went with him. We were lovers."

She had told him in order to experience again, as she was

doing now as he followed her, the delight of being both desired and desirous as she had known it then. She had told him in order to experience again that greater awareness of herself, of the shifting and floating of the weightless silk around her thighs, of the threads of her hair that, glimpsed from the corner of her eye, were like flying spider silk in the sun, seen and not seen. She had told him in order to experience again that woman she had been years ago, followed by the man, the father. When he came alongside her she glanced at him to see her effect upon him, and saw the face of a sick child.

They stood in the shade of trees; and all things, the fragrance of the flowers, the tang of the limes from the drinks on a table close by, the voices in conversation among the trees and flowers, the heat of the day, some dust in the air from somewhere on the other side of the high, wrought-iron fence, everything served to make his face that of a boy taken sick at a picnic. "I remember you," he said, pressing at the leaves on the path with his heel. "I don't mean that I met you. I just mean that I remember you."

"How?" she asked.

"The time, I mean," he said. "I remember the time."

"The time?" She felt the loss of herself, as if she no longer existed even in anyone's memory, her features, her voice, all forgotten. Only the time remained as a frame empty of its picture of a woman.

"My mother used to cry," he explained. "She seemed to be crying all the time. And they would quarrel when he came home. Sometimes the mascara would run down her cheeks and make black tears."

"But they weren't getting along even before he met me."

"Yes, I suppose," he said. "But she cried anyway about you."

He lifted his eyes in the silence he had enforced, and they were a child's accusing eyes, the eyes of a boy troubled by his mother's troubles, seeing his mother's face streaked by the mascara, hearing the quarreling through a wall, through a door left open.

"You shouldn't have told me," he said.

"Or committed the crime ten years ago?" she asked, the wise, ironical woman.

"No, no, I know more about people now," he said, defending his store of wisdom. "I just said you shouldn't have said it," trying to tell her that he was ashamed for reacting as a child, thrusting his mother between them, and that she should not have forced him back into the past, into the child loyal to the mother, when he was experiencing the pleasure of her company, the company of a strange woman giving him her time and gracefulness and wit, gifts that implied his maturity.

The shame he felt for reacting as a child and the love aroused for that memory of his mother struggled together, forbidding any further ease with her. They walked side by side past guests who fell silent as they went silently by, much like lovers who have had their concluding quarrel. They made a circle of the garden and at the table nearest the porch she stopped to chat with a friend. The boy went on before she could introduce him, and, glancing after him, she saw his long legs hurrying across the shallow brick steps, saw that his body was tense again, that he was no longer persuaded by her into a belief in his desirability as her companion.

The woman she was chatting with drew out from behind her a round, yellow cushion and tossed it into the empty chair. She sat down and continued the chatting, smoking and smiling, and seeing the face of his mother weeping black, bitter tears. She sat with her bare arms on the table, observing how the circle of trees and round white table and the soft, pointillistic light through the leaves all gave the group around the table the intimacy of a group in a painting, but seeing, all the time, the face of the weeping woman. There was unhappiness and tears for that woman long before she, the mistress, appeared in their lives, there was nothing that could have been done even if this feeling for the other woman had been experienced at that time, but the fact of her indifference then, of her inability to probe the other woman's suffering struck her now as a tragic thing. She felt that she was a hundred years old, discovering that the person in her memory who affected her the most was

not the one she had loved the most but the one she had understood the least.

She turned partly away from the woman she was talking
with and, reaching over the back of her chair, picked a red,
velvety leaf from a small tree blossoming with purple flowers,
and with this activity concealed the weeping face of the other
woman that was discernible, she was sure, on her own face.

Around the Dear Ruin

My sister married Leo Brady because he was a merchant seaman and made good wages, and because he was gone most of the time. She and her five-year-old boy had been living on the sales of her cable car etchings that tourists to San Francisco picked over in the little art galleries and bookstores, and on the sporadic sales of her oil paintings. They were married a few days after he came from sea, and a week later his ship sailed again for the Orient. In the six weeks he was away, the steamship company sent her, at his request, all his wages. But the day that he returned was unrewarding for Leo.

Clara had her studio in an old building on Columbus Street. The first floor was occupied by the Garibaldi Club, whose members assembled every evening for cards; above her, on the top floor, lived two young men, a bank clerk and a window dresser. But she knew Leo's step on the bottom stair, and, lifting her head from the pillow, she said, "Why couldn't his ship have cracked in two? All the others did."

I was kneeling to help Mark, her boy, undress for bed, and I paused with my hands at his waist and lifted my head to hear her above his prattling. "Did you want anything?" She had been lying in a fever all day.

"Listen, listen!" she admonished me.

And I listened and heard the steps.

Swinging the boy lightly up, I sat him down on his bed. That day I had crew-cut his hair because he had wanted to imitate me, his Uncle Eddie, and his shorn skull sparked the tiny, blue confetti eyes that were like mine, like Clara's, and gave a malapert air to my red-striped T-shirt that I'd been wearing under my sweater and had slipped over him to sleep in; but it wasn't the moment to carry the boy out for her to admire. Wrapping him in under a couple of army blankets and a Mexican serape, I stepped out from behind the screen just as Leo set down his suitcase outside the door.

"Tell him I ate poisoned pigs' feet!" she cried in a desperate whisper. "It's called botulism. Tell him I died, Eddie," she begged. "I'll pull the sheet over my head and he'll go away."

Leo knocked shyly at the door as he opened it. When he entered, his bigness and his suitcase lent him a proprietary aura that he did not want. Up went his hand to remove his old black fedora, revealing beamingly, deferentially, his young, bald head.

"Clara's sick," I told him, when we had shaken hands.

Leo's brown eyes swelled sharply and his hands at once hung limply, unable to administer, in the artful way he felt necessary, the sympathy they held. With the contempt she had implanted in me, I thought: Why did he include himself in their marriage? If he really loved her then he would sacrificially send her his wages and never appear in person.

"She catch something?" he asked, his voice low and longing.

"The flu, I guess. She got me out of art school this morning."

"Did you call a doctor?"

"She doesn't want one."

As if walking in loose slippers, he tiptoed to her, and his throat and his eyes were full of love and of reluctant pleasure from the thought that she was helpless and he could help her. She was lying with her face toward the wall and she did not turn or move a muscle. Her long mane of coarse, unshining hair, the inert color of walnuts, lay out upon the pillow, and the very tip of this he bent twice to kiss.

"She's asleep," I said, taking my coat from the chair. "Mark's already in bed."

But he couldn't speak, so full of her presence was he, and bending again he kissed her hair for the third time.

"Eddie," she called.

The silence she ought to have kept overcame me.

"Going?" she spoke to the wall. "Okay, and always remember to contradict your teachers. It makes good biography." In spite of her dismay at his return and in spite of her weak condition, her voice took up again for Leo the thread of seduction, like a long-lost bad habit.

Leo was listening above the bed, his large body, in a leather jacket and black frisco jeans, solemn with his yearning toward the impending moment when she would realize, now that she was awake, that he had come home.

Imposed upon me as I ran down the two flights of stairs was the memory of all the delicacies Clara had been serving the past few weeks, the Sunday evenings I came to supper—things bought with Leo's money, like Italian pastries, lobster and crab, crème de cacao. The uneasiness I'd felt when partaking of that food struck at me now on the dim stairs like an accomplice Leo had left there. But I found justification for her exploiting him by recalling that all our years had been lean ones. In the town of Monterey, our father (his patron a real-estate woman, gross and canny, in whose house we all had lived) still sat in taverns, his duck pants colored by oil paint and spilled brandy, telling like an immortal Peeping Tom of intimacies of famous men from Biblical figures down through the centuries to Mussolini. At sixteen Clara had come up the coast to San Francisco and modeled at the art schools to pay for her tuition. A plain girl, short, long-waisted, heavy in the legs, she had seemed, contrarily, to be burning incense to herself; wrapped in a Japanese cotton kimono and wearing copper earrings like cymbals, she would ascend the dais, and the dropping of the kimono was always graceful and positive. Two years ago, when I graduated from high school and followed her, I arrived just in time to make the acquaintance of Mark's father, with whom she had been living for six years and who disappeared a few weeks after I met him. Small, dark-eyed, he had reminded me of a Shetland pony—any child could own him. All he left behind was a packing job in a ceramics shop and, like a guest departing, a copy of a highly literate quarterly containing two pages of his poetry. Leo Brady, a seaman with allegiance only to artists and a desire for talented women, came on the scene a year ago and had bided his time until another of her affairs had frayed and torn. The marriage, on her part, was an act of panic. The week he spent with her before his ship sailed she was drunk day and night, a half-nude, hanging-haired drunkenness that he mistook for celebration. My recall of these things and the sympathy for her evoked by them absolved me of the guilt of complicity, leaving me free to slip out unburdened into the cool evening and to forget even her and her fever.

At noon when I knocked at the orange door there hung within the studio an atmosphere of drowsing tension. Leo called for me to enter. He was sitting by the window, and the glare of noon revealed strikingly the shabbiness that had accumulated since his return. Hope had ebbed from his eyes, in the way a mirage leaves the air empty; the pinstripe shirt was partly out from his jeans and open halfway down his chest; and the black socks he'd been walking around in had fallen at the ankles and their soles were dusty. He put his finger to his lips.

"Who's there?" Clara asked.

"I thought you were asleep," he said.

"Not till I die," she replied, her voice like green brass. She turned on her back, laying her arms above her head, but saying nothing more. Her face was opalescent, wedge-shaped by pain, and my heart turned over.

"Did you call a doctor?" I asked, sitting by him.

"She won't let me."

"Did she sleep all right?"

"With her eyes open."

I shrugged. "Maybe she knows what's wrong and has her own remedy." And to comfort him: "When she gets a little better, she'll realize you're home."

"She knows it," he said loudly, snipingly, in spite of himself.

"Oh God, I know it!" There was always an unpredictability about her, and when she rose onto her elbows, flinging her hair back, she gave me the same shock as would the sight of a mermaid rising from the waters of a public beach. "It wouldn't be so bad if I could just forget him when he's gone, but it didn't work." She dropped her chin toward her chest. "Eddie," she wailed, "I feel terrible. Call Dr. Larson and tell him I'm dying. Tell him to save me."

But when I stood up she stared at me with a ponderous frown, her eyes deep inside her head, like pebbles. "Where you going?" she demanded. "You just got here. What the hell is the matter with you, you didn't have to come at all." Her strangeness poked a sharp finger into my chest, and I sat down again for a complying moment.

"You asked me to call your doctor."

"You been directing all your questions at him," she complained, "and he doesn't know a damn thing." She lay down again, staring up at the ceiling. "How simple are his wants. All he desires is to identify himself with artists. He married Clara Ruchenski because she'd had an exhibit in some dank little gallery and sold a painting once a year. How happy he was on our wedding night. I thought people didn't get that happy anymore, not since before the Flood when everybody was a brute with a big, smiling face. No, no, I'm wrong!" she wailed, tossing her head from side to side. "I take it all back. I never did think like that about Leo. I'm not a snob. Please, Eddie," she begged, "you know I'm not. You know me, don't you, Eddie?"

Leo and I stood up.

"I don't hate him, Eddie. I mean I wouldn't if I weren't married to him. He'd be a big, sweet guy with a respect for artists. That's the way I used to think, and I slept with him a few times, too."

"Be quiet, be quiet," I said.

"You shut up!" she cried, rising again on her elbows. "You're so good, aren't you? I hate to take you along to a party, always hanging in a corner like a tintype of a great artist in his youth and obscurity. If there's anything I hate it's hang-cheek people." She tossed her hair behind her and, thinking it was still falling forward, went groping for it with a blind hand over her breasts.

Leo was putting on his shoes and coat, his movements the sibilant, busy ones of a hurt person departing.

"Leo Brady! Don't let me hear you walking on tiptoe anymore," she cried. "I listen to your quiet and it's a terrible din."

"Lie down, Clara," I said when Leo had closed the door after him, and her hair was grimy damp to my palm.

"Eddie, Eddie!" she wept dryly, lying back and clamping my wrist in both her hands, and her bared teeth were coated with the suffering that she had concealed from us.

When I got down to the sidewalk he was standing with his hands in his pockets, squinting up at the sun, his small, flat, pocked face grayed by the slashing pain in his heart. "Is it time for the kid to come home?" he asked. "I could buy him a meal in a restaurant so he wouldn't have to go up."

Together we walked the few doors to the bakery, and he stared bleakly at the Italian pastries while I called her doctor on the pay phone. Then for a few minutes I waited on the sidewalk with him for the woman who took Mark to kindergarten in her car, along with her own son, and brought him back.

"Why in the hell didn't she marry Picasso, then?" he said.

Shrugs were becoming habitual with me. I was unable to tell him what I had discovered, that she had married him at the nadir of her life. She was twenty-six already and none of the dreams had come true. Leo beside me, a sailor home from the sea, a motherly young man, was unaware that he had been inflated into a grotesque figure, beyond anyone's recognition, by her terrible fear of the anonymous and the unsung.

Leo sat down on the stairs just inside the entrance, and I went up again. The door was open and inside the studio, Mark, who had returned while we were in the bakery, was leaning against the wall, crying. At first I thought that Clara was comforting him from a distance, urging him to come to her. But she was complaining about the Chinese boy who sometimes sits on a crate full of blue pigeons in front of a poultry and fish shop in Chinatown and, lifting out a fluttering bird at a time, cuts its throat while its wings stretch fanwise across his forearm. She was pleading with the boy to stop, her voice thin, bewitched, like that of a pigeon granted a human voice in the last moment of its life. Mark was crying because she did not recognize him.

His back was to her and in his hands he held protectively from her his red oilcloth briefcase in which he always brought home his crayon drawings for her to see.

Leo rode a bus across the Golden Gate Bridge to Muir Woods, carrying the urn in a paper sack. Under the big redwood trees he spilled her ashes, on that spot where he had first kissed her, the day they had picnicked there and she had painted a water-color. On his return to the city later in the day, he gave the urn to a junk dealer on McAllister Street, and there was nothing more to attend to. Mark had been taken up to Santa Rosa by his paternal grandparents, owners of a chicken ranch, responsible people who, whenever they drove down to San Francisco, had always brought money for Clara, and fresh eggs and poultry. Leo trudged down to the hiring hall, sat for a day and a half, and signed aboard a Pacific Far East Line freighter sailing for Manila, Yokohama, and Hong Kong. The night before he left he came to my room, and I served him sherry and panettone. He sipped and chewed awkwardly, ashamed in my presence, unable to formulate a reason why she had so frantically wanted to rid herself of his child that she had undergone surgery performed by nobody knew who, some man or woman in a shaded kit-chen whose window we could never identify in the city's hun-dreds of vertical lines of windows.

With a slice of panettone balanced on his fingers, he said at last, "We could of afforded a kid. We could of afforded nine of them. She didn't need to worry." His face was set forward as into a smarting wind. "I got three brothers and two sisters. We didn't live on caviar, but we loved each other. My father was a skilled mason, laid the steps on a lot of those civic center build-ings in Los Angeles."

A raisin from the slice he held fell to the floor, and he leaned over heavily, apologetically, picked it up and placed it deli-cately on the table's edge.

From Yokohama he wrote me a short letter, asking me to take good care of his record collection and the puppets he had brought from Italy after the war, armored knights a foot high that hung on the studio walls. His letter was like a note of greeting and reminder that a connoisseur, traveling, might address to the caretaker of his apartment's treasures. On that last evening he had persuaded me to move out of my one room and into Clara's studio. "If you don't mind," Leo had said, "I could leave my things there and when I come in between runs maybe you could put me up for a couple of nights." But when his ship docked again in San Francisco he didn't call on me.

Once in a while when Clara was alive and I had an evening free from the janitor work that paid my tuition at the art school and from handpainting silk blouses for a wholesaler, the labor I lived by, then I used to go down to Vesuvio's and have a glass of wine with Clara and her friends. But I never went anymore after Clara died, for mourning's sake and because of the pity that overwhelmed me whenever I remembered her lying demented and dying, and I remembered often. Since I kept away from her friends, I heard next to nothing about Leo. In January, eight months since the evening he said goodbye, I received a second letter, from Kobe, inquiring about Mark and about my studies. But he gave me no address where I could reach him, so I gathered he didn't care for an answer. Then one midnight in March I met him on the street near Vesuvio's, and a woman was with him.

Leo saw me approach and waited, blinking resignedly.

"Well, Leo," I said, shaking his hand. "Why don't you let anybody know when you get into town?" Glasses clarified his eyes now, and he wore a navy blue suit, doubly buttoned across his heaviness.

Leo introduced the woman as Evelyn, and she smiled at me nimbly, her crowded teeth curving out from under her upper lip. She was a red-haired, attractive woman, her full bosom snugly wrapped by her green silk dress. Leo asked me to accompany them to Vesuvio's, and the woman walked ahead of us, a precise, quick, ballet walk in low heels, her long coat swinging smartly. A day or so later I heard from someone at school that she was the estranged wife of the psychiatrist, Irving Eidel, and that she was engaging in an affair, in imitation of her husband.

Over the first pouring of wine, Leo clasped my shoulder. "Saw a painting of yours at the museum," he said. "You're doing all right, kid . . . And he's only twenty-one," he said to Evelyn. The fear of ridicule took a quick sidestep across his face. "You don't paint like your sister did," he said to me. "You got human beings in yours. Her pictures all looked like broken glass. I always felt like I was walking barefoot in broken glass."

"If you'd wear shoes you wouldn't get hurt," the woman said.

"I'm not talking about art," he replied, coloring. "I'm talking about Clara. I was married to her."

"*That* I've heard before," she said, sharpening. "Is it your only claim to distinction? Haven't you even got a battle ribbon to talk about?"

Behind his glasses his eyes went small in humiliation. I put my hands against the table to move it away from him, for his anger was jamming him in between the table and the wall. But the woman slipped her arms around his neck, kissing him on his throat. "The trouble with you, Leo baby," she said pawingly, "is you don't love yourself."

"Don't give me any of that crap," he said, straining away from her. "You want me to kiss myself in the mirror every night?"

She began to laugh, her teeth springing forward handsomely, her sloping shoulders shaking. After a moment her laughter lost its erudition and became simpler. With her quaking body against his chest, he drew one arm out from her encircling arms, turned his face up and lit a cigarette. Then he gave way and laughed himself, a contrapuntal laugh, high in his nose, deep in his chest. While this was going on, four of their friends filed through the swinging doors and drew up chairs around the table. None of them had I met before.

"He's Clara Ruchenski's brother," Leo said, introducing me to one couple. "They're from New York," he explained to me. "They never met her." And of them he asked, "When did you come out to the Coast?"

"Last August," the woman replied.

"She died a year ago May," he said.

Evelyn Eidel was chatting with the other couple and didn't hear. After a few minutes I left, because I had to be at the school early to help open doors, I said. But my impatience with Leo was growing unbearable and it seemed to me that I pressed my elbows to my sides not to make room for other persons but to keep myself from jolting everyone away from me.

One Sunday morning a month later, I was wakened at six o'clock by Leo knocking at my door. Defensively, he wore the preoccupied, hounded look of a fiction detective who can intrude upon anyone at any hour. Sitting before my drawing board, he remarked on the changes in the studio. My untidiness prevailed. The chartreuse velvet spread that Clara had laid over the broad couch was worn away in spots; and only one painting remained of Clara's, a small red and blue abstract that I had chosen to keep. The others, big and small, had been sold at an exhibit of her work at the Contemporary Gallery. But the four Italian knights in armor hung on the wall still, and his record collection was neatly upright in its section of the record case. He didn't comment on his belongings.

"Did you hear that Evelyn and I broke up?" he asked when we sat down to breakfast. "No, you couldn't of so soon. It happened last night. Nobody's heard about it yet." He picked up his fork. "I been walking around all night."

Oh, I see, you want the parting to break the Sabbath calm, I accused him silently. You can hardly wait until the word is spread around among your artist friends and you are the subject of animated conversation.

"She took a liking to me at first," he went on. "Practically hog-tied me. I figured she saw me for myself, saw me with angel eyes. You know how you always wait for somebody to come along and see your heart of gold, right smack they look into your eyes for the first time?" He gave one short, great cough to clear his chest. "But she only wanted some guy to sit at her feet. No intellectual. She was roughing it." He removed his glasses and the flesh around his eyes was puffed to receive a blow.

I said, "You should have learned something from Clara. I was only an eyewitness, but I learned that you kneel too much."

Expertly his eyes jabbed at me. "Be an eyewitness to this too, Eddie," he said coldly. "You'll be an eyewitness to a lot of things before you're my age." Again he slipped his glasses on, his careful, trembling hand foretelling how he would be in his old age, and, reaching into his coat pocket, he brought out a tiny, enameled box, the kind for carrying pills in. Blue roses were painted on it.

"Never showed this to anybody but you," he said. "Don't get scared, but in this box is all that remains of Clara Ruchenski. The rest of the ashes are already part of the leaf mold and people have picnicked over her. But there's a little bit of ashes in here, took it for myself when I scattered the rest. Want to see?"

With false aplomb he bounced the box in his hand in an attempt to forestall his collapse, for his voice was breaking and falling in his chest. All at once I crossed my arms against my chest to keep down my own sorrow over Clara.

"She's in the palm of my hand," he said. "That's why I kept this. She's harmless. She's nothing. If I took the ashes between my fingers, it would powder off into air. But I'm alive, God damn it, and that means something. There's a big difference between alive and dead. This is what they come to," he said, shaking so much that he had to stand up, and precisely he set the box down by the salt and pepper shakers. "This is what they come to. They're the stupid ones. They go crazy. They go crazy and eat dirt."

Jerking the chair far out with an elaborate gesture, he sat down again, pressing his forehead against the table's edge. After a while he spoke to the floor. "It's over me like a ton of water, the things I don't know." When he lifted his head to see my face, there was a red mark across his brow from the table.

Myra

On the weedy floor of the valley lie the mudbrown matchboxes, each a row of ten rooms under one flat roof, and a narrow wooden porch runs the length of it, each man's porch his neighbor's also. Four boxes face each other to form a square, the earth of it hard as rock in summer, rutty with holes in the rain, and the many boxes and their squares are a maze that covers the valley. A few small trees, straggling lines of them hardly as high as the low dwellings, prettify the roads that intersect the project. Sometimes a loud, topheavy flickering and haggling of sparrows make a tree's presence known, or they make themselves known in the spring by their sungreen foliage, but for most of the year they are lost in the barren scene, under them stripped cars rusting or new ones, red and pink and blue-jay blue, reflecting the sun in their chrome.

The hills rise around three sides of the valley and thick upon them are more dwellings, but up here the houses are in pairs, family houses, standing back to back, and crowding in upon the highest of them are groves of oak and eucalyptus and madrona. Up here, the tenants can see the islands and the bay, can see, across a narrow inlet, brown hills casting brown reflections and the white egrets standing on their hairpin legs in the shallows; can see, farther out, the high cliffs of Belvedere with the raw, flesh-colored frames of the new houses hanging out over the water; can see the traffic on the highway that runs past the project—the huge trucks with their names read half a mile away and the cars swerving around the trucks on the long climb up to the bridge.

On Sunday, the men who dig the earth for the foundations of the houses all over the county, pour the concrete, carry the lumber on their shoulders, light the early morning fires for the carpenters to warm their hands by, on Sunday, some of them, some of the younger ones, lounge in their cars way up on the rim of the project. They sit in their cars and drink from beer cans and bottles, and their high–low laughter, their richly loud voices sound among the trees behind them, along with the fall of the cans on the carpet of wrinkled pods and acorns. They sit up here and survey all.

Their women are left to themselves. They do their household tasks as they do on weekdays; they go to church in the morning, and in the afternoon they visit next door, an hour or so over a beer, with the door open onto the common porch, a rock for a doorstop, to let out the heat from the room and the smell of mustard greens and the kerosene that feeds the stove, and then they go back and lie down on their beds and nap, and the sweat breaks out in rings around their eyes. In the hot weather there is no current of air, and in the cold, the high, capricious heat is piped along above the ceiling, all along the rooms. This Sunday abandonment happened to Myra Hall, young as she was, comely as she was, slender, hipless, and tall, with her head high and her eyes always down, her skin red-brown and smooth like the madrona trees when the bark peels away.

It began at the end of the first year of their marriage. Before that, she and Lionel did things together on Sunday. They drove up to visit his brother's family on the outskirts of Petaluma, spending the day there, and when they walked around the yard, holding hands, she would scuffle up red chicken feathers with the toes of her high-heeled sandals. She was a city-bred girl, born in San Francisco and never away from there in her nineteen years. The country delighted her, and sometimes, because she liked to see her hands clutching his shirt, she exaggerated her response to a garter snake, a tomato worm, a spider with a body like a cherry. On other Sundays they went fishing in Sausalito, out on the old ferry slip, picnicking on fried chicken and pie. All around them the sea gulls sat on pilings or walked close on the planks to see what was to be done with the bait and the fish. The seawater thudded and smacked around the old timbers, and far across the water the white fog blew in, its feathery edges melting in the sun and the shining towers of the city floating above it; and once in a while he would duck his head and kiss her nipple, take sweater and nipple into his mouth, and her eyes would narrow down and all she could see was a long glitter, like a glittering wave. Or they stayed in their room all Sunday, the door still locked from the night and the green blinds down and the lace curtains closed, and while people passed along the wooden porch and cars pulled in and out of the lot and dogs tumbled and growled together against the door and a mixed-up cat meowed at the crack and the heavy, dusty Sunday weighed down upon all the flat roofs, they stayed in there to love. With the covers thrown down at the foot of the bed, they slept. They took turns fixing something to eat, and when she stood in her dark nakedness by the stove he would say, "Come here, come back, forget that." All those Sundays belonged to the first year; then he began to go out without her.

Along about eleven o'clock in the morning, as she was washing dishes in the narrow kitchen that was filled with the smell of bacon and shaving soap, he would open the door and go out into the coming noon, and she never knew where he was going. He didn't know himself, he said, "So how can I tell *you*, woman?" She swore at him when he left and when he returned, and if she was out to a movie or visiting a girl friend and returned and found him playing solitaire or already in bed, she swore at him then. He would tell her where he had been, with this fellow or that one, as if it were the most natural thing in the world for him to be with his men friends all day Sunday.

When she got pregnant, unable to express to him the secret pleasures of the experience and, in a way, not wanting to, she fell silent, was sullenly, spiritedly silent, hoping that the pleasureless part of it, the leaning over the toilet bowl and the shuddering return to bed, would rouse his love. But he seemed to think that her bearing a child was the most natural thing in the world and undeserving of his attention. In the early months she almost miscarried. Opal came in from two doors down the porch and did her chores for her; she said, "You cry, you fidget so much, no wonder you gonna lose that baby. You as itchy as a worm in hot ashes," and left her alone. She lay in the dimmed room with nothing upon its partition walls but a sky-blue placard with gilt letters *God Bless Our Home* left by tenants before them. A salmon pink upholstered chair, a coffee table, a kitchen table, and the bed on which she lay, a walnut bed with its dark green spread—a room both crowded and bare. The windows were closed against the high winds that blew up after hot weather, the blind clicking in the stream of wind that came in through a crack. She lay alone in the room between two other rooms, the one on the west side burnt out, its tattered green blinds hanging at the paneless windows—months ago a kerosene stove had exploded, and the black, damp wood was still like pepper in the nostrils—and the other, an old couple's room, the man lying all day on a sofa by the door, his long, handsome body in soft and clean, yellowy long underwear, tended by his woman with her Old South kerchief on her head that was bent over the Bible she read to him or the bowl of food she fed him. She heard the cindery silence on the one side and the celled-in voices on the other, and remembered a sleep-walking night that Lionel had told her about, laughing, a night that had happened to him when he was a boy on his father's farm near Baton Rouge. He had killed a cricket, and that night the cricket was on him; he had walked in his sleep and seen rabbits swarming up out of the well and woke up out there bawling for his mother. But nothing was on his conscience now for stepping on a woman.

When the cramps weighed like an iron inside her, she went out to the green telephone booth standing like a sentry box by the road and phoned the clinic in the city. "Go back to bed," her doctor commanded, "and stay there," and she hung up without asking him about the other method of saving babies she had heard about—they gave the woman a hypo or something—and found her way back, a clothesline making a welt across her face. A colored baby was dirt to them, those smoothy doctors.

They didn't care whether a colored baby got born or not. When she went again to the clinic, as she did each month, and told the doctor that she had almost lost the baby, he said to her, "Calm down or we'll tie you down to a bed here and keep you down until delivery," and for a while, there in the examination room, in the reception room as she went out past the rows of waiting women, and part of the way home on the bus, she believed that they could do that to her, keep her prisoner because she could not calm herself.

One evening, as she stood by the stove, stirring up potatoes in the frying pan, her hand with the spatula in it was stopped by his slowing down as he took off his jacket; she sensed from his slowness that he was *seeing* her. "Maybe you better refuse them jobs," he said. "You don't want to be losing it. What you about now, six months?"

She was struck by his concern as by a blow. As if he had slung his hand across her face, she began to wail. She spread her hand over her rounding belly, closed her eyes, threw back her head and began to wail with all the agony of desiring to be close to him again. She stepped to him and clasped his body around, and he, after a moment of surprise, put his jacket on the table and tried to calm her by stroking her back, but it took a long time for her to feel his hands upon her. While he showered, she sat on the toilet cover, clasping her hands in her lap in a confusion of anxiety and relief, and when he stepped from the stall, drying himself with his army towel, she caressed him to prevent his returning again to ignorance of her. She stroked his back, she kissed his thighs, she made a mystic ceremony by getting down on her knees and kissing his feet. He was smiling foolishly, sparring her away, a sense of shame and delight in his eyes.

Confined by her behavior, he stayed home that evening. With a small comment about her condition he had triggered an avalanche of hysterical affection and he was pinned beneath it. He carried himself cautiously, stiffly, his eyes glancing away from hers. At eight o'clock a friend of his rapped at the door, and awkwardly he invited him in, a fellow with a loud body

and face but no voice. Myra sat at the table with them while
they drank their beer, her eyelids stretched far down over her
shifting green eyes that rounded out the lids in the way her
pregnancy rounded out her breasts and belly. Only Lionel
talked, rubbing and crossing his legs as he told a funny story.
The visit was short, but somewhere in the midst of it Lionel
slipped out from under her mood. He went out on the porch to
say goodbye to his friend, and Myra, still at the table, heard
their voices rising released into the night. Just at the moment
when she thought he would enter the room again, she heard his
voice farther out in the parking lot. For an hour he sat in his
friend's car and when he returned she knew by his face, which
was remembering banter, remembering gossip, remembering the clues given him to future joys, that she was again only in
the margin of his sight. She sat with her forearms out upon the
table, catlike, watching him sit himself down on the big chair's
edge and riffle the cards for solitaire on the coffee table. She
knew in her heart that he had no other woman, but she also
knew that he might have one soon. His return to the company
of men stirred up in him the need of pursuit again, and the
woman would be somebody else's wife, someone whose husband was in the army or away in Alaska working in the canner-
ies, because having himself a married woman was the next step
above having himself a girl. And she knew the way he'd treat
that woman, because she'd seen it done by other men: *You can
cling to me all you want, woman, clasp me around with your arms and
your thighs, but I ain't yours, I ain't nobody's,* a way that would
drive that silly woman crazy, whoever she was. But *something*
had got hold of him without mercy, something he liked as well
as he liked that woman waiting for him shamelessly in public
places, and it was his freedom to come and go, it was that
freedom of a man who is trapped by his color and will not be
trapped by anything else, by job, by children, by woman.
That's a puny thing, she wanted to scream at him. *That's a puny
thing, that's a hell of a kind of freedom you got.* But she didn't know
if she was right about him or how to say it if she was right, and
the only way she could tell him was to spit on the table. She spat

on the yellow flower of the oilcloth, wiped her mouth, and crawled into bed with her dress on.

Opal rapped at the door a few minutes after Lionel had left for work. A woman in Ross was asking Myra to come to work that day, Opal said, leading the way back to her room, her blue satin mules knocking annoyed against the porchboards, her behind moving like a nest of snakes in the tight, shiny nightgown. "Why'n she call you last night 'stead of this mornin'?" Opal complained, spitefully speaking forward instead of over her shoulder.

Myra sat sleepily at the foot of the bed, the phone in her lap. The caller was a woman she liked, an elderly, strong-voiced woman, an ex-nurse who lived in a two-story house within an acre of garden. She always felt friendly toward this woman, and she responded now without resentment to the masculine voice explaining that guests were coming that evening to stay for several days, that she had just learned late last night. Please, couldn't Myra come today?—a little ironing, a little cleaning up? "Yes," she said, yes, she'd come, she'd be there by nine o'clock, and heard the woman's laugh, an elderly, harsh, and broken laugh, the kind a person puts on to make you think she was at your mercy and you granted her her life. But when she hung up she remembered the weariness that came after her last job for another woman, a couple of weeks ago; she had stood all afternoon on the concrete floor of a basement, ironing fine sheets, frilly blouses, little girls' pinafores, linen napkins, while a tall gray poodle wandered in and out, out into the flowers and sun and up the high porch steps, his nails clicking on the floor above her head, a dog possessing the run of the house and the air. *What do you care if I die, you bastard?* she said to Lionel. *What do you care if I come back and die?*

Opal had humped in under the covers again. "What you say yes for?"

"I like that woman."

"You like her better'n your own baby?"

She went back along the porch on her bare feet, feeling apart from everyone, feeling jagged in her mind after last night's hysteria, hating the woman she had agreed to work for, that woman telephoning at half past seven in the morning, sure about claiming a colored woman's day, and she wanted to beat her breasts, for nothing fitted together anymore.

On the way back from the job, almost the moment she climbed down from the bus at the depot shack, the pangs began. She ran across the yards, the sooner to lie down, ducking under empty clotheslines, grappling and flailing her way through hanging laundry. By the time she got to her door, she was already tearing at the buttons of her blouse. She lay down in her slip and drew the covers up over her mouth.

Lionel fixed the ice bag for her the minute he got home. After he had showered, he cooked supper and brought her a plate of rice and leftover stew, and she leaned on her elbow to eat it, her head in her hand. The unshaded light above the table where he sat, facing her, deprived his narrow, bony face of its contours, flattening it into a newspaper face. "You strain yourself?" he asked her. "What you do to yourself?"

"I did my chores," she told him, and he felt the meanness in her and ate on without talking anymore.

Oh, get rid of this meanness for me, she begged him. *Why do you clam up and make it seem like meanness is my true nature?* No words from him, just the tink of his fork on the plate and the stuffed-nose way he breathed when he ate. Her arm began to quake with weariness, and at that moment she wondered if even her half-up position was risky. She leaned over the side of the bed to put the plate on the floor and lay back, and her disgust with the few forkfuls she had eaten and with his happy drudgery way of eating and with the nothingness between them in this hour when the child was losing its poor, watery-handed hold of life rose up in a long wrench of a wail.

"Jesus," he whispered. "What do you want of me?"

She stared up at the stains of rain on the ceiling, the pictures of bears and monkeys they had picked out long ago as they lay there. How could a man change like that? His entire body aware of her, even the soles of his feet against her feet, and then be that person no more? And why was it she could not tell anybody of what it did to her, though it sat day and night in her mind? Even if her mother came alive again, came back on a nightmare visit and knocked at the door, she could not tell *her,* though she came wearing her black faille dress and gloves and hat, came to be *told.* Was this swelling of herself the thing she couldn't say to anybody? No child, but the misery of his ignorance of her?

"You want me to get Opal?" he asked.

"Don't bother yourself," she said, and turning her face to the wall experienced a great longing love for the abused child within her, the child that was only becoming and that was treated so cruelly by its mother even so early, so soon. She wept, and her weeping calmed his fear — she could not weep, he thought, if she were in pain — for she heard again his fork against his plate.

She dozed, wrapped in the quilts and in the heat that was forced into the room and into all the rooms down the box and all the boxes in the valley, until heat and quilts and pain became one, an unbearable, strangling quilt that brought her awake in terror, and she called to him. She heard a chair pushed back and saw him stand, and knew by the slouch in his body, by the quietness in the yards, that early evening had passed and it was night. "Go get somebody," she told him, and felt no love anymore for the child or for anybody.

Opal came, and the old woman with the pale yellow scarf tight over her skull, and a grin of sorrowing exertion whose center was a tooth's gold cap, perforated with a four-leaf clover, a cap gleaming like the hope of prosperity. They eased the protest from her body and disposed of it for her. The thing she was rid of, she saw now, was her complaining against him, and she was ashamed of it, as if she had wrung her hands at every door along the porch. The real child would be born in the afterwards of this one, born to a woman. They washed her bent legs and feet, and she felt that the knuckles of her fingers were like brown, empty snail shells through which the light would shine if she held up her hands, and that the lashing-out had quit her tongue forever, that there were no more words and no more anger to spit out on the table. By the time a stranger-doctor came, almost an hour after Lionel had phoned him, she was falling asleep under the women's ministrations, even as they were wiping her face of its sourness and salt.

Like a Motherless Child

The old woman crossing the street had a blue scarf drawn over her head and tied under her chin, and the string of lights at the market entrance so enlivened the color, that the men drinking their beer in the row of cars at the curb transformed her for a few alert moments into a girl. When a car's headlights came fast down the hill, she darted to an island in the road and told her age in the shadowy scoop in her skirt made by the space between her scuttling thighs, a cradling bare of comfort.

Jennie Griggs wasn't one to wait for a car to pass, she always ran when she saw one coming, not in panic but because her own intentions came first. The ground was caked in this area around the market. A week ago a heavy storm had filled it with water; the muddy water ran down from the hills all around and filled it like a bowl, and cars bogged down and branches floated on it. After seven days of hot sun, the layer of mud over the asphalt curled up into patches of dry crust like the bark of a tree, and hop-skipping across it in her gray tennis shoes, Jennie thought: It's nice for children to jump on and crackle, but for old people it's only confusing.

In she went among the eucalyptus trees towering behind the market, a midnight area in the green light of early evening, with a clearing in its heart for the padlocked red kerosene shack where tenants filled their jars and gallon cans, and came out, after a high, gaspy step over a ditch, onto the road that led her up to the houses among the hills. The April evening had settled down only half an hour ago, waiting until everybody had eaten supper by daylight, and waiting, even, for some women to remember their washing and gather it in, but not waiting, it never did, for children to come in from the roads and the grassy

slopes. She heard them around her, taking leave of one another
by climbing the porches of home and running down again,
by wrestling with arms that wouldn't let go, and the fennel
they had trampled in the day's roaming was fragrant on the
cooling air.

She paused in the grass by the turn of the road, by the porch
of the house that was the nursery school by day and used at
night by whatever group wanted it, to listen to the stamping of
feet and the women singing. The flat-roofed, redwood house
was like all the others, but over the lower half of its windows
red paper was glued, and the light from within transformed
the panes into the ruby red of stained glass. The women rode
along upon the pulsation, upon the stamping and clapping
beat, like faraway women carried along a river, waving their
arms, and she thought if she had lived among Negro people
when she was young and had heard this beat of this never-
ending river, she would surely have given in to it and got
religion, gone to prayer meeting six times a week, hung a
colored picture of Jesus above her bed, and crocheted *Jesus
Saves* for a front door curtain. It was too late now, but she
might have learned some humility then, she mused, stumbling
back onto the road. Now she liked to manipulate things herself
too much, she had a little bit of Jehovah in herself, a bit of His
cunning and His domination, and she didn't want to give it up.

Her legs were toughened from climbing the hills for twelve
years, calling on her friends, but she took more time than she
had taken in the early years because now her breath was traitor-
ous. The more infirm she became, the less tolerant of infirmity,
and whenever she lay sick or was hobbled by arthritis, she
accused the parts of her body of betrayal, and right along with
her spirit's alienation from her body she feared betrayal by her
friends, a scorning of her wisdom, a gesture of ridicule at her
departure. Once in a while she glimpsed this trend in herself
and was afraid of it, but it was out of hand like the brittling of
her bones. God must have been awfully old and shaky when
He created Man, she thought, because in the Bible He was
always accusing people, always coming up behind them.

Up among the houses by the highest road she sought for the

shadow of the apricot tree that was thrown upon N. T. Gatewood's door by the porch light of the house facing his. She had ways of finding the houses of everybody she called on, for it was easy to knock at the wrong door. All the houses were alike, and a dim bulb here and there didn't reveal the faded white numbers painted on the walls.

N. T. Gatewood rose from his green plastic lounge chair—she saw him through the window to the right of the door—and in his elderly surprise knocked askew the rosy lampshade. N. T. never called out for anyone to enter, he preferred the formality of opening the door himself, and he took so long this time, pushing his slippers across the room, trying to get his stockinged feet into them as he walked, that his daughter came out into the hallway to help him answer the knock, drawing her white satin robe around her.

N. T. was not a petty hypocrite; if he was not pleased to see you he did not smile and greet you, he gazed at you with glum curiosity. Jennie Griggs always countered this reception by becoming offensively forward, like a small, nervous dog that does not distinguish between the learned and the unlearned when it barks at people. In the doorway she bristled up at him, "You seen the notice they got posted over by Keever's office?"

He nodded, opening his mouth to say something.

"Let me tell you what it says," she went on.

"I read it, I tell you," he broke in, greatly irritated, and flapped his hand toward the sofa.

"You read it?" she asked the girl, and the girl shook her head. They had never met, and this was the spontaneous, irreverent way Jennie liked to meet a person. Only a few days ago the girl had moved over from the city to live with her father. He was ailing, and he wanted the comfort of calling to his daughter in the night.

N. T. folded up inside his chair, saying that this was Jennie Griggs and this was his daughter Vida, and old Jennie, already crossing her legs on the couch, nodded at the girl, who nodded back in an efficiently lovely way and disappeared down the hallway.

"My daughter is a social worker," N. T. said. "All my

children are doing well," he went on, since his visitor did not agreeably remind him of it. "Darcey, that's my oldest boy, he's a lawyer in Chicago, got some big clients. Clyde, he's a news-paperman in Los Angeles." He chuckled mechanically, as if she were clucking her tongue with envy. "I used to be in the newspaper game myself, got the job for him. Vida, she inter-views people over at the University Hospital. She helps those that need help and she weeds out the dishonest ones."

His shirt was too large for him, the collar rose higher as he sank lower. A wine wool shirt of expensive cut, it had proba-bly been sent as a hand-me-down by the Chicago son, and the color of it put a coppery fever in the old man's dark skin, as from an agitation of parental pride. His narrow slippers were of fine leather, glowing with wax, a recent gift, perhaps for Easter, and the chair—that, too, was a gift from some time back. That's why you've gone to seed in your old age, she said to him silently—your children turned out well and things aren't as bad as you thought they were when you were young. If my children sent me a big slick chair I wouldn't be using the edge of your sofa.

She untied the blue scarf. "Well, you seen the sign," she said, spreading her hands over her thin tangled hair to feel for hang-ing hairpins.

A click of contempt in his nostrils, like the sound of beetle wings folding. "What's the matter with you that you didn't expect it all along?" he asked her, carefully enunciating as for a lip reader. "We've known for years that someday we'd be told to remove ourselves and all our earthly possessions from this place. Do you wish to remain here forever?" He waved a long, limp hand toward the kitchen. "The houses will soon be falling down around us. The time we had the storm, the rain filled up a roasting pan we put in the corner under the drip, filled it up in half an hour. We called Keever, and he sent a man over to fix it. But there's other things wrong, too. Afflictions seldom come one at a time. It's the same way with a person. My heart is not my only trouble."

She smoothed her skirt over her knees to keep her eyes away

from the inward musing of his face, for she knew that in his manhood he would never have complained about anything physical. Somewhere along the line, she thought, we begin to give in to the things we detest.

"You think that's bad?" she countered. "The rain came in so bad down in the flats where we are, we had to move Henrietta's bed, and then we couldn't sleep all night for the rain pounding in the buckets. She don't see well, you know, and everything sounded double bad to her, and she says, 'Sounds like Noah's rain must of sounded in the pots and pans of them wicked people.' But you think it's going to make us happy to get kicked out altogether? It'll rain just as bad inside some other place we go. You think I ain't lived in those basements over in San Francisco? Dark in the middle of summer like you're walking around in your grave. Say, I lived over there. And the walls like a big map of the United States, all made by water seeping in. And I lived over on Larkspur Creek in this county, when my daughter and her husband had a houseboat over there. Shook and rocked in a storm, and everything green mold, even your nightgown when you got up in the morning. If you're poor you're wet wherever you go."

The lag of defeat in his eyes, N. T. gazed at her large hands flying now to the scarf in her lap to shake it and smooth it, now to her sweater pocket to stuff the scarf away.

"But in nice weather," she went on without delay, "there's things here you can't find anywhere else. Look out your own windows, you can see the green hills all around, and the oaks. I can see them when I hang out the laundry, I got to go out in the yard, but you can see them standing on a rug."

N. T. picked his newspaper off the floor and folded it up. "You look at history," he said, "and you'll see people have got to move along, move around. Some people move three miles and some twenty, and some people plant apple seeds in the wilderness, they set up their tents on alien soil."

Nodding vigorously, she cried, "That's right, that's right. That's what I mean when I say the government got no right to kick us off this land, because most of us we come from somewhere else, we come here to build Liberty ships, and they was good enough to put up houses for us right above the shipyards because they wanted us here. And some of our kids, the first thing they ever saw was the green hills around. That's right," she said, still nodding hard.

Now with fitful fingers he unfolded the newspaper, spreading it across his lap and bending forward to see if he could do anything about the edge that extended beyond his knees. "What're you coming to me for?" he asked.

"You got pull," she said. "Take a man like Keever, he hops for you. Whenever somebody needs a faucet or a pane of glass or the oil stove don't work, and they can't get Keever to do anything, don't they come up and see you?" And don't you always, she thought, explain like a lawyer that it's not Keever's fault that the government don't come through with decent appropriations anymore for the upkeep, before you put your hat on and go see him? And if he's got no excuse, you figure one out for him. You hop for Keever, that's why he hops to get your roof fixed. You're his apology man. "And that congressman—what's his name, McMahon?—he'd hop for you, too. He's a friend of yours, ain't he? You was handing out his picture to elect him, you was in charge of getting him votes in this project. Write him a letter for the people who live here and ask him what he can do to see the people don't get kicked off the land. So if there's a law that says the government is going to tear down the houses by June next year and sell the land, you can tell him that houses may of been built for temporary but people never was built that way, they was built to last a lifetime and what's the government going to do about the folks that got no place to go? Where *you* going?" she challenged him, and before he could answer, "Henrietta's niece, she says to me—she's got three kids—'Where'm I gonna go? Over in the Fillmore in the city that's the only place we're allowed, and they're tearing that down because it's slums and they got a hard enough time settling the families that's evicted.' That's what she said to me." She was sitting stiffly as if on a leather chair in the office of the congressman, afraid that to relax was to compromise.

N. T., as she harassed him, pretended to peer down the columns of the newspaper. "By the time it takes to get a new law passed," he informed her, "we'll all be cleared out anyway, long before."

"You ought to write that letter, anyway," she said.

He slapped the open newspaper with the side of his hand, wedging the paper down between his knees. "What I'm saying is this," he cried, his voice rising over hers like a larger bird. "When they pass a law it's got a lot of reasoning behind it, and nobody there in the nation's capital is going to be in any hurry to do away with a law that got put on the books after all the hearings and that sort of thing. I'm not saying there aren't some laws that should never have got passed, and I'm not saying there aren't some wicked men who get themselves elected to public office, but someday they've got to answer for their sins, and if the people don't punish them, God will. What I'm saying is that you're not going to move mountains with any letter. There are only a few of these projects left, and Congress isn't going to change any law just to take care of one or two. The people who were made to go from those other projects, they'd be sore." After speaking, he struggled to un-crease the newspaper, swatting at it and spreading it out.

Jennie wiped her dry, limber nose with the blue scarf. "It don't matter and it never did matter how many victims go before it's your turn or your children's turn. If you got any heart in you, you still try to save them from whatever they been condemned to. You don't say let 'em go because you don't want to hurt the feelings of them that are dead already."

The scarf, left by Joyce on her last visit, was rippled with the odor of cologne, and she wished that she had not worn it, for if N. T.'s daughter had got the scent of it, the girl would remember the scarf as verification of the story her father was sure to tell her, of Jennie's daughter. She rose, shook out the scarf flauntingly as if it were a square of sky, biblically blue, tied it

under her chin again, and turned the doorknob, her agility
denying the despair caused by her ramming attack upon an
ailing old man who could do nothing more than write a letter
in longhand. They were flattering each other with abuse and
that was all they could do.

Out on the porch, she saw, beyond old N. T. in the doorway, his daughter coming down the hallway. The girl was in a
slim black coat over a flowered dress, silver earrings tingled
with light, and she was plunging her hand into a large leather
purse, searching for keys to the smart gray car parked alongside the house.

Padding her way along the dirt road with two small dogs
sneezing and snarling at her bare ankles, Jennie found the porch
with the pots of plants along the rail that marked the shortcut
down the hill. It was a risky descent, the steps hewn into the
earth by children's leapings and women climbing up and down
to visit. She ought to have kept along the road, she chided
herself as her foot felt out the depth of a step, but the girl would
have stopped the car to ask if she wanted a lift to the flats, and
she didn't want to sit beside the girl, folding her hands in a
posture of gratefulness. The girl had the quality of a finished
product; she was—Jennie was sure of it—dominatingly slow
in explaining things to the ignoramuses and failures who came
to her for help, the way most of the social workers were who
had questioned her through the years. The girl aroused in her a
sympathy akin to that she felt for small and lovely, thin-legged
birds, but in this retreat from Gatewood's presence, Jennie felt
the need to damn them both.

From up here she could see the city, glittering hard as glass
in the night with all the soft colors of sun and air and mist, and
the pink streamers of light that the city sent out into the black
waters of the bay almost touched the shore at the foot of the
hills where the dark remains of the shipyard lay like pilings
of timber. The only light down there shone above the auto
wrecking yard that occupied an acre of the deserted place.
Sometime soon, she said, they won't allow no pensioneer old
lady to see around from up here. The sight of the city will

belong to those who can afford it, and no little black faces will wonder at windowsills at night about the blinking red lights on the tips of the towers of the bridges. Gutturally she said, "Get away, get away," to the dogs that had left her heels way back on the road above.

She passed close to houses, hearing the aerated voices from the radios and TV sets, her descent relayed by the barking of dogs and the rattling of the gates that confined them to the narrow porches. Along in the grass by the lower road she bent over, her hand on her knee to brace herself, to pick up a child's tinny trinket glinting, a birdcage no larger than the cushion of her thumb that was rubbing dirt from it. Oh, say, wouldn't Orville like this! she crowed. Or Joyce or Hamden or Justin, placing her children in her room in the flats, all waiting cozily in a circle on the floor, telling stories in low voices and laughing high at the end of them. And their faces were long ovals, their sandy hair scrubby where her scissors had cut, and their eyes in the lamplight like the black cabochon eyes of little animals in the forest, and each of them thin and loud and surprising to her as the triangle that rings out in an orchestra. How many trinkets had she brought to them, and shells and bird feathers, beach pebbles and gold-veined rocks? Although she had picked them up matter-of-factly, as though compelled by her tidy nature to clean up after molting birds and geological shiftings, she had given them to her children with an air of mystery. Some benevolent spirit had dropped them in her path, conveying to her, with these many small gifts, the news that her children were to be favored by fate, were to be beautiful and great, humane and beloved. She had no child at home now, but she cocked her head at the trinket.

Say now, look at that, Justin! she cried. Inside the cage was a tiny green parrot on a perch. More than the rest of her children, Justin had perceived the prophecy in the things she brought home, the richness of existence that the things foretold, and he had died the youngest. In the Philippines, bombed to the bottom of the sea. The names of the islands were cruel words, untranslatable except in the sorrow of the bereaved. She squinted at the trinket turning in her fingers and knew that she had climbed to Old Man Gatewood for a selfish reason, no matter how she had barked at him about saving his own people. For she had come in her old age into a fertile valley and she had no provisions for the wilderness. She was an old woman afraid of another room, another street, another cashier in another market, afraid now, almost, of the people of her own skin, finding comfort among the ostracized. She was an old woman, seventy-one, stopping to pick up a trinket in the belief that it was a token for her to take home to her children. But Justin was at the bottom of the sea; and Orville worked in the Texas oil fields and wrote to her once a year, and his children had never seen her; and Hamden—nobody had heard from him in twelve years—and, sometimes, when she got her pension check and went into the city with her paper shopping bag to look around in the basements of the stores, she'd go into a cafeteria, after, and be afraid that she'd see him among the unshaven men hanging their poor wino heads over their bowls of navy bean soup; and Joyce—it wasn't her husband who had been with them at the Creek, for she had no mate and no children, and she might as well have been born to another mother, there was no spirit in her for her own rights, only the rights of the men who wanted her. They were lost to her, her children, every one of them, and she was as timorous, in this moment on the road in the night, as a motherless child.

She pocketed the tiny birdcage in her sweater and, as she went on, kept it with two fingers from jumping out. But it was only a trinket from a penny gum machine, and she ought to have left it in the grass for the child who lost it to find it or another child to find it and claim it. What shameful thing was she doing, stealing from children?

The Birthday Party

The boy, wakened by the sound of his mother's heels as she went past his door, ran out into the hallway. She turned when he called to her. She had her coat on; her face was without makeup, and pale.

"Where you going?" he cried.

"Get back in bed," she called back. "You're old enough to be left alone."

"*You* get back!" he shouted.

She went on through the living room, her head down.

"It's very late," he pleaded. "I'm already in bed."

"When you wake up I'll be back already," she said. "Call Grandma if I'm not. If I'm not, then I'm never."

When the room was empty he heard, from where he stood in the hallway, the faint music from the radio. In the past few weeks, she went out often during the day or was not home when he returned from school, but she always came back before it was time for supper; she left him often in the evening, but the girl from the apartment downstairs always came in and did her homework at the desk and stayed with him; she wept often and brooded often, but she had never left him late at night and had never threatened not to come back. Though she had wandered the apartment all evening, saying no word to him, her jaws holding back the furor so forcibly she could not open them to eat or speak, he had not expected her to go out in the middle of the night.

He ran into her bedroom. It was untidy; a dresser drawer was out, her white negligee was on the floor, and the big, black marble ashtray on the bed table was filled with cigarette butts. The bed's silk spread was wrinkled and there were small de-

pressions where her fists had pounded. He crawled under the
covers and lay down in the center of the bed, and the return of
sleep was like her return.

The sun, and the lamp still lit, shocked him awake. Afraid
that she had not returned, he leaped from the bed and ran out
into the hallway, calling. She answered from his room and sat
up in his bed when he went in. She was in her slip, her coat and
dress on the chair.

"You said you weren't coming back!" he shouted. It sounded
like an accusation that she had not kept her promise.

"That's all right," she said. "If I hadn't, you're seven years
old, you're old enough to do without me. That's a sign of
maturity, to do without a person."

"You said you weren't coming back!" he shouted again. He
stood in his pajamas in the doorway, terrorized by her troubles
that had driven her out at midnight and detached her so from
him that her return seemed imagined. The man she was going
to marry—who was going to be a more fatherly father, she had
said, than his own had ever been—had not come by to see her
for many weeks, and it was to see him that she had gone out in
the evening so many times, and it was probably to see him that
she had gone out last night.

"I always come back," she said. "Like the cat the man was
always trying to get rid of in the song. He tied her to the
railroad tracks and he threw her into the ocean with a rock, but
she always came back the very next day." She reached to the
chair, her fingers digging into her coat pockets. "Well, no
more cigarettes." She shrugged. "All I did was drink coffee at
the places that stay open all night. You would have enjoyed it.
Saw two motorcycle cops eating hot apple pie. They had their
helmets off and they looked human. And I slept in the car a little
while, but my legs got cramped. You should see the stars out
there at four in the morning."

She tossed off the blankets, hung her clothes over her arm,
and walked past him in her bare feet to her own bedroom. He
followed her, unwilling, now that she had returned, to let her
go from his sight.

"Who's going to take me to Molly's party?"

"I'll take you," she said. "Grandma's going early, and it's out of her way to pick you up, anyway. But, my God, it's not until two."

"We've got to buy a present," he said, afraid that nothing would be attended to from now on, that everything would be neglected; using the party to urge her to look after him again, to distract him again, and engage him again.

She picked up her negligee from the floor and clasped it around her and roamed the room, looking for cigarettes. She gazed into the oval mirror above her dressing table, while her fingertips felt among the jars and bottles for cigarettes. "Oh, don't you fret, don't you cry," she said to him mockingly, gazing at herself as if trying to accept as herself the woman with the swollen eyelids. "We'll be there on time and we'll bring a present, too. You're an anxiety hound," she said. "Oh, the champion anxiety hound."

He began to prepare himself for the party, searching for his shoe polish kit and finding it in his closet under a stack of games. He sat down on the floor and polished his best shoes. He was not fond of Molly, who would be nine, and he saw her seldom, but he prepared himself now as if he and Molly were the best of friends. In his pajamas he went into the bathroom and combed his hair, wetting it until it was black and drops ran down his face, and combing it over and over. He slipped on a shirt, put on his suit and turned the shirt collar down over the collar of the jacket, the way his mother always did. At noon he called to her from her doorway, waking her.

In the jewelry store, where he had gone with her a few times to buy presents, they looked at a tray of bracelets. Around the walls were large, colored pictures of coats of arms; on the counter tops were silver trays and bowls and candlesticks. When she asked him if he preferred a silver chain with charms or a silver chain with one small pearl dangling from a silver claw, he did not balk at a choice, as he had done in the past when he had not cared and had known that even if he cared she would have made her own choice. He put his finger on the one with the pearl. Like himself in the past, she did not care, or else he had persuaded her with his decisiveness, for she nodded at the salesman, who smiled as if it were the most appropriate choice anyone would ever make and caught it up with graceful fingers.

He followed his mother down the few stone steps to the terrace above which strings of red and blue triangular flags crossed from the upper windows of the gray stucco house to the balustrade. Under the flags, a throng of children wandered in twos and threes and clustered together over games, their voices rising high on the warm, still air. His mother had a little swing to her walk that implied that parties for children were what she liked best in life, and, walking this way, went into the midst of so many children that he lost her. At the moment he saw her again, his grandmother clapped him over the ears, lifting his face to hers and kissing him on both cheeks. Above her head, as she bent to him, the flags burned their colors into the clear sky.

With her hand on his shoulder, his grandmother led him away to a corner of the terrace, where Molly's mother was trailing her bare arm above the long table, dropping colored candy, tiny as seeds, into the red crepe-paper basket at each place. He could hear the small sound of the seeds falling because the commotion of the children was far enough away.

"We filled them all last night," she said. "Tons. But today they look half-filled. Up to the brim, that's the way," she said, motioning him to cup his hands and pouring candies into them. He began to help her, awkwardly, following her to drop a few more into baskets she had already filled. "Where's your mother?" she asked.

"She just stayed a minute, to kiss Molly," his grandmother said. "She's coming back later to pick him up."

"Is that you, Elsie?" somebody called to his grandmother from the kitchen. Because his hands were empty and Molly's mother seemed to have lost all sense of his presence, he followed his grandmother. She was small and quick in her coral dress, and her large, yellow beads made a faint jangling. In the white, sunlit kitchen, Molly's grandmother, in a smock stitched with a large, red rose whose stem was as long as the smock, was sticking tiny pink candles into the high, pink cake. Her hand, small and bony, covered with brown spots like freckles melted together, was trembling. She was his grandmother's best friend; they were so close they were like sisters.

"Tell me if I ought to use the white candles, if you think I ought to use the white candles," she begged.

"You can alternate," his grandmother suggested.

"Oh, that's strange, don't you think? Who does that?" the old lady demanded crossly. One pink candle fell into the thick frosting. "Oh, pick it out!" she cried to him. "Your fingers are littler!" But while he thought about the possibility of his clumsiness, she darted her hand in among the upright candles and picked it out herself. "All the same color!" she cried decisively. "Little girls like pink." But in a moment she was undecided again. "Elsie," she wailed, "is pink all right?"

The old woman's wailing over the candles alarmed him. He wondered if his mother was gone already, and he went out the back door of the kitchen, down a narrow passage overhung with vines, and out onto the terrace again. She was not there among the children; he leaned over the balustrade, and she was not with two other mothers standing and chatting in the small garden below, and again he felt the terror of the night before. He was afraid that she would not return for him, that her threat of the night would be carried out that day, and he wished that he had not gone off with his grandmother and that he had not reminded his mother of the party, and he imagined himself fighting her, if she had remembered the party herself—clinging to the bedpost and to the railing on the front steps and to her.

A little girl passed by, ringing a bell, and he was jostled along by the other children toward the birthday table. In the throng roving around the table he looked for his name on the triangular paper flag above each crepe-paper basket. There were so many names that, after a time, he got confused and found himself going around behind the same chairs, now with children seated in them. Then he read only at empty chairs and found his place. Under a high, red paper canopy affixed to her chair back, Molly sat at the head of the table. At her elbow, the many presents were piled in a red paper cart with blue wheels. The cake was carried in by Molly's mother, followed by his grandmother bearing a great, cut-glass bowl of pink ice cream. Molly's grandmother went along behind the children, pouring pink juice from a large, white china pitcher into paper cups; another pitcher, of glass, frosted from the cold liquid, waited on a corner of the table.

Molly braced her hands against the edge of the table and blew at the candles. Seven stayed out, two flared up again.

"You're too excited," her mother cried. "You're gasping." Although her voice was amused and loud, he heard an edge of annoyance. Molly, after a calm, deep breath, blew again, and the two little flames became rising wisps of smoke.

Molly's grandmother sat down beside her to eat a bit of cake. He was next to her, around the corner of the table, and her bony knee knocked his. "Oh, I think this is the nicest party I've ever been to!" she cried, beating the edge of the table with her fingers as if rapping time to a tune. Her voice seemed to him deliberately quavery, appealing to the children. "Isn't it, dear? Isn't it?" she begged him, patting him on the knee with rapping fingers.

Molly, under her canopy, lifted the presents one by one up from the ribbons and rustling papers. Each time she swung to the side to take a present from the cart, or clapped her hands, her long hair bounced against her back. The children nearest her, himself among them, fingered the gifts piling up before her—a long bow and a leather quiver of arrows; a small doll with a bald head and three wigs, dyed red and yellow and black, each like a puff of cocoon silk; a lifelike poodle dog of dark gray wool; a white petticoat with blue ribbons entwined in it, for which she kissed her grandmother, whose restless hands rested for that moment on the wrapping papers she was folding. The transistor radio she turned on at once, and the tiny, crackling voices of the singers went on and on under the tissue paper and other presents. She held up the bracelet, shaking it high above her head, as if it were something musical, and dropped her hands to open another present. There was a gift from each one at the table and from other people who were not there—uncles and aunts who lived in other cities. There was such a profusion of gifts that it seemed to him the reason for the party was more than that the day was her birthday. The party, he felt, was to take care of any crying to come.

On the terrace a puppet tent had been set up, a rickety frame draped with red cloth. Up high in it, like a small window, was the stage. The children sat on the ground, and behind them sat the women in bamboo chairs. From the corner of his eye he saw his grandmother in her chair; he saw the coral dress and heard the beads jangle whenever she shifted her body or clapped. Last night his mother had told him to call his grandmother in the morning, and her presence now, a few feet away, at this time when the party was tapering off and some mothers were already returning and watching the puppet show, was like proof that his mother would not return. Up on the little stage the jerky puppets with cawing voices, the Indian chief with a feather headdress, an eagle, a bluebird, and a pioneer boy with a coonskin cap, shook their arms and wings and heads at one another and sometimes collapsed over the edge of the stage. The laughter around him startled him each time, because he was watching the steps from the street and each mother coming down.

When the curtains jerkily closed, a young man with a beard, wearing a tunic of coarse cotton embroidered in red, and a woman with long hair that hung down her back like a little girl's, came out from behind the stage. The man bowed; the woman picked up the sides of her wide, flowered skirt and curtsied like a good and proper child. Some of the mothers slipped sweaters over their children's shoulders and guided them across the terrace and up the steps, and some gathered in a cluster with Molly's mother while their children gathered around the puppeteers to see the puppets put away in the tapestry satchel, each one waving as it went down. From a chair he watched the women and children climb the steps, until only one mother was left, chatting with the three other women while her two daughters wandered the terrace with Molly. He was watching the red tent carried up by the couple, swaying between them, when he saw his mother coming down, nimbly sidestepping. He saw her change the expression of her face, smiling at the couple and expecting to smile at whomever she saw next. She waved to him, the only child among the empty chairs, a wave that implied she knew the party had been wonderful, and crossed before him to the women. She had a sweater on now, as did the other women whose circle she joined. He saw his grandmother kiss her on the cheek, grasping and shaking her elbow, and his relief was expressed for him a little by his grandmother's emphatic claiming of her.

"So, Molly?" his mother called to the girl. "How does it feel to be nine?"

"What?" called Molly.

"To be nine? How does it feel?"

"Oh, I feel the same, I guess," Molly called back, a slight wonder and vexation in her voice. She went on wandering with the other girls—some purpose to their wandering that only they knew—their heads bent over something in her hands. The light wind picked up the ends of their hair and the ends of their sashes.

Molly's mother laughed. "In a few years she'll begin to feel the difference," she said.

"When she begins to feel it," her grandmother said, "you won't need to throw any more parties. She won't let you. Isn't that so, Molly?" she called, but her voice was too frail to be heard far.

"She can't know if it's so," said her mother, again with that loud voice that was both amused and annoyed.

His mother motioned to him and began to move away from the others, and his grandmother joined her. He got up from the chair and was a step ahead of them. All over the terrace the seedlike candies lay scattered, and a few ribbons, here and there, were blown along an inch at a time.

"You act like you want to get away," his mother said behind

him, raising her voice a little to make sure he heard, but keeping it too low to be heard by the women they were leaving. "I came down and saw him in that chair as if he were suffering punishment," she said to her mother. "This morning he couldn't wait to go. He was ready at six."

"It wasn't that early," he said, hurt by her ridicule.

"No, he wasn't ready at six. I was out till six," she said, and the sound of the anguish remaining in her throat from the night silenced the three of them.

"Is it over? Is it all over?" his grandmother asked her as they climbed.

He turned, because he no longer heard their heels on the stone steps, and saw that his mother was covering her face with her hand, and with the other hand was clutching her purse to her breasts. The way her chest bowed in and the way her fingers spread, trembling, over her face made her appear as fragile as her mother.

"Ah, not here, Lovely. Not here," his grandmother pleaded, touching his mother's fingers. So much love went out to her daughter that her old body seemed depleted suddenly. "The children, they can see you," she warned. "They can see you, and they've had such a nice day. Ah, not here." With her arm around his mother's waist, she made her continue up the steps. Before he turned away, he saw the three girls gazing up at them curiously from under the strings of red and blue flags fluttering in the wind.

The Search for J. Kruper

On the plane from New York to Phoenix, where he was to stop over for a few days to enjoy the sun before going on to the coast, the novelist, Robert Klipspringer, chatted with the stewardess and with the passengers nearest him, a congressman and a manufacturer of a plastic racetrack game, all of whom had recognized him. Although he knew he erred and was engaging in a grandiose comparison, he felt that the three were cognizant of the murky and turbulent weather with which the plane was contesting as his, Klipspringer's, kind of weather, for had he not, in his novel, contended with his past, with his life, as the plane with the storm? He drowsed a while, woke to find the plane swimming in the white sunlight of the desert, and, again against his will, he likened the approach of the plane toward the myriad swimming pools of celestial blue, each in the shape of its owner's desire, to his own approach toward his rewards for that scouring of his past he had chosen to undergo. A taxi carried him and his slim suitcase to one of the larger inns and, a few minutes after his arrival, he walked out, in swim trunks and zoris, across the rose terrazzo and lay down on the edge of the swimming pool.

He had flown East to confer with his agent and to sign a contract for the paperback publication of his latest novel—now and for six weeks past in a mighty lead over all others and acclaimed by the entire spectrum of the nation's critics—for such a spectacular sum that a small news item to that effect appeared on some front pages, and so he found the desert sun more enjoyable now than he remembered it from twelve years ago when he and his second wife had rested a day in Phoenix on a summer trek into Mexico. They had dared the trip on a morsel of advance royalties for his first novel and the meager savings from his salary as a philosophy instructor at a minor college in New York State. She had been taciturn and unloving in a motel room where the rattle of the air conditioner affixed to the window screen kept them awake all night, and, speaking only to quarrel, they had gone on into the Mexican desert where the heat stripped the recaps off their tires, vultures danced on burro carcasses beside the road, and for miles their headlights picked up a vast migration of toadlike creatures across the desert night. The convoluted misery of that marriage he had related in his novel, along with that of his first marriage. Was he exposing his back to the sun too long? He pushed up, dangled his legs in the water and rubbed his arms to spread the oil, and found beside him a young man who had been considerately waiting for him to sit up.

"No doubt you're exhausted after your Herculean efforts," said the young man.

Klipspringer accepted a cigarette. It was the brand that he preferred, the preference stated many times in the novel. On such a congenial basis, akin to a friendship over a decade, with his, Klipspringer's, foibles and follies and depths known, most casual encounters now began. As expected, the young man related his own past, his own life, as though over the time of their friendship he had so far failed to reveal himself to the extent that Klipspringer had done and was now in haste to attain an equality of confession. Very slender, his face fragilely handsome, his dark hair partly bleached by the resort sun, the young man revealed that he was at present employed by a socialite from the East, whom he had met in Acapulco. Inasmuch, he said, as he spoke five languages, he was to serve as her interpreter on her trip to Europe. He told of his childhood as the son of the French ambassador to Spain, of his affair in Rome, searing and extravagant, with the wife and constant leading lady of a famous Italian director, of his sojourn up in the Sierra Maestra with the forces of Fidel Castro as correspondent for a Paris daily, and of his journey through the jungles of Mexico with the great novelist, J. Kruper. While imparting

this last bit, which was for Klipspringer the crowning bit that
gave him, the companion of Kruper, a reflected glory as tangi-
ble as his glowing tan, the young man gazed over the pool, one
leg in the water, the other bent in order that his knee serve as a
rest for his elbow, smoking his cigarette from lax and graceful
fingers.

Never had Klipspringer met anyone who claimed even a remote acquaintance with Kruper. It was more credible to claim,
instead, an acquaintance with someone who had run across
someone else, an oil driller in Tampico, a seaman in Hamburg,
a prospector on a desolate mountain, who claimed to have
worked side by side with a man he swore was Kruper. A claim
of acquaintance with Kruper himself was not only suspect, it
was an almost unforgivable undermining of the legend of that
elusive man. Klipspringer, afraid that his curiosity would silence the young man, also gazed out over the pool asking at
last, idly, "You say you know Kruper?"

"I'm in love with his daughter," the young man replied.

"He has a daughter?" asked Klipspringer.

"Of course. He has three."

"Which one?" asked Klipspringer, not wanting to ask that
question but forced to by his confusion as to which question,
among countless, to ask next.

"The youngest and, of course, the most beautiful. She has
hair as black as the wings of the devil, way down to her knees."

"Does he live, as they say, in Mexico?"

"As they say."

"Born there?"

"It is his refuge."

"Ah, refuge, yes." He nodded as if he knew from what
pursuit, from what tempest.

"You have heard the latest theory?"

"Which one is that?" asked Klipspringer.

"The Czechs advanced it first, after which the French translated it, then the Germans from the French, and the Mexicans
from the Germans. The theory is that he killed a man. In an
elevator in New York City, forty years ago. The man found in

the elevator had on him the papers of a young Czech writer. But the dead man did not comply with the Czech's description. Not the age, nothing. What, then, happened to the young Czech writer? He becomes J. Kruper and flees to Mexico."

"Did he do it?" Klipspringer asked.

"He doesn't say."

"No, of course not," he agreed, in hasty apology.

"I myself don't believe that he did," said the young man. "In the first place he is not a Czech."

Klipspringer waited in silence for further revelations. Speculation was appropriate in a conversation with someone who had never met Kruper, but with a friend of the man it was like asking for betrayal.

"If you care to meet him and are someday going down to Mexico, as far as Cuernavaca, say, I will be happy to give you a letter of introduction," said the young man, still gazing out over the bobbing heads.

While the young man and his woman companion sipped cognac at the bar, after a supper as Klipspringer's guests, the writer excused himself and went up to his room to telephone his wife in Carmel. In his coat pocket was a letter to Kruper that the young man had composed at the supper table; it possessed for Klipspringer as great an urgency as a summons from Kruper. Ila, his third wife, was called to the phone by her daughter from a previous marriage. She agreed that he ought not to postpone the trip even for a day, for who knew where the man might be the day after that? She urged him to accept as true the young man's claim, for it was entirely possible that he, Klipspringer, was the one to persuade Kruper to reveal himself, he was the one to write Kruper's biography, and that the young man had sensed this possibility. She could see the book jacket now: Kruper photographed at last and with Klipspringer, his reverent biographer, beside him, both men under a Spanish arcade on Kruper's villa.

After he had reserved a seat on the plane to Mexico City and replaced the phone in its cradle, he continued to lie on the bed,

his shoes off, his shirt unbuttoned, the cool air from the lou-
vered windows wafting to him the laughter and music from
the night and the pool. The numbness, the faint buzz in his
right ear seemed to be due not to his hour-long conversation
with his wife so much as to his surprising decision to believe
the young braggadocio.

From out in the pool, which he knew to be beautiful in its
illumined state, green-blue and filled like a harem pool with
women of various shades of brown from the desert sun, the
voice of one woman came to him above the others, this one
both sweet and raucous. If he strolled out from his room to the
pool, all of them, each in her strategic time, would turn to gaze
at him, having heard that he was at the inn and recognizing
him. And if it was what he wanted, this recognition, then he
ought to go and claim it, it was his. But once his clothes were
off he did not reach for his swim trunks on the back of a chair.
Instead, he bent to his suitcase, found his leather kit containing
a miscellany of personal things that he had listed somewhere in
his novel, among them Band-Aids, two extra pens, flashlight
batteries, aspirins, cuff links, eyedrops, sleeping pills, and
earplugs. In the years before he overcame his fear of barbitu-
rates, a fear he had examined in his novel, he had used earplugs
on noisy nights away from home. He had not used them for
years, but now he stood before the mirror of the dresser to
watch himself swallow a pill with habit's ease and also slip a
pink plug into each ear.

Since he did not care to go to the trouble of transferring to the
bus, he proposed to the driver of the taxi carrying him from the
airport in Mexico City that he continue to be carried on to
Cuernavaca, and so he was—out through the city and up into
the mountains above deep, immense valleys from which wisps
of smoke rose high into the silent afternoon. They arrived in a
rosy sunset. He took rooms in a small and exclusive hotel and
ate his supper in the garden where peacocks and cranes stalked
over the lawn and flew up with a clapping of wings to roost in
the lower limbs of the trees whose large, fire-colored blossoms

fell to the ground with the sound of a small, soft fruit. The moon rose, a warm erratic wind rose, and excited by the enchanting conditions which he interpreted as propitious he strolled out through the lobby to the taxis. The woman in the cafe, where he asked to be driven, was to act as his liaison with Kruper. Twelve years ago, even five years ago with three novels to his name, he could not, he mused, have approached so confident of his welcome as now. Surely a man of wide and eclectic ranging through the literature of the world, classic and current, Kruper would recognize the name of Klipspringer and think twice, think six times, before turning him away.

"*Aquí?*" he asked as the taxi swung up before the open door of a dim, hole-in-the-wall cafe with three tables, lopsided cloths, and four customers, three of whom were sprawled around one table, one with his head down beside his plate.

"*Aquí,*" said the driver. On the other side of the street rose a massive stone wall, along the top of which men sat with their backs to the street or, since they were so high, to the night sky. "*A la izquierda,*" said the driver, "*es el Palacio de Cortés.*" So it was obvious the cafe to the right was his destination. He had expected it to be brighter, cleaner, but might it not, just as well, be dingy and with a narrow staircase in the kitchen leading up to a room where the great man paced the floor? Or was he the squat, elderly man alone at a table, with his grey hair shaven close and his jowls hanging over the collar of his soiled shirt and his small, pale eyes fixed in austere curiosity on Klipspringer's head poking out the taxi window?

Shaken by the conviction that the man was Kruper, Klipspringer sat down at the empty table, unable to speak, likening his abashment to that of a young novice ushered into the presence of Conrad. A number of flies flew up from the cloth and beyond their darting bodies he saw emerge from the kitchen a girl who met the description of Kruper's youngest daughter given him by the young man in Phoenix. One thick braid hung over a shoulder and lay on her large bosom that swelled against the embroidered blouse.

He ordered a beer. Then, before she turned away, he detained her with an appealing face. If she did not recognize it, she would at least suspect that he was somebody of intelligence, somebody who intended no flippancy, no flirtation either with her or with life. "You are *amiga con Felipe*?" he asked, limited by his scanty knowledge of her language. "I am also a friend of his."

The name of the young man caused such an agitation of her plump face that he could not make out whether she was smiling or weeping.

"He told me," he said, "*su padre es* J. Kruper."

"Who is her father?" the man with the jowls demanded, his voice on guard, deep and rumbling, and, as if he had commanded it to be silent, the far-off music from the band pavilion in the plaza ceased at once on a flourish of trumpets.

"Forgive me," Klipspringer began. "I am looking for her father. You are her father?"

With the stolidity, the expressionless calm of a man who has sired twenty children, and an unknown number beyond that, he nodded. Unable, any longer, to contain the anguish aroused by the name of Felipe, the girl ran wailing into the kitchen.

"Then you are J. Kruper?" Klipspringer asked.

With his forearms on the table, the man meditatively turned his bottle of beer between his palms, taking the time that a dog takes to turn around a few times and lie down. "No, but I am his brother," he said and smiled a narrow smile of yellow teeth and gaps.

Klipspringer introduced himself, observing, as they both rose halfway from their chairs and gripped hands, that his name meant nothing to the man.

"He is here?" asked Klipspringer.

The brother shook his head as one does humorously for a child who has asked for too much.

"Where then?"

The brother shrugged. "The last letter is from Ixtilxochit-chuatepec, but that means nothing. By now he may be back in Veracruz."

"Veracruz is his home?"

"Let us say," said the brother, "that the earth is his home," and smiled again his narrow smile. "I am sure you know," he said, gesturing Klipspringer to sit closer, an invitation Klipspringer accepted at once, "that many countries claim him as their own, each one claims his place of birth. But if the earth is his home, what is the difference where he first opened his mouth to bawl?"

"Yourself, you're from. . . . Let me guess," said Klipspringer as if for camaraderie's sake alone.

"Amsterdam," said the brother. "Our father was a ship-wright. It was a big family, he was the third from the oldest and I was the third from the youngest, so if you want to know what kind of child he was, if he whined or if he laughed, if he did good deeds or sulked in a cupboard, I can't tell you. At the age of ten he shipped as a cabin boy and by the time I went to seek my own fortune he was already away for many years. But I met him again on a freighter to the East Indies. To make a long story short, the ship went down in the Atlantic. The captain and the rest of the crew all went down except my brother and myself."

Klipspringer sat in confounded silence. The story the man had told derived from one of the early novels of Kruper. Was the man Kruper or Kruper's brother or simply a reader of Kruper's novels?

"You are yourself a writer?" the brother asked.

Klipspringer nodded, reaching for a cigarette in his breast pocket.

"And what is it you write about?" asked the brother, offering a cigarette to Klipspringer and lighting it and his own with a finesse that was strange for the large blunt hands whose cuts were filled with black grime. Or was it ink?

At the risk of sounding melodramatic, hoping that the man would accept his words as honest and significant, he answered, "Of my life."

"Of your life," the brother mused, seriously enough, impressed enough, settling back and stretching his short, heavy legs in their baggy trousers. He gazed at Klipspringer's clean-shaven plump cheeks and, for a longer time, at his coat, at its fine cloth of subtle stripes. "Not every man has the courage to turn over his own stones," said the brother. "And because you have that courage I will give you the name of the woman who translates my brother's works. Since she does not care to be tracked down by searchers after Kruper, her name never appears on his books. She lives not far from here but you must phone to set an hour as she is a doctor and has many patients. It's possible that my brother is with her now for a few days and—who knows?—he may be acquainted with your life and rush out to embrace you."

On the paper that Klipspringer slipped across the table, and with Klipspringer's pen, the brother wrote the woman's name in a cramped, laborious script.

At four the following afternoon, the hour of his appointment, Klipspringer, in high, anticipatory spirits, pulled the rope to the side of a small, carven door and set a large bell to clanging above his head. The street on which the taxi had left him was narrow, full of stones and ruts. A manservant, an Indian, admitted him, and Klipspringer entered a tiled hallway whose opposite end opened into a small court struck with sunlight. On the straight-back chairs in the hallway several Indian women waited, wrapped in brown and black rebozos, barefoot, one with a child in her lap.

He waited for the *doctora* on a bench in the court and was certain that the woman whose simple and benevolent household this was would not fail to respond to his plea. He began a conversation with the manservant, and since the servant was attending to the luxuriant plants that edged the court, watering them with a hose and picking off beetles, Klipspringer described for him the garden of the hotel. He knew the place, the servant said. The *doctora*'s husband, the servant went amiably on, had collected many plants on long trips up into the mountains and into the jungles, accompanied by the *doctora* who took care of sick Indians. Klipspringer, at this unfolding, was struck by the conjecture that the *doctora*'s husband was Kruper, whose avocation explained the man's firsthand knowledge of the Indians and the country's varied terrain. A great, unbounded desire to find Kruper was now in possession of Klipspringer. If his search had begun from curiosity alone, it had become a matter of immeasurably more than that, and at this point he was convinced that Kruper was in one of the rooms that faced the court, perhaps even inspecting him from behind a curtain, and that this was the arcade, shading the windows, under which their picture was to be taken together.

Quick of step and apologetic for her delay, the *doctora* sat down beside him on the bench. She was once a comely woman; her large, dark eyes and her dark hair, grey at the temples, were evidence enough. He was confused by her, attracted by her remaining beauty and rebuffed by her own unconcern with it. She was untidy, her hair in a straggling knot and a spot or two of some tincture on her blouse.

"Your husband is a botanist?" he asked.

"He is dead," she said.

"Was he Kruper?" he cried.

"No, he was not Kruper, he was an English botanist," she assured him, and Klipspringer was both relieved and surprised at his error.

Over the phone the *doctora* had recognized his name; although she had read none of his novels, she subscribed, she had told him, to several periodicals from the States and had heard of him. But she did not, now, reveal anything about Kruper. Her answers were elusive of Klipspringer's questions. He saw that she regarded him as she would a patient, both respectful of his person and ruthless with his ailment, and under her influence he was convinced that an ailment had brought him here.

"Kruper visits you?" he asked.

"Never."

"So he is not here now?"

"Never," she repeated. "Even his agent in Mexico City he never sees. That gentleman deposits the royalties in the Banco de Mexico and forwards the mail to a box in the main post office. Neither he nor I are ever visited by Kruper. The one and only time I have ever seen Kruper was in the jungle near the Guatemalan border. It was the first trip that my husband and I made into the jungle, years ago. Kruper was, then, a peddler, with burros, from one mahogany camp to another. He asked me if I would consent to be his translator, and a short while after we returned home there arrived his manuscript of that novel of the Indians in the camps. I am the one who translated it into English. I did it in the evenings, as I do now. The evenings I devote to Kruper."

"He writes in Spanish?"

"Sometimes in English. Does it matter, when eventually it is translated into twenty-seven languages?"

"Isn't there a courier who brings his manuscripts?" he demanded, pacing the court that a few minutes before had seemed so exemplary, so giving in its lush yet precise beauty; now he felt unbearably deprived. "Isn't there a courier? A man whom you could follow, whom you could send someone to follow?"

The *doctora* crossed the court, disappearing through a door under the arcade, leaving Klipspringer to speculate elatedly that his desperation had persuaded her to plead with Kruper to reveal himself. She reappeared with a large envelope of heavy, brown paper. "You will see," she said, "that he mails his manuscripts and that he lives in a village so small and so remote that the postmaster, if he can be called that, does not even own a rubber stamp with the name of the village. He dips his thumb in ink and smears it across the stamp."

Klipspringer held the envelope that Kruper had held, on which Kruper had written in a scrawling hand, with a thick-nibbed pen, the name of the *doctora,* the number of her post office box, the town and the state, and up in the left corner his name and nothing more, and which he had sealed and bound— there were the marks of it—with twine. It was not, he noted, the cramped handwriting of the man in the cafe.

In despair he sought out his hotel on foot, climbing the hill where his hotel was situated somewhere along the endless walls of villas and of ancient churches. When at last he stood in the blue-tiled shower cubicle, his head bowed under the onslaught of tepid water, he expressed his despair with a long howl. Toward the end of his howl he was interrupted by a rapping at the door to the hall. He twisted the shower handles and in the silence, punctuated by the water dripping from his body to the floor, shouted through the wall, "You got a *problema?*"

"Señor Klipspringer, I come to solve *your problema.*" It was a man's voice, low, urgent, authoritative, uneasy but not unpleasantly so, a voice familiar or perhaps not familiar. Kruper? Was it possible that Kruper, hearing that Klipspringer was searching for him so guilelessly, so earnestly, so hopefully, had decided to spare him further torment and appear in person at his door? With his towel grasped around his waist he flung open the door and saw that his visitor was the *doctora*'s servant, pressing his sombrero to his chest and solemnizing his face.

"The *manuscritos* come by mail, that is true," the servant said as he stood in Klipspringer's room. "But it is not true, also. Do you yourself believe that *manuscritos* so valuable he would give to the *custodia* of the mailman? No. I will tell you what happens. Kruper gives the *manuscritos* to a man who brings them in his hands to the post office in this town. The man gives them, with a few pesos, to the clerk who puts the *manuscritos* into the box of the *doctora.* Kruper has much *confidencia* for the *doctora* but he is afraid, also, that the *doctora,* who, you understand, is in love with him, will ask a few questions of the man. She will tell him to sit down and bring him coffee and *pan dulce* and ask him if something hurts, his foot or his heart, and soon she will know everything and arrive at the house of Kruper with her black medicine bag and her nightgown."

"Go on," Klipspringer urged as he dressed.

"Once I sat down to drink pulque with him," the servant said. "He is *norteamericano,* like yourself. He was born in El Paso and has white hair and a scar on his face. But I waste time to tell you these things when you can meet him yourself. We can go now to the man that brings his *manuscritos.* The sister of this man was the wife of Kruper. She died in childbirth and the child also."

Since the servant had come on foot, Klipspringer and he
went by taxi into the heart of town, to the edge of the labyrinth
that was the marketplace. With the servant leading the way
with rapid steps and a skilled serpentining through the throngs
in the narrow streets, Klipspringer followed over ruts, some
filled with black water, and under canopies of grayish cotton
squares, ducking his head to avoid the low ones. The evening
sky was still light above the canopies but everything under
them was suffused with a blue dusk: the piles of fruit, the trays
of yellow and purple and red beans, the pots and shoes and
hanging blankets, and the peddlers, men and women, some of
whom were packing their wares away. The turnings they took
were innumerable but at last his guide came to a halt before a
row of medicinal herbs in great variety, filling baskets and in
mounds on the ground, each kind with its sign claiming its
specific cure. The young man who emerged from among these
herbs possessed, at least in the twilight, as innocent a face as
Klipspringer had ever seen, as though a daily imbibing of brews
from all his herbs barred from his system all diseases of the
body and the spirit.

With his mouth to the ear of the herbalist, the servant explained the purpose of Klipspringer's presence. The herbalist
smiled and nodded and, in turn, spoke a few words into the
servant's ear. "He says," the servant informed Klipspringer,
beckoning him to come closer, "that he will do it for you
because I ask him to do it. I have told him that you are the man
that Kruper will be happy to see." Again he spoke into the
herbalist's ear and again the herbalist spoke into his. "Kruper,"
said the servant, translating, "lives in a house between the
house of this man's mother and the house of his uncle in Iguala.
If you will give him paper he will make a map so you do not
become lost."

On a slip of notepaper, the herbalist drew a map consisting
of a line with one small square at the end of it and, across from
the one square, three more small squares, with an X in the
middle square. So now it was Iguala, Klipspringer mused; it
sounded like a lizard in the middle of a desert. Only God—and,

he hoped, some bus depot clerk—knew where it was. The herbalist gave over the map with a smile whose respect made it difficult for Klipspringer to dispute, to himself, the belief of these two that he was the man whom Kruper would welcome. For this respect and for their guidance Klipspringer laid several twenty-peso notes across the palm of the servant and as many across the palm of the herbalist and was led out from the labyrinth and into the plaza, where he shook hands with the servant and was left to himself. The lamps were now lit and hundreds of black birds were streaking in from all over the sky to shriek and squabble in the trees of the plaza.

On the bus to Iguala that he caught early the next morning, or barely caught, as he had permitted the crowd of people in the cavernous, fume-filled depot to rush up into the bus before him, he stood at the rear, forced there by latecomers filling the aisle, his face at a level with the shelf that was laden with baskets and rope-bound suitcases and, close to his eyes, a sack that moved. When the bus, grinding and roaring down the street, was stopped short by traffic crossing its path and he was thrown onto the lap of an Indian woman in the last seat and, rising, was thrown again to her lap, another seated passenger unfolded a spare seat into the aisle and Klipspringer sat down, facing front. When he gazed ahead his eyes were confounded by the close and far legs of the many men in the aisle. When he glanced to the right, his face was six inches away from the back of the head of the passenger in the aisle seat who was gazing out the window; it was the same to the left, and both obstructed his view of the countryside. Occasionally, a passenger got off at a village or along the highway; more often, someone else climbed aboard. Some passengers struggled with stuck windows and failed. The sun beating on the roof of the bus made the interior even more malodorous until, after a time, it seemed to Klipspringer that the bus was panting a mixed odor of poultry droppings, ripe squash, exhaust fumes, and odors he could not identify, and that this exhalation was inhaled by the passengers in lieu of air.

He sat with his suit coat on his lap, his shirt wet across his back, unable either to lean back against the woman's knees or to stretch his legs forward, and growing more alarmed each mile with his gullibility. It was incredible, he thought, that he had allowed himself to be duped into the belief he could find Kruper and to be machinated onto this bus to Iguala with these strangers oblivious of the task he had set for himself, four years ago, of baring his life, and oblivious of how he had accomplished the task, neglecting nothing and withholding nothing, baring all: verbatim revelations to his psychiatrist; the scenes with his wives, the spoken and the unspoken and the unspeakable parts, and with his father, mother, mistresses, friends and enemies; the journals where the dregs were, the journals without deletions, without change. Not one of them knew that in his own country hundreds of thousands held in their hands at that moment the chronicle of his life, eight hundred pages encased in a jacket bearing seven poses of the author, a large one on the front and six smaller ones on the back, and with his name three times larger than the title.

A sensation of suffocation convinced him that he was expiring and set up before his eyes the item to appear on the front pages of his country's daily papers: died in Mexico on a second-class bus to Iguala. But only he, the expiring man, knew it was in the midst of fears and fumes and in search of J. Kruper and that he searched for Kruper because he, Klipspringer, as his fame had grown, had found his own life more fascinating material than any other man's and now was obsessed by that life, confined way down at the very bottom of that life, that he searched for Kruper because to find him was to find the means by which Kruper forgot the self that bore a name and became all others, became nobody and anybody and everybody. At that moment, with death upon him, he became suddenly and terribly intolerant of his own name. If he threw his wallet under the seat of the man to the left or the right he would, he reasoned slyly, die without a name, unidentified, unknown, a *norteamericano* in an expensive suit and shoes whose body nobody would know what to do with. Would a consul send an underling to Iguala or order the body transported to the capital? Of course not, for dead and without papers he could be, as well, a Canadian, a German, or an affluent Mexican who had hopped aboard the wrong bus.

Iguala's dust rose in a cloud as the bus rattled into the depot lot, denying him further time to throw away his wallet and to die. His coat over his arm, his handkerchief to his eyes to wipe away the attacking dust, and gripping his suitcase, he staggered down, knocking over a pail of hot water in which several ears of corn were floating. Down on all fours, the Indian woman whose produce it was picked up the corn from under the passengers' trampling feet. He paused to make amends, then went on, observing how, on the instant, a thick dust coated his wet shoes. Out in the street, that was like an adobe passageway, he turned to the right, as directed by the map. The sun was incredibly hot. He was hungry and thirsty and wished that he had bought a tangerine or two from a peddler in the depot lot, but a superstitious hope that some repast would be offered him by Kruper, a repast for a pilgrim who has at last arrived, had dissuaded him. The herbalist's map was simple: at the end of the street and across from a *tienda* stood three houses, the middle one the house of J. Kruper. Yes, far away was the *tienda,* its soft-drink sign and cigarette sign bright spots of color on the side wall facing the town. By its door two dogs lay on their sides, unmoving. An impatience even stronger than he had known before the other doors where Kruper was to be found, an impatience so strong and so delightful it was an exultation, gave him the eccentric energy to run a few yards between every few yards of trudging. Yes, there was the row of adobe houses, small, yardless, undecorated, but not until he stood in the street with his back to the *tienda* and the dogs did he accept the fact that the house in the middle was not there.

He set his suitcase in the center of the empty lot, sat down on it, and for a long time gazed out on the endless earth, across tremendous, barren valleys to a far rim of craggy mountains and to the milky-blue sky, rippled with the heat, that swept back over all. The absence of the house and of Kruper was, he thought, all, all as it should be. A yellow dog with one ear slunk around him, its lip lifted, its eyes sidelong, touched its nose to his shoe and returned to the street.

At the airport in Mexico City, after he had wearily fumbled his papers before two of the battery of immigration clerks, he entered the waiting room and, since it was crowded, sat down on a bench near two women already sitting there. As he gazed out through the glass at the field and the plane with its attendant figures, he was aware that the women near him were now silent. Then, as he expected, he heard his name and felt his arm touched, and turned toward them an exhausted yet benign and grateful face.

  They were attired in pastel suits; their hair, also, was pastel, and clusters of gold and glass baubles hung from their slim wrists. One, he learned, was the wife of a dentist; the other, her sister, the wife of a storage company president. Since a few minutes were left before departure time, he ordered a round of drinks from a white-jacketed young man and as he drank, now with a sister on each side, he laughed with them over their jaunt, enjoying their obligingly pliable voices, happy when called for and reflective when called for, enjoying their appreciation of his presence. At the loud speaker's bilingual call he went out with them, still with a sister at each side, along the covered passageway and into the sunlight and, after them, up the steps and into the plane.

The Diary of K.W.

February 7
Often a young woman will marry an old man just because she likes his soul. But you don't see this happen vice versa. You don't often see a young fellow marry a 63-year-old woman. When this happens, which is once every 20 years, you see their pictures in the newspapers all over the country. They live in Oskeegee, Georgia, or some place like that, and he looks moronic. Nobody marries an old woman because she has a soul.

February 9
At noon today I was fired from my job of cafeteria substitute helper at the Eunice B. Stratton Grammar School. I was told by my supervisor to go and see a psychiatrist. But I would rather argue with God. God costs nothing and His arguments are weightier. But I confess that after I was fired, this very afternoon, I strolled into a clinic but the social worker told me it would have to be group therapy because so many people came for help and I was not a desperate case, so I strolled out again without leaving my name. I don't want to talk about my quirks to other people with quirks. It wouldn't be so embarrassing if we were all alone together, but a psychiatrist sits there listening and I've heard he doesn't say a word. You get the feeling that the ones who talk about themselves are the crazy ones and the one who sits silent is the sane one. Contrary to what I said above, God doesn't answer either. It's myself answering myself and sounding weighty, doing the job for Him. In my room I talk about my quirks to God with no embarrassment or not much. I threaten Him or disown Him, and then I answer for Him. If He'd answer, I'd die. But a man

with a college education, why you expect an answer. I would rather write things down as I've decided to do in this diary and, besides, that immortalizes me, like Leonardo da Vinci. The psychiatrist takes notes, I hear, but that's not the same as keeping a journal by yourself. He can't take down the real meaning, just the cryptic stuff he swears by. He translates the quirks into a code and never knows he's forgotten something.

February 11
Speaking of Leonardo da Vinci (I speak of him because I can't bring myself to speak of what is closest to my heart) I was looking through his journals down in the basement of the City Lights Bookstore today and I came across one thing he says that goes I Never Grow Weary of Being Useful. That got me between the eyes. That's what I'd like to be. Useful. But nobody has any use for me so I am useful just to the two cats from upstairs and some pigeons that all look alike when I go to feed them crumbs in the park across from the Catholic Church.

February 16
No more delays! It's time to go back. No more sidetracks! (I began this diary with an O because it looks imposing, but no more flourishes!) It's time to go back to the day he moved in upstairs, two weeks ago, and misfortune began to fall on me like bits of plaster falling from the ceiling as the ceiling prepared to fall in from his footsteps up there which I hear like a giant's footsteps. They are quiet but of such meaning to me! The young couple upstairs who sublet the apartment and the cats told me he was Dutch and an architect and they hoped that the young man and myself would get along fabulously together. The girl uses words like that because she is jaded and must make life seem fabulous because she has only begun it and to think otherwise would be disastrous. They are a polite young couple and I know when they return they'll come down the back stairs with a little gift for me from Scandinavia or Italy, which is where interesting gifts come from that cost next to nothing. No more delays! The day he moved in I saw him

from my window, I looked down at him from behind my curtains as he got out of his Fiat and lifted out some luggage, and my first thought was Now if I had a son that is how he would look, that is who he would be. How do you know? I asked myself. How do you know a son of yours wouldn't look like your father as you remember him, more like a plucked turkey than a man—Poor Father, Forgive Me!—gawky and sad, a plumber with a lower lip like a pitcherspout, same kind I've got. Or like your brother, a hulk with little hands that smelled of bay rum because his father's hands smelled of honest underground. How do you know a son of yours would look like that stranger down there? The son idea left soon enough, left me with an ache in my heart that was my recognition of him as more unmentionable than son. I have a lot of old magazines under my bed and I went through them for clippings that might interest him. I have art magazines and architecture magazines, all printed on slick paper, magazines I found two for a nickel and smelling of dampness at the Salvation Army, rummage sales, old bookstores. Well, I snipped out pictures of beautiful buildings in Brazil, in Israel, I snipped out page after page of articles that I didn't fully understand because I'm no architect and folded them neatly and put them in his mailbox which is next to mine by the front steps. Then a day later I wrote a little note, or to be precise about it, I printed it because I print nicely, almost professionally, like the print you see on architectural drawings at the museum, and I said I hoped he could make use of the articles and pictures I'd left in his mailbox, the note just an afterthought, as if I'd thought that he might be wondering who put in the clippings and it was impolite to keep him guessing. But I couldn't make myself sign my name. My name meant too much when I imagined it at the bottom of that note. It made me wonder too much who I was. I even left a painting of mine leaning up against his front door, a portrait that I did at Galileo Adult Night School, of a woman in a black lace mantilla, and it had my initials on it. My initials on that picture explain everything but he hasn't come down yet to ask me, "Are your initials KW, by any chance?" If he did come down I wouldn't tell him I lost my job as cafeteria helper. Because he would want to know Why and how can I tell him it was because of him? That would be the last thing he'd expect to hear, that an old woman he never saw before lost her job because he moved in upstairs above her. I can't even explain it to myself in this journal.

February 21
There is an old man I chat with whenever I meet him on the street. On a leash he's got a dog the size of a dried pea. Without a leash he wouldn't know where it was. Today I saw him coming a long way off. He walks so slowly because he went to extremes in his youth. He has pores deep as craters and a nose like a purple onion that is further evidence of extremism. Today he says, "Did you see in the paper this morning where 9 out of 10 men interviewed say they can't understand women? Women live by their emotions and men live by their minds and we shouldn't even try to figure out what you're going to do next?" "Crud!" I shout, thrusting my flubby old face in his flubby old face, and I pull up my rummage sale skirt to show him my varicose veins under the black stockings that hide the veins but not the lumps they make. "You think I got these lumps from my emotions dancing me around? I got them from mental conscientiousness," I said. "Standing-up jobs all my life, elevators, counters, cafeterias. I got a record of 63 years stability." And he laughs in a spitty way because he's got no answer he learned from a newspaper.

February 24
Every night he's got a woman up there. Maybe it's his sister visiting him because he's emotionally disturbed and she comes by at supper time to bring him cheeses and chocolates and pastries to cheer him up. Or maybe it's his very wealthy mother who because she is so wealthy and swims a lot in her swimming pool and wears Helena Rubenstein cosmetics can sound so light and so young up and down the stairs. She is up there now, I can hear her heels tap-clacking around up there. Some-

times in the morning he comes down the stairs singing and I have to clap my hands over my ears, I can't bear to think he comes down happy because the woman was with him the night before. It's his sister, I'm sure of it, and he sings because he has Dutch chocolate in his pockets to eat while he sits at the drawing board. Why doesn't he investigate? Old fool, what does he care there is an old woman down below who lost her job? You could never convince him it was his fault. What I should have done is write down what happened the day it happened. Now it is confused in my memory. Besides the intervention of time, which is a bad enough intervention, I haven't eaten well. The money from the last check went on the rent and the utilities and some small items of food in addition to the chicken necks which I cooked up for the two cats although I ate the broth myself. Not only do I feed myself but I feed the two cats that he forgets to feed. He is too busy feeding the girl! the girl! whatever it is she wants to be fed. Great God, what a wonderful thing to be a girl and be fed! fed! fed! until you are plump and sleek and sassy and delirious!

March 2
It's wise to get down the day I was fired at the Eunice B. Stratton Grammar School, because I need to try to remember why for my own good. When the reason gets away from me I get scared and wonder what crazy fault in me did me out of a job. Why was I fired? I refused to serve the children their hot lunches. There were all those trays, there were all those little faces moving along above the trays, gazing down into the containers of vegetable soup, mashed potatoes, cream corn. Everything was as it always is in every school where I worked as substitute cafeteria helper. But I refused to serve them. Why? Well it occurred to me that food was abominable and that if they continued to eat, the kids at the Stratton School and every school in the city, if they went on eating their hot lunches every day they would only be preparing themselves to suffer, they would only grow up to suffer. The pity for them stopped up my mouth. The pity had been in my mouth for days already

and I'd given up breakfast and was feeling nauseated over that variety of foods. So there I stand in my white uniform and my gray hair all neatly tied back in a skimpy pony tail with a bit of green ribbon so my hair doesn't get in the food, my hands washed, my bony hands antisepticized by the strong amber soap that drips down from a glass ball in the lavatory, and a bit of cheery lipstick on my thin lips, there I stand with the children piling up, piling up, and I can't lift my hand with the ladle in it. No, I can't hop and skip to the piping little voices from the little heads on the trays. "Serve! Serve! What's wrong? Serve!" I hear the voices of my co-workers, of my supervisor, who is a large, sloppish woman even in the neat uniform. She is hissing over my shoulder as she shoves me aside and grabs the ladle herself. We make a pair, I think, she with her busty waist and me straight as a uniformed stick, she the talkative, ladling, eating kind (it always made me queasy to sit opposite her after the kids were out of the cafeteria and see her talk with watery mayonnaise on her lower lip) and me the untalkative, unladling, uneating kind. Why right then I thought to myself that I had no business in the food industry even if it was seeing that children got a hot nourishing lunch. So I was not surprised when I was notified after all the kids were served and I was still standing there with my hands hanging down that I was dismissed. It was the pity for them that wouldn't let me use that ladle. No, it was pity for myself because the young man moved in upstairs and if he came down to ask me about my initials what difference would it make since the initials belong to an old woman? The pity for them and for me is all one pity and it's got to the point now where it won't let me talk to anybody. It's difficult for me to tell the vegetable man who's in charge of the stall outside the Buon Gusto Market what I want, ten cents of broken asparagus, a wilted lettuce for a nickel, mainly because I don't want anything but you have to eat to stay alive. Sometimes he sells me what I don't ask for because he hears nothing from me. It seems to me that there is not enough communication to be had over small transactions like the sale of vegetables and that all my life that was all I ever had, small transactions.

But he can't hear a thing so he pops the vegetables into the bags and when I get home I find myself with cauliflower and chard, things I never eat, that the very smell of sickens me. So I throw it all away. I can't bear the sight of food anyway so it's all to the good that it's not what I asked for. When I pass Stella's Bakery and see the cakes and hot cross buns, when I pass the Safeway Market and see the big red letters about juicy chuck roasts, when I pass the restaurants and see through the glass the customers eating rich soup or cutting steaks or sipping wine, or when I read in the gossip column that at the Taj of India the gossiper was served fowl covered with gold leaf as in the days of the Moguls, why I think of the part in the Russian novel where the poor student sits in the railway compartment, starving, and the fat Kulak couple who are facing him take out their bread and sausage and eat without offering him any and without any embarrassment. When I eat my toast and drink my tea I feel the eyes of the poor on me. I don't feel poor when I eat so I don't like to eat. I can't seem to think about all the hungry people in the world because there are too many to think about at one time, so the student on the train—he is everybody, he is the children at the school, he is myself, he is hungry of body and soul. No, I don't like to eat anymore. Even if I had a job I think I'd eat less than I used to . . . The above reason for losing my job sounds like a reasonable reason when I write it and read it, but I'm afraid that in a little while, when I'm doing something else, the reason will sound like nothing but that crazy quirk I was afraid to admit to.

March 6

The upsetness is with me again. The day I was fired I wasn't upset in this way even though it was an important job and they make you sign an oath about not being a member of an organization that seeks to tear down the government. The upsetness began when I learned there aren't any jobs around for a woman who's 63 years old. I knew this before but it didn't mean much because I had a job, but when I didn't have a job anymore then the fact there wasn't any upset me. I am in the habit of stealing old Sunday newspapers from the woman who lives upstairs across from the architect. She is a mouse-sized woman who works in a dime store. She leaves the papers outside her back door intending to throw them away later, so it's not really stealing on my part but it would be polite of me to ask for them. However, I don't like to humble myself mainly because I don't care for her. It began, my not caring for her, the day I was taking an oil painting of mine down the front stairs to see if some gallery would hang it up, and she passes me going up and asks to see it, but all she can say is "Isn't that pretty?" Does she think I'm a fool that I like my work called pretty? I concluded then that she was the fool if she thought I was fool enough to fall for a word like pretty. There are fools and fools, and some you can become fond of but she is a fool that you avoid. Anyway, they insult you to your face, the want ads. They say Girl Under 25 or Must Be Young and Attractive. I used to say Crud To You, meaning the employers, but after I got fired I read the ads and got upset. Maybe I ought to go over to file for my unemployment insurance, but since I was only a part-time worker and that not regular and making close to nothing I'm not sure if anything is coming to me. Besides, there are so many people in lines and so many spaces to fill in, so much milling around and so many faces that don't know one another. The thing to do is not be upset and the way to do it is to let pleasure set in. You can make yourself glad you've got no job and glad you're not looking forward to any. This is better than being upset. Besides, since I may decide to not eat, it doesn't matter whether I've got money coming in or not . . . It's 9 p.m. I can hear the faraway noise that comes up from the ships and the piers down the hill when they work all night and the sound of the air-conditioner that goes day and night in the Roma Macaroni Factory across the street. Upstairs I hear the woman laughing.

March 9

They are quarreling across the hall, the taxi driver with the Hungarian name whose grandfather was a count and his sweet, naggy wife. They have a black poodle named Valentina. They also have an old dog shaky in the legs that some family in the neighborhood abandoned when they moved away and it's got a sad, resigned look such as I've never seen on any face before, man or beast. It lies at the foot of the front steps and you have to step over him, coming or going. I wonder if I have the same kind of face with some anxiety mixed up in it. Whenever I see sad faces on cats and dogs I wonder how I look myself. Today is the first hot day of the year, it came unexpectedly, and they are getting ready to go to the beach. It's 3 o'clock already. He's carrying out canvas chairs to the car and an armload of odds and ends and he's shouting at her to "Hurry, for God's sake, or the best part of the day will be gone!" "Please! The umbrella!" she cries. "The umbrella!" and runs back up the stairs and unlocks the door again. Great God, the day is gone already and when they get to the beach, a strong wind will be blowing, cold and gritty . . . They're gone, thank God, with their two dogs. It's a warm day, the acacia trees are dropping their tiny, rusty yellow puffs, I see sweepings of them in the sidewalk cracks whenever I go out, and the blossoms on the few fruit trees in the neighborhood smell like white mice. Tonight I'll go up the backstairs and knock at his door. He ought to feed those two cats himself and not leave them for me to feed because I've got nothing to feed them with and I can't bear the sad faces of all the animals around here on the front and back stairs.

Night of the Same Day
Maybe I ought to have a cup of hot tea to warm me up and settle my shaking legs, but my mouth doesn't want to open. My breath nowhere around when I want it, I went up the backstairs. Wusto! he opened the door with his brown hair up in tufts as if he or she had been running fingers through, with a dishtowel tied around his waist, with a puzzled, surprised look on his face that said, Who comes up the backstairs, Who? "You forgot to feed your cats and they beg at my door. Cats," I said, "got to eat regular, like human beings." That humbled him.

It's always wise to forget the formalities if you feel yourself ill at ease and begin with the criticism. "Oh my, oh my!" he cried, striking his brow with the back of his hand. "The cats! I forgot to feed them!" and he turned sideways to say to the girl, "I forgot to feed them!" and I got a fair look at her from a distance. She was sitting at the table by the window, and the paper lantern of a lamp above the table glowed off her buttersilk blouse and off her red hair. I saw her dimly because my eyes had come up the twisty dark of the backstairs. She was sipping wine from a tumbler and reading a magazine and she gazed at me, that girl, with a little bit of interest and a little bit of puzzlement and that was all. She gazed at me, that girl, with no kinship in her eyes, creature of my own sex but oh so different from me, so young and so well fed with love and delicacies and the stares of strangers. Maybe she's a clerk behind a jewelry counter, maybe she types all day in a tight little office, but she's only beginning. But me, I felt that even when I was a child not elongated into gauntness yet, with the pitcherlip that wasn't a caricature yet, that was still a quaint child's lip, even then I knew that someday I'd come knocking at the back door to have the young man open it and let me see what kind of woman was privileged to sit at his table and swing her foot and sip his wine and make herself at home, at home, at home. "When you see them next time tell them to come up," he said just as the two cats ran in, and to the cats he cried, "Forgive me! Forgive me!" and smiling and nodding, nodding and smiling, he closed the door, opened it again instantly. "Can you see? Can you see?" he cried. "Here, I'll leave it open until you get down," and he did and the light was on the stairs until I got to my own door. That was kind of him, he was kind, he was somebody else's kindly lover who leaves the door open for an old woman to get her light by as she retreats down the backstairs on her love-shaken legs . . . One of the upstairs cats came down again and scratched at my door and now it's walking over my journal leaving paw prints made of something resembling licorice gum. Upstairs all is still, all is shuddering with love.

March 15
Maybe I'm feeling magnanimous tonight because in last Sunday's paper which I picked up yesterday on the backstairs I read an article by an eminent psychologist in New York by the name of Reik who said in the title that Men Love Work But Women Love Men, and down in the article about how When Women Claim Equality Then They Renounce Their Superiority. That made me feel good for an hour or less. It made me feel superior. But after a while I began to suspect that statement. I wondered what it was I ought to feel superior about because I didn't seem to have what he implied I had. So I went to bed sad and lay there wondering why I've always been afraid of them if I was superior. I look the other way and always have, all my life, because even when I was young they looked right through me. I was afraid of their indifference which is a worse kind of cruelty than laughing at a woman because she's odd. At least being odd you're being something more than nothing. So I went to bed sad and slept sad, but this morning I got up and began to count my superiorities because I find it upsetting to be at loggerheads with an eminent man in the Sunday papers. So I counted 26 paperbacks, a can of evaporated milk, a loaf of bread, and 5 withery apples. These are not special superiorities belonging to women alone but they were the only superiorities I could find so I counted them.

March 29
All my life I never gave Life serious thought, like the people who write books about it. Oh they get all wound up, they write 1,000 pages or they condense it down into four lines in a poem. That's the way I used to feel when I was young, that I had a lot to say. But I couldn't say it like the others and that turned me against them, it turned me away because they had so much to say that was so complicated that I felt like a simpleton. Worse, like an eavesdropper. So I read only a few things in my life. But now I feel the opposite, I'm not intimidated any more.

That's a laugh, trying to find out what I'm doing here when I've already been here 63 years. The basement of the City Lights is a good place. You can read down there, they have tables and chairs, and you don't have to buy anything, nobody bothers you. Down there I read lots of great people. Not that I read them from cover to cover. I read a page and then when I lose track of a man's thoughts I skip a page, but I manage to collect a lot of insights for myself. For instance, one poet I was reading, one of his lines hit me between the eyes, I felt as if I should have read that line when I was born. It went He Never Supposed Divine Things Might Not Look Divine. There's more before and after to support that line but that's the part I remember, that's the part that made me feel not so queer all of a sudden. "Hell!" I said to everybody who all my life had looked through me as if I wasn't there. "You don't know the Divine when you're looking right at it!" Today I read a Spaniard, a philosopher. Maybe it's really my own idea but I've got to give credit to somebody else because it's too good an idea for me to have made up myself. But this is the picture I came up with, that made me feel complicated and calm at the same time. I got a picture of my Soul. Suppose there are three heads, and the one in the middle has two faces, like Janus. The two-facer in the middle is the Soul, and one face is looking at The Person You Are and the other face is looking at The Person You Might Have Been, and both the other faces are looking at the Soul. All these heads are contained within you, but you're not the first head and you're not the third, you're the two-facer in the middle looking at both. The Soul is me. I'm not the woman I could have been under more congenial circumstances and I'm not the woman I am, old growly-gut who can't look anybody in the eyes because she's ashamed of who she is and ashamed for them for not seeing her Soul instead of her. I was able to keep this picture of my Soul intact until I got home, but once I got here and smelled the old magazines and the cat spray and the cold rubbish smell that comes up from the basement and saw I had one last teabag, some dried beans, and 7 prunes that I found at the bottom of a canister it was hard to remain the observing Soul. I found myself becoming the old woman again with her stiff hands and her hunger and the next minute becoming the person I might have been, a wise old lady with eyes like Christ's, with supple hands with antique rings on them, my place of residence the mansion across the street, up on the corner of Chestnut and Grant, that nobody lives in, that belongs to somebody in Italy. The macaroni factory is at the lower corner of the block and the mansion is at the upper corner and in between is part of the earth that's vacant, that rises as high as the roof of the factory, with long slicks of grass and clumps of ferny fennel and, up at the top, scotch broom. One day I climbed up that mound to peer through a wrought-iron gate in the stucco wall at the back of the mansion and saw a little statue of a youth above a waterless fountain in a tiled courtyard. On top of the high walls are arches and doorways like afterthoughts loaded on, and stuck in the walls are lions heads that gaze out over the mound and the macaroni factory and the bay. That's where the woman I might have been would live in her wisdom and wealth and eminence. I try to believe I am the Soul in the middle but the other two keep getting the upper hand . . . The cats are driving me crazy. They're yowling on the backstairs of the building next door because there they can look into my kitchen window and me at the table. Maybe they think they press me more with their hunger when they stare in from outside like the poor children in Hans Christian Andersen staring in at the rich eating their feasts. They curl their tongues at me and warble their throats, begging, begging, and their yowls are magnified in between the buildings like in a cavern.

April 7
How pale I look whenever I catch a glimpse of myself in the mirror over the basin. Sometimes I splash warm water on my face but I purposely avoid looking into the mirror when I do that. I only catch glimpses going by. Every time I glance in I'm reminded of something I read by a French woman philosopher who was very religious and wrote about God, and she said

When A Beautiful Woman Looks Into The Mirror She May Think The Image Is Herself. An Ugly Woman Knows That It Is Not. So that way I try to make myself feel better whenever I look, but I make myself feel worse again by suspecting that the girl upstairs looks in the mirror and knows the image is not herself. Yes, I grant that further advantage to her, that she is not taken in, every time, by the image. Sometimes I feel that woman philosopher by my side whispering to me how human is my face and sometimes that humanness is nothing that does me any good. No, I feel too many ways whenever I glance into the mirror, so I try to avoid it. Mirrors should never have been invented. Maybe the thing to do is hang a towel over it.

April 9
If I lived in the Middle Ages they would have burned me for a witch. But they would have made a mistake. I'm the extreme opposite of a witch. That's what I'd like to be, a witch—things would be at my mercy instead of me being at their mercy.

April 11
Yesterday at noon I saw her again. I heard them come down the stairs and waited behind my curtain to catch them when they reached the sidewalk. She walked from the lowest step to his car and I saw that she had her red hair done up in a pouf with a big, sharp curl on each cheek pointing to her especial face like a finger saying I'll Have That One, and I saw that she had a tiny waist with roundy hips, and pointed shoes whose heels had made a feminine click and clatter on the stairs for how many weeks now? Made them going up at suppertime and coming down late or the next morning but never at noon on a week-day. I began to think about those curls on her cheeks and for the fun of it I made myself a cardboard hand, one of those old-fashioned hands you used to see pointing, and I pinned it on my straw hat with a safety pin so that it was pointed down at me. Maybe it was God's finger pointing, maybe it was God saying Look At This Woman In Her Aloneness. She's Got A Soul

Because I Gave It To Her. She's Not Dead Yet Even If Some People Look Right Through Her As If She Was. She's One Of My Living Souls. But I didn't get up enough courage to wear my hand of God until today when I went out for a minute, not any longer because my legs don't carry me. I was weak from my hunger and my eyes were dazzled by the daylight on the pavement. I went around the block with my hat on, down Francisco, up Stockton, and down Pfeiffer to Grant again and into my door again, so weak that I fell onto my bed and couldn't rise again for an hour. There was one of those Matson liners blowing its horn before it sailed, a blasty, bleary blow. One of those sending off parties was going on and the horn sounded tricky as if somebody was having fun while he was warning people to get off or get on. The blowing accompanied me around the block and I took it that God was blowing a trumpet for me on my journey, or asked Archangel Gabriel to blow it for Him, so people would look at me as I walked around the block with His hand on my hat pointing at me. But what was happening was the opposite. The Dutch architect and the girl were on that ship taking off for Hawaii. I knew this because he came down last night and knocked at my door and asked me if I'd be kind enough to look after the two cats until the other couple got back from Europe, and I said that I would. Here I had dreamed, in spite of the girl, in spite of knowing he wouldn't, of him standing there kind and forward and noble and asking me if my initials were KW, at last. But all he wanted was for me to take care of the cats for another two weeks until the couple got back and he didn't even offer to give me the money for the catfood.

April 12
She knocked at my door with lilacs. The mouse woman from upstairs. She said her sister brought her a whole big bunch from Orinda and she wanted to give me some. "You can paint a real pretty picture of them," she said, but this time I knew what she meant by pretty, and I was sorry that I'd been so

snobbish the first time she said it on the stairs. Maybe she's only got a few words at her disposal and maybe pretty means wonderful to her. I said "thank you" and said I'd paint a picture for her of the lilacs, but I don't have the strength even if I had enough paint in the tubes. I put the lilacs in a mason jar. The thing about flowers is that when you inhale them it's like putting your face into cool water. The fragrance is like perfumed water. She meant wonderful. That's what they are. Wonderful.

April 13
Carpenters are working on the roof of the macaroni factory. On the roof there is a small frame structure that looks like a square house with one door in it and they hammer inside the door, they draw up their lumber to the roof and into the door. If they're up there tomorrow and if one of them glances across the street and into my window he'll think I'm napping, an old woman lying on her bed napping. Tonight I'll leave the curtains open so in case I can't get out of bed in the morning whoever is on the roof can see in. The caretaker at the mansion can see in if he wants to, and the boy with the spade who climbs the little hill after school can, and the people who take their dogs up there and look out over the bay and down at the ships between the piers fanning out into the water. I've been up there myself to pry around and I know it's a view to see while they wait for their poodles to relieve themselves. Anybody up there will be able to see the woman lying on her bed and someone may say to himself that the old woman has been lying in there for 3, 4, 5 days . . . Or maybe nobody will think anything's wrong because that thought would disturb the even tenor of their days. Maybe it will have to wait until the young couple come downstairs with their gifts. When nobody answers they'll come back the next day and then begin to make inquiries about me from the Hungarian couple, then from the landlord to see if I moved out as they have friends who would like to move in. The landlord will come over from his house with his key and as he is turning the key in the lock the girl will get a premonition and take her husband's arm and wonder if she ought to tell their

friends about the apartment or not tell, because if a person died
in there they might not care to be the ones to move in right after
and that would be putting them in an embarrassing position.

April 14
It makes no difference, your name on a gold cup or on the social
security records or on the census records. Today I remembered
that my name is on the gold cup in a glass cupboard at the
Eastside High School in Los Angeles. I was surprised to remember that I was valedictorian of my class. It was nice at the
time in a strained way, I think I looked like a scarecrow in a
peach-color lace dress and made a lot of promises for the class
about what we were going to accomplish. It makes no difference, your name. Who knows who you were?

The Next Day
On the other hand it isn't his fault. It's the years' fault. The
years are too much for me, the years are full of the prevailing
public opinion, and what's a few days of coming up Divine
from the basement of a bookstore? He moved in upstairs at the
end of the years and I blamed everything on him because an
excuse was what I needed, a match to set fire to the pile of years
in my chest. I hate to think that prevailing opinion wasn't as
prevailing as I thought it was. Come to think of it, I remember
seeing lots of homely women with children around their skirts
and lots of old women laughing. But that little doubt makes
me feel like asking somebody for food and how do you do that
without shame?

The Last Day
The ceiling will fall in, it can't bear the weight of his footsteps.
The ceiling is about to fall in. All I feel is the fall of the ceiling
about to fall.

The Houses of the City

On some days he longed to be with his mother before the hour of her return to their rooms, and in the afternoon he would seek her out at whatever house she was cleaning that day, even though the place was halfway across the city, up in the heights where the big houses stood apart like rich merchants' wives watching their husbands' ships entering the bay below. In his small body was the quality of the pointer dog. He walked slightly stooped, pushing forward, his feet going down in a plodding way.

It was late in his tenth year when he began this practice. He would be in the midst of a scuffle after school, along a sidewalk somewhere, and suddenly he would think of her and at that moment offer nothing further to the struggle. This silent urgency was more effective in breaking his opponent's grip than was his fierce, animal strength. Always in the morning she told him where she would be that day, so that if anything happened to him at school his teacher could call her right away. He felt that it was impossible for anything to harm him; but anything could harm her.

She was alarmed the first time she opened a door to him. He was not sick, he told her. But he had no other reason to give. Of his fear of her dying he could not tell, because to give words to this fear was like pronouncing sentence upon her. If he kept it to himself, the fear might prove groundless. After the first time they said nothing on his arrival. He made no demands upon her, and sat in the chair she pointed to, his hands folded obviously away from the lure of knick knacks and magazines. He listened to the sounds of her cleaning in other rooms, and was not restless.

Certain women were fascinated by him, as if, in his silent clinging to one chair, he were a large moth, its intentions unknown. Once, as he sat in a glass-enclosed sunporch, a large-leafed plant growing from a blue, glazed bowl on the carpet fingered his cheek, touched his elbow each time he fidgeted, but he did not move to another chair, hypnotized by the plant and its curiosity as if it were the lady of the house. Then one afternoon he was sitting in the hallway of an upstairs apartment, facing in a dutiful way the opposite wall and taking a small liberty in examining minutely the oval piece of wood that hung on the wall, a yellow horse painted on it, the long, white tail of the horse touching the green grass sprouting up. Aside from the sounds of his mother at her tasks, he heard another person astir in the bedroom beyond the oval picture. He heard the sluggish movement of a person turning under blankets, then the sound of slippers scraped along the floor. He heard a man talking to himself with the voice that is acquired while the body is lying down: a voice pocketed deep in the throat, granular, caressing, complaining.

From the half-open bedroom door came a young man, not much older than a high school boy. His hair was red and stood up in curls, as if startled in advance, and he paused there in the doorway, staring in exaggerated surprise at the boy in the hallway chair. He was tying the tasseled belt of his bathrobe, which was a jewel-green silk, and one end of the belt he held in surprise across the palm of his right hand.

"Fran!" he called. "Who is this you let in?" His voice was cajoling and demanding; he listened to his own voice like a violin pupil listens to the music he makes. "Do you want to see me?' he asked, dropping his head in a pointing way. "If you have any business with me, speak up! If it's a debt I owe, let me congratulate you on getting past the door. Most of my creditors sit on the steps outside. Well, how much do I owe you? Whatever it is, I can't pay it."

Now he placed his hands on the arms of the chair, leaning over the boy, and the boy turned his face away, embarrassed, from the corners of his eyes meeting the young man's eyes.

"I can't pay you for this reason," explained the young man. "Do you see this house, how clean it is? Well, you should have seen it before that woman took a mop and vacuum to it." His close face was sleepily plump, and his hair, so near, was something to be puzzled out, something with an answer to it, its curls were so many and entwined. "If anyone is going to be paid," he said, "it's her, and you'll have to wait your turn. She works like a dog and stands for a lot of abuse from her employers, and she's constantly worrying all the time about that son of hers. She's got to keep him decently clothed, you know, and fed." Their eyes met again, forced by the young man's eyes to a mutual comprehension of her plight. "But I'll tell you," he said, laying his hand on the boy's shoulder. "Come into the kitchen with me and settle for a cup of chocolate."

Under the spell the boy slid off the chair so abruptly that his head hit the young man in the chest. With the nape of his neck in his host's hand, the boy was marched down the hallway. In the kitchen his mother was seated on a high stool, polishing silverware at the sink, a scarf of many faded colors wrapped around her head. She glanced over her shoulder at them, an absentness in her eyes as if she watched a dog or a cat, a household pet, saunter into the kitchen. Afraid suddenly that his presence jeopardized her job and that she was not going to recognize him, he stumbled as the young man pressed him down into a chair. For a moment he did not know who he should be, her son or the bill collector.

From the refrigerator, the host drew out a bottle of milk and poured some into a pan. Then he stirred in several teaspoons of cocoa and several of sugar, in this process spilling some of both on the waxed linoleum, and his leather slippers made a sticky, rasping sound as, uncaring, unhearing, he walked about.

"He don't need no chocolate," she said.

Up went the young man's spoon in a gesture of disbelief and dismay. The young man was startled by this rudeness. "Is that the way to talk to a guest of mine?"

The boy laughed out loud because he was sure now of who he was, and he shifted in his chair, granted a freedom of movement in the chairs of this house.

"For that," said the young man to her, "you can't have any. She can't can she?" he asked, but he asked it of her, bringing his face close to hers, delicately close, the two profiles, presented to the boy in the chair, reminding him of the approach and ascent of butterflies, touching and yet not touching. At once he was left out of the game. He had thought the game was for him and he learned that it was played only to accentuate some knowledge between his mother and the young man. And the boy was caught in the midst of his laughter, his elbows lifted eccentrically behind him like wings going up.

They had hot chocolate together, the young man and he, the host sitting with his legs apart, his robe falling away from his bare thighs, not at all embarrassed that a woman could see so much of his body. The young man drank in a hungry, nervous way, bobbing his head down impatiently to meet the cup on its way up. It was when he was lifting his head, swallowing elaborately in his haste to continue what he was saying, that he spoke the boy's name: "Matt," he said, "you've got catchall ears. Listen to this," and went on with his story. But the boy glanced up at his mother, unbelievingly. She had told his name to the young man, but of the young man the boy had been told not a thing.

When the host said, "Well, come along," Matt followed him up the hallway and into the bedroom. The curtains were closed, and the young man switched on the lamp by the bed, got down on his knee, and rummaged through a pile of magazines that lay under the bed. This room hadn't been cleaned yet. It smelled of cigarette smoke, of night perspiration, and upon the lamp's table were strewn a number of little things: theater tickets, manicure scissors, a red glass ashtray, a man's handkerchief, a lifesaver candy, a dime and four pennies. Was the young man an actor? he wondered, for he had heard that actors slept all day. There was something dramatic in the young man's bowed back, covered with the slick green robe, and in the leg, stretched out behind the bent knee, with its white knot of calf and its quivering heel. Rising, the young man placed in the boy's hand a thick magazine, a photograph of a Dalmatian dog on its cover, and gently prodded him to turn around; and the boy, lifting his head so that he could find his way out through the dimness beyond the lamp, saw his mother's black coat thrown over the back of a rocker, and on the seat of the rocker lay her small red hat.

Again he sat in the hallway, turning the pages of the sports magazine, while in the bedroom the young man poked about, getting dressed. The magazine had pictures of men in hip boots, fishing, of dogs carrying ducks from reedy water, of horses; and the smell of the paper was clean, strong as lacquer, the pages satin smooth and weighted in his hands. He turned up the palm of his right hand to see if it were dirty and would soil the white luster. Usually, he thought, she left her coat and hat in the kitchen. Once, in another house, when it was time for them to go, she had brought her coat from the back porch, where a late afternoon rain had flicked it through the screen; it was too shabby, she had said, to hang in the hall closet, because, if a guest came, he would not want to hang his coat next to hers. But in this house her coat was lying on a chair in a bedroom. His right hand was again on the magazine, but he still could not say whether his hands were clean or grimy. Lifting his hand again, he decided that it was not clean enough, and he closed the magazine, placing it on the floor beside his chair.

Closely, he listened to the sound of her in the kitchen, his hands clasped in his lap. By such devout observance of her presence he was proving to her that he was a more loving son than the young man could ever be, no matter how hard the other tried.

They would ride home together in the evening, boarding a trolley or a cable car, depending upon which neighborhood she was working in, and something in the waning day and in sitting beside her, watching the tall, narrow houses slip by like boards in one long fence, caused him to become tired of pre-monition. With the onset of evening's soft glamour, she would become for him quite alive and everlasting. On their journey home that evening, he sat beside her in the trolley, clasping between his knees her shopping bag, and each time she laid her hand on his knee, the love and shame of the betrayed wrinkled across his face. If he was unduly frightened by the way her hands were turning translucent, by the way her veins were rising along her forearms, if she was, after all, not going to die, there was, he thought another way she could be lost. When they climbed down from the trolley and walked along the street to their apartment house, he swung the shopping bag in his left hand so that the bag separated her and himself. But when the bag, light as it was, scraped against her ankle, his heart contracted with remorse as if he had deliberately hit her.

When she unlocked the door, he slipped in before her and lay directly down on the couch. Since their kitchen had no window, she switched on its ceiling light, and gradually as the street grew darker, as the sun, shining eastward down the street, withdrew its flame from the lamp at the corner, leaving a dark gray smudge in the globe, the panes of the bow window in which he lay became black mirrors and he saw in the one that was near to his face the reflection of the kitchen doorway and his mother by the stove. The picture was miniature, unreal, and when she spoke to him he answered her by speaking to the reflection, but this disturbed him and he turned his face to the rooms.

She came from the kitchen carrying plates, but instead of placing them on the table she continued to hold them in her hands while she faced him, pressing her hip against the edge of the table. Her face and down the front of her were obscured by the darkness of the room, but the sides of her thin body and some outer strands of her short hair were lit by the light from the kitchen behind her. She laughed a bit, in a wry way that did not change the set of her head.

"What do you want to follow me for?"

He put his hands over his ears.

When she had set the table, she came and stood above him. Into this room whose cold was not yet dispelled by the warm air from the kitchen, she brought in her body the heat from the stove and on her skin the steam.

"Well?" And, hearing no answer, "Come, sit down and eat."

Obediently he sat up, but as he got to his feet she put her

hands against his chest, pushing him down again; before he knew it, she was lying beside him and they were holding each other so closely that to breathe he had to turn his face upward.

"What do you want to follow me for?"

With his arms around her, he found himself listening to her body and heard her listening to his, and it was comical, almost, like two persons staring at each other through the same key-hole. In that moment he changed his reason for following her. It was not the possibility of her dying that troubled him, but something else he had picked up just an hour ago. The young man was pretending to be her son, and she did not object. This disloyalty of hers became so loud in their bodies that she had to let go of him and sit up.

"How did he know my name?"

"I told him," she said. "Can't I talk about my own son?"

"But you never told me you told him my name."

"Do I have to tell you about everybody I tell about my son?"

Was it something he had exaggerated all along, he wondered, their alliance against the persons she worked for? Although she came home bringing stories about them, describing them and their visitors jabbingly, vindictively, had he believed mistakenly that with these stories she bound herself and him together?

"Come now," she said. "Get up and eat."

But he made no effort to rise. She was standing away from him, weary of her own guilt, but he knew she was uncertain over which side she was on, his or the young man's with the crudely bared thighs.

Felis Catus

When they awoke their first Sunday morning in their very
own house and slippered across their sea-grass rugs to eat their
breakfast on orange pottery, with the soft blue bay and the dark
green trees and the houses farther down the hill all blurring
together beyond the bamboo screen like an impressionist painting; when now, after four years of apartments, they were settled at last, they talked together about finding a cat to live with
them.

Mayda, chatting with the girls under her supervision at the
telephone company, let it be known that she and her husband
were in the market for a cat. After all, it was one of those
homey, prosaic subjects that she was always looking for to
maintain common ground with the girls, ground fast slipping
away; for they were resentful, she knew, that her interest in the
arts had procured for her, tall and homely as she was, a tall and
cultured husband, and they suspected that he had sat down and
planned with her, like a military strategy, a cultural life together that ruled out her fraternizing with the girls. But when
one of the switchboard operators showed up in the morning
with a gray-striped kitten in a shoebox, Mayda regretted having touched upon the subject. Unable to refuse it, she grew
quite attached to it in the first week, for it did have a great deal
of whirligig energy that one would never have anticipated
from the *paleness* of it. Afraid, however, that their friends
would think them indiscriminate, they drove up one weekend
to a Siamese cattery near Guerneville and returned home with
two seal points, adolescent brothers. Charles, watching the
lean, beige brothers slide under the furniture and step high and
bouncy upon the piles of cushions, said, with satisfaction, that

they were losing no time in making themselves at home. But Mayda was a bit intimidated by the formality of their purebred bodies and went into the kitchen to get down on her knees and try to coax the gray one out from behind the stove.

In his browsing in the secondhand bookstore a few blocks from the London Men's Shop where he clerked, Charles came upon many a reference to cats in books that, topically, were in no way concerned with them, and he began to buy books that he would not otherwise have cared for—a Victorian era travel book on Italy because of some wonderful passages about the cats of the Forum Romanum, and a biography of a famous English surgeon because of the photograph it contained of that bearded gentleman with a huge tabby cat upon his lap. For the first time he was made aware of the predilection for cat companionship on the part of many renowned persons who had made their contribution to society in every field from entomology to religion, and the resemblance he bore to those persons in that respect increased his dissatisfaction with his job and reinforced the tantalizing idea, always in the back of his mind, of trying his hand as a novelist or an art critic. In Chinatown one afternoon he spied, in a window crowded with kimonos and carven teak boxes, a hanging glass shelf holding an assortment of tiny, painted ivory cats that overcame his antipathy for bric-a-brac, and he bought one—a yellow-striped tomcat on its haunches, a dazed, lopsided, pugilist's look in its face no bigger than an orange seed; and at the Museum of Modern Art one evening they bought two Fujita prints of feathery young cats, and Charles matted them on black silk.

When they had been living in their new home for six weeks, Mayda found time to reply to her sister Martha in Sacramento. She told how happy they were to be breathing what Charles called "green air," tending their garden and their cats, and told what a relief it was to drive out of San Francisco every evening, what a pleasure to drive back across the bridge to their charming hill town of Sausalito and contemplate across the bay the city where they worked all day; and she commented wryly that Charles' mother, in leaving him a sum of money large enough to make a down payment on a home, had finally contributed something to his comfort. Martha replied promptly, as usual, glad to hear they'd found a house "all cut out for them," and in uncomplaining comparison told them about the disrepair into which her own house had fallen. She'd taken a lot of time off from her work, she said, because she hadn't been feeling well for the past few months, and the money she had set aside for repainting and reroofing was used up. *Oh, well,* she wrote, *it doesn't look any worse than its neighbors, and that goes for me, too.* One of the items in her letter was about a college girl who had taken a room for a while in Martha's house. The girl had followed a state assemblyman to the capital, Martha wrote, but just before the assembly recessed the fellow must have broken everything off, because the girl cried all night long, so loudly that the children kept waking up and whimpering. *She was a strange girl,* Martha wrote. *The next morning she said she was going to Mexico and that we could have her cat. Then she packed her clothes and drove off in her foreign car. Peter tells me it's a Jaguar. You can have the cat if you want it. It's a handsome sir. She told me once what kind it was, something rare, but I can't remember. The kids always forget to feed the poor thing. Usually, I wouldn't mind seeing to it myself, but my chores seem to be piling up on me lately. Did I tell you I was down to 109 pounds?*

The following Sunday they drove up to Sacramento, leaving early in the morning and knocking at Martha's door at ten o'clock with tender, surprise smiles on their faces. Martha, in a faded housecoat, was eating breakfast alone, the children having run out to play. She pushed aside the dishes and served the visitors coffee, repeating what a nice surprise this was—How long was it now since they'd visited last? A year come August? They said they had come because they were alarmed by her letter, and Mayda, pulling up a chair to the table, thought her sister's appearance gave them ample reason for a visit. And when Martha, her eyes rickracked by teary eyelashes, reached spontaneously across the table to pinch Mayda's cheek, to plump it out as one fondly does a baby's cheek, crying, "Maydine, you rascal!" utterly forgetting that her younger sister's every letter in the past four years had been signed by the new name Charles had chosen, even the displeasure Mayda felt over the discarded name was quashed by the pleasure the ailing woman took in saying it.

"Charlie," Martha said, when they had hardly lifted their heads from the first sip of coffee, "why don't you poke your head out the back door and call the kids? Just call loud, they're somewhere around."

He got up reluctantly. "Don't they come home for lunch?"

"But they've just had their breakfast," Martha said.

"Well, why can't we wait?" he asked querulously. "We're not leaving so soon." And he sat down again, frowning.

"Never mind!" Martha cried hastily. "If you'd rather just sit and talk that suits me fine. Once they come, we won't get a chance." Then with sincere concern she asked him, "And how is your asthma these days?"

He shrugged, surprised that he should be questioned about something that had not bothered him for almost four years, not since the early months of his marriage. But Mayda, perceiving that her sister was tracing his petulance to some lurking illness, cried with obliging cheer, "Oh, he's much better now. But we keep our fingers crossed."

The sisters took up again, as if their letters had been actual conversation between them, the news about themselves, and, stimulated by this sitting face to face with each other, they recalled their parents, recalled their friends, and soon Martha was recalling again that rainy day, six years ago, when her husband, a taxi driver, had lost his life in the streets not far from the capitol building. They had heard it all before, but, to Mayda, it was more tragic now than it had been even the first telling, because of Martha's thinly striving voice. And so she was dismayed when she felt Charles' hand upon her knee, and, glancing at him, saw that he was sorry about his disagreeableness. His hand was reminding her that he was always upset to the point of surliness by the suffering of others, by their physical deterioration. It was because he wanted so badly to express his sympathy and yet sympathy seemed so inadequate. *Darling, you know how it is with me?* his hand said. She did not respond. All this under the table apologetics was an affront to Martha, who could see that he was not listening. But when, a few moments later, a cat brushed against Mayda's ankle and was gone, her own eyes lost their listening, she moved her feet searchingly.

The cat leaped onto Martha's lap and from there onto the table, where it stepped knowingly among the dishes in the manner of a prince slumming along narrow, winding streets. Martha feigned a sideways brush-off, rising from her chair and crying, "Did you ever?" But Mayda reached for it, lifting it from the table and setting it down on the floor, not attempting to take it into her lap, for it had the inviolable weight of someone else's property. It belonged to the girl in the Jaguar.

"What kind is it, Charles?" she asked eagerly.

"Peter knows," Martha said. "He remembers brand names and things like that."

The cat elongated itself toward a cracked white saucer under the high-legged stove, found the food there not to its liking, and sat down with its back to everyone, musing in the heat that still remained in the region of the stove. Never had they seen a cat with fur of rich brown, and the combination of topaz eyes and glossy brown coat and long, thin legs was the height of elegance.

"How old is Peter now?" Charles asked, lifting the percolator from the hot pad and shaking it.

"Here, here, I'll make some more!" Martha cried, reaching for it.

"No, no! I can do it!" Charles rose, glancing up at her cupboards. "Just tell me where you keep the coffee."

"Peter's nine now," Martha said, while Charles was filling the percolator, jostling the aluminum parts around and making himself at home. "And Norine's seven. Could I borrow a cigarette, I wonder?" she asked, leaning back and smiling a pale flirtation. "I'm not supposed to smoke, and so I've got none in the house. Peter caught me smoking once and he really had a tantrum. He's terribly worried about me, that boy. They're both as nice as pie, it almost makes me cry. They're so tidy! But you know the way kids tidy things up? Everything looks kind of odd, like there were little shrines all over the house." She leaned forward to accept a light from Mayda, holding the cigarette clumsily to her lips. "They're angels, but I'm not going to brag about it."

"Suppose we call them?" Charles suggested, setting the percolator on the flame.

"Wait'll I finish this cigarette," Martha begged, and Charles put his hands into his pockets and strolled about the kitchen, gazing at trinkets and potted cactus plants on the windowsill, and he leaned against the door frame, gazing out through the screen and remarking about the huge fig tree in the yard. Then he was purposefully gone, and they heard him calling. A few minutes later he held open the screen door, and under his arm, as under a bridge, the children entered, and he came in after them, smiling.

"God, they've grown!" he exclaimed. "They didn't even remember me, they couldn't imagine who'd be calling them. You should have seen their faces when they came through the hedge."

"It's Uncle Charles," Martha assured them. "Don't you remember Uncle Charles and Aunt Maydine? How can you forget so fast?" she cried. "He got afraid of a man's voice," Martha explained. "He thought something was wrong, he thought it was the doctor calling."

"I'm sorry, old man," Charles said, and Mayda shot an unbelieving glance at him, never having heard him use that term before. The triteness of it must surely, she thought, go against his grain. "I didn't mean to frighten you, but your mother was telling me all about you. About how tall you are and what an enormous memory you've got. She said you know what kind of cat the girl left."

"That cat? It's a Burmese," the boy said, not yet able to look Charles in the face. Beckoned by the sound of the children, the cat, having wandered up the hallway, now wandered in again and poked its muzzle at the food in the saucer, this time eating it reluctantly, its tongue smacking a delicate distaste. Ambivalently, its slender body seemed to be backing away from the saucer, for its front legs were in a low crouch while its hind legs were up straight and shifting weight, as if the cat were unwilling to admit to spectators that it was finally accepting this gray, crumbly food.

"Its name is Rangoon," the boy said, warming up. "She called it Baby all the time, and I asked her if that was his real name, and she said it was Rangoon. I thought that was a funny name. I'd never call a pet of mine a goon like that. I didn't say that, I just asked her why she wanted to call it Rangoon, and she said Rangoon was the name of a river in Burma and Burma was where the cat's ancestors came from. She said a guy who loved cats, he was in Burma when a war broke out, and he escaped with the cats with bullets flying all around him and brought them to the United States." He had slid from his mother's knee and was standing in a pose of jaunty authority, his ankles crossed and his hand on his hip.

"I should think she'd want to keep it," Charles asked, "with all the history it's got."

"She was spoiled," Martha said.

"She cried all night," Norine told the visitors.

"That's because she was spoiled," Martha explained to the child, who was leaning against her. "Norine feels sorry for her, but I say it did her good to lose that man. You couldn't contradict that girl one little bit."

All at once Peter and the cat were wrestling amicably in the hall doorway, and no one knew whether Peter had intercepted the cat's flight or whether the cat had seen Peter moving toward it. After a moment the cat hung down from Peter's hands, the long body tentatively resigned, the tail swishing.

"If you want that cat you take him," Martha said to Charles.

A grimace wrinkled up Peter's face. It wasn't a prelude to a weeping kind of frown but had a senility to it. He looked, Mayda thought, like an old man attempting to read fine print.

"But you never take care of it," his mother reminded him.

"Never mind," Charles said. "We've got our hands full of cats."

"But this is a rare one," Martha insisted above the sudden rattling of the percolator as it shot up jets of steam.

Charles fumbled the pot to a cold grill, all the comfortable agility gone from his movements. "Rare, smare," he said. "At night all cats are gray."

"Take it! I don't want it!" Peter had dropped the cat and turned his back on them, and was standing rigid, shouting up the hallway as if to someone at the other end.

Not at all dismayed by her brother's shouting, the girl said recitingly, "Once we had a cat that ate clam chowder. But this one can't keep nothing on its stomach. Peter told me he'd rather have a tabby cat because they can eat anything. He said he didn't think this one could even eat a mouse. He said he wasn't sure it was a real cat."

"Well then, it's good riddance, isn't it, Peter?" his mother asked, and chidingly, "People like you more when you're generous."

The jagged atmosphere was soon dispelled by Charles's blandishments and by the children's desire to be swayed by him. After a while the girl took his hand and led him into the backyard to see her vegetable garden. Peter followed them out, and towed Charles back through the kitchen to examine the boy's collection of rocks and gems, and, emerging from the children's bedroom, Charles informed Mayda that Peter had given him the name of a firm that sold Arizona rubies for 25 cents a packet. At lunch they sat crowded around the kitchen table, and Charles made jokes, the halting way he had of relating an anecdote or posing a riddle interfering to no degree with the children's appreciation of him, expressed in whoops and sputtering attempts to tell as funny a joke. In the midst of it, Mayda wondered with an unpleasant shock if he appeared naturally comic to the children. Sometimes children saw things and people disproportionately, and perhaps they misconstrued his tall, thin body and the sharp contrast of his black crew cut with his large, pale eyes. Even the pink shirt, so popular in the city with young career men, might appear to the youngsters to be comically inappropriate for a grown man, and part of a clown's costume. After a time, the children got overexcited, and Martha's weary voice darted in among their cries. She clasped Peter's wrist, and to force him to pay attention to her, shook his hand until it was limp and tractable.

At three o'clock they left, after an hour or so of parlor sitting with Martha. Under his arm Charles carried Rangoon, and as soon as they were alone in the car and the cat was leaping in leisurely curiosity from Mayda's lap to the back of the seat and down again, they were immediately silenced by their feeling of uneasy gain. The fact that they were taking Rangoon home with them made their whole visit suspect, even in the stronghold of their mated minds, and there was nothing they wanted to say to each other.

Within a few days, Mayda wrote to her sister, addressing the letter placatingly to Peter, too, and to Norine, and reported that Rangoon was getting along famously, that a friend of theirs who was a reporter for a daily paper and who had covered a cat show once had been over for supper, and he thought Rangoon was championship quality. But they weren't going to enter the cat in any competition, since they had no record of its ancestry. Can you imagine?—there was a studbook for cats wherein cats of known ancestry through four generations were listed, and another listing called the Foundation Record for cats of less than four generations of traceable ancestry? Wasn't that a kick? The reply came from Peter. It was written with pencil on lined tablet paper, and folded crookedly into the envelope, and he said that he was writing because his mother thought he ought to because Rangoon had been his cat; he told them about his and Norine's trip to a swimming pool and how they came home with their hair wet, and closed the letter on the same page he had begun it, hoping it found them in good health and signing it, *Your dear nephew, Peter.*

"Martha dictated it," Charles commented, and later, when the bomb had exploded, he remembered that casual observation of his and was able to say with sickly triumph, "What did I tell you?" Two weeks later, a letter from Martha came, the longest she had ever written to them, and following the news that her doctor had called in a bone specialist for consultation and that they had persuaded her to enter a sanitarium, *They think I'm such a rare duck, they don't want to lose hold of me;* following the information that the few silver serving spoons left to her by her mother, and the family photographs, were being sent to Maydine railway express, for she didn't want to be leaving precious things to the mercy of the tenants who'd be renting the house; following the details of upheaval, and the prediction, *You wait, Maydine, I'll bet my new boudoir slippers I'll be waltzing out of there in no time,* she at last asked them, Charles and Maydine, to take her two children into their home until she was well and could fetch them.

As customary on their return from work, they had taken the mail from the box that stood at street level, and, climbing the long flight of brick steps, had opened first that which promised to be most interesting. On that evening their choice was a letter from a couple vacationing in Spain and from whom they had expected no letter at all, being, as they were, on the outer edge of that couple's circle, and they had paused halfway up the steps to read it, this recognition of them arousing on the instant a sharp delight in their home up ahead of them and the feeling of the bay at their backs. It was not until they were already in lounging clothes and sipping their wine that she opened her sister's letter. They ate their supper with no appetite, and Charles asked, picking at the casserole and green salad on his plate, "Do we have to decide tonight?"

"Don't be silly," she said, feeling an impending annoyance with him. "She's not leaving for three weeks yet. We've all that time."

She recalled to herself with a kind of pain, with a feeling of lameness, how plain the children were. If they were beautiful, they'd be a little easier to have around; the admiration of visitors would compensate for the trouble of caring for them, and their beauty would reflect, in a way, upon herself, for they were her sister's children. But they were as plain as the rest of the family, as she herself had been, and now that she had taken the edge off a bit with the way she bound up her dark hair, with the wearing of Mexican silver necklaces that sometimes seemed as heavy and eliciting of favor as a religious ornament between her breasts, did she want to be constantly reminded by the children of her own essential plainness? Idling her fork around her plate, she was overcome by an irrational anger against Charles, and drew her feet in farther under her chair. What was the matter with being plain? What was the matter with being big-boned, lanky, and plain, as long as your heart was in the right place? Why must he be so particular about how she appeared to other people?

"This place isn't big enough," he was saying.

"There's an extra bedroom," she said, not to be persuasive but simply to state a fact.

"That's not an extra bedroom," he bristled. "It's got a north light, and it's going to be my studio. There's no *bed* in it, is there?"

She made no reply, scourging herself for her rural mentality that called a room a bedroom just because it was empty. But at once she felt allied with Martha, with her own dear sister, her own dear, honest and uncomprehending sister who continued to call her by her real name, and she stood up, choking on her misery.

He followed her into the front room and stroked her bowed head and made her get up a minute from the chair so he could sit down and take her onto his lap, and he comforted her and said he was sorry and if she wanted the children to come and live with them, it was all right with him. They were nice kids and old enough to take care of themselves after school. It was all right with him. But she didn't *know,* she wailed. She had a closeness with him, she told him, that she had never had with anyone, with her mother or father or even with Martha, and she didn't want it destroyed by any relatives of hers imposing on them, by the children who would probably shatter this affinity by denying it nourishment like time and seclusion and the indulgence of happy, little idiosyncrasies. She didn't know, she wailed. She didn't know.

Only once did they bring themselves to mention the problem, when one evening Charles, bending over to set down upon the floor the large blue platter spread with canned mackerel, asked Mayda, "Where'll they go if they don't come here?" and gently with his foot pushed aside the cats who were rising up on their hind legs or running against one another just beneath the descending plate.

"Go? They'll go to some neighbor, I guess," she said. "If there are any that generous."

"Will they wonder if we don't take the kids?"

"Who?"

"The neighbors, the neighbors," he said.

"They're not *your* neighbors," she replied acridly.

That night he came down with an asthma attack the like of which he had not experienced since his childhood. He sat bolt upright in bed, his chest hollowed out by his long, hoarse breaths that drew her up beside him in terror. She switched on the lamp above their bed and saw that the four cats, bedded down over the expanse of comforter, had already been watching him in the darkness, their heads high and alerted. So frightened were the animals by the sounds he was making that when she slipped from under the covers and ran in her bare feet to fetch his nebulizer, they fled the room. She sat beside him on the bed, fervently kissing his shoulder, and when at last he had some relief and lay back, she asked him, "What could have done it, darling?"

"My life's slipping by," he replied in hoarse sarcasm. "It worries me."

"It might be the cats," she speculated.

"The cats?" he cried, tossing her cooling hand off his brow. "Why not pollen, or eggs, or anything? That little lost cat we smuggled up to our apartment that time—it slept on my neck all night, it liked to sleep there, and did I get an attack?"

Already shaken by his spell, she could only stare down at him timidly, her long hair falling around her arms like a shawl protecting her from his cruelty. He softened, stroking her arm and explaining to her that he was sick of his job, literally sick of it, that he didn't have it in him to be a salesman, no matter how well he was doing at it. He tried hard to be capable, he said, just because he hated it so. She agreed that it was time for him to quit the London Shop. If he wanted, she said, to take a few months off and look around for something more congenial, or even do a critical article, why they'd get along for a time with just her salary. They'd meet the house payments and the car payments all right, they just wouldn't be able to bank anything or buy clothes or things like recordings.

The next evening he told her that he could not bring himself that day to give his notice of resignation. Maybe he wouldn't have another attack for a long time, he told her. Maybe the one last night had been a fluky thing. But a few hours later, when he had barely laid his head on the pillow, he came down with an attack the nebulizer was not equal to, and she called in the local doctor, who gave Charles a shot and left some pills and told him to drop by for a checkup when he got the chance. In the morning he was too weak to rise, and he agreed to her proposal that she would phone his shop as soon as she got to work and inform the manager that Charles was suffering from asthma and suggest that, since she didn't know how long he'd be away from work, they'd better interview some other man for the job.

When she came home that evening she sprawled in the canvas butterfly chair. No words spoken, he brought her a whiskey and water as if she had ordered it, and sat down on some pillows on the floor, sat awkwardly, his long bones at odds with one another. Whenever, before, he had revealed a momentary fear of her, her vantage had put her into a panic, but now she took a cloudy pleasure in seeing him uncomfortable. He was leading her by the nose into a conspiracy against the children, and he *ought* to be uncomfortable about it. He *ought* to be feeling guilty. She slid farther down into her chair, stretching her legs out like a slattern into a position he had chided her about in the past and cured her of.

Not long after supper he retired to the bedroom as if he had been banished there. Until it grew dark she busied herself in the garden, troweling here and there, and three of the cats kept her company. Enlivened by the cool of the evening, they were scuffling together, or calling throatily, or darting at insects she could not see in the dimness. She had no view of the bay from this rear garden, but the absence only increased her appreciation of the place, for she knew the bay was there, waiting, while she occupied herself within this garden that was filled with absolving fragrances and enclosed by plum and madrona trees. Charles had closed the bedroom windows against the garden with as much finality as if a decree had been read to him, denying him the pleasures of the evening; the bamboo screens and tan silk curtains were both in use, and through this double film she saw only the glow of the lamp above the bed and that was all. She thought of him propped up by a mountain of colored pillows from the living room and suffering pangs of guilt, and her resentment of his maneuvering against Peter and Norine was dispersed by her gratitude to him for the composite gift he had given her—for marriage and this home and this garden. She troweled under the bedroom windows, thinking of her childhood and what she had learned of his. They hadn't been happy, either. No happier than Peter or Norine. Charles in military school, seeing his mother once a year and his father never, and herself going to work at fourteen, passing for eighteen because she was so tall and overgrown, and crying at night for all the things so bountifully possessed by the small-size girls. Now, for the first time, they were on compatible terms with life. They had each other and they had this house that, although it was built to the specifications of the previous owner, seemed built for themselves, and in its interior decoration expressed Charles' talents that had been so frustrated by his years spent in stuffy, small apartments. After an evening at a concert, they could return here and find a certain leisure in which to remember and assimilate. They had no more time than they had before, but they had room and graciousness in this little house that gave the impression of being time. And did they not deserve this?

She stood in the doorway of the bedroom, clasping the

lapels of her sweater across each other as if she had caught a chill in the garden, and said to him, "I'll write Martha tonight. I'll say we're sorry, but we can't possibly take the children because we're having some trouble . . . you've got your asthma again, and this time it's so bad you've had to quit your job. I'll explain it as a kind of nervous breakdown, and say that we'll just be able to make ends meet for a while."

He said, "Oh, God, Mayda, I feel like a dog," and laid his book on the comforter and could not look at her, and then, in a moment, broke, bowing his head and rubbing his hand over his face, saying to her, "Come here, come here."

She went down on her knees by the bed, and they embraced, and he stroked her hair back to kiss her brow, while she assured him that it was not his fault he was laid low by his desire to do more than just sell clothes for the rest of his life. It was not his fault at all that they couldn't take the children. They wept together in relief, for now they were again in accord, and they wept for Martha and the kids and the whole tragic situation in that little family.

In the days that followed he set himself a regimen of reading and researching for the article on Paul Klee he had in mind, and this activity, and Mayda's enthusiasm about his project, had a calming effect upon his nights and he slept well. But on the fifth night he was again victimized by his asthma; not so severe a spell, but distressing enough, and he coughed, off and on, until morning. In the last gray hour before she arose, she suggested to him that he really ought to go down and see the doctor for some allergy tests, and, feeling that their accord was certain enough now that he would not think she was belatedly accusing him, she again brought up the possibility that the cats might be causing his spells. Lying upon his back, his hand spread appeasingly upon his chest, he considered this at length, and they agreed to experiment. They would prohibit the cats from entering the bedroom, and twice a week she would brush the cats thoroughly and throw away the brushings in a paper bag, precautions that would rid the air of the irritant, to an extent. And to further convince her of his amenability all along, he began to muse upon who, among their friends, would be most glad to receive the cats, if the experiment did not work and they might be forced to give the cats away. The Siamese brothers could go to that young couple who had bought the house on upper Broadway in the city and who said they were going to get around some day to buying a Siamese; they were just acquaintances, but at least he knew them well enough to see that they would be appreciative. The gray cat Grisette could go to the child next door, and Rangoon? Well, Rangoon could go to Lizbeth, that elderly photographer who kept the most exquisite cats. It was six months now since the evening they'd been introduced to her at her exhibit in the Museum and had gone up to her studio afterward. She hadn't been by to visit them, and they'd phone her once more and say they had a surprise for her.

So when, a few days later, Charles strolled down the hill to the doctor's office and the doctor told him to get rid of the cats that had been underfoot that night of his house call, Charles was able to say that Mayda and he were already experimenting. And when he told Mayda about it that evening, repeating what the doctor had said—that the asthma was only a symptom and that what he really had was an extravagant fondness for cats, a disease, said the doctor, called Felis Catus—Charles laughed pleasurably in the manner of one recalling a compliment.

They needn't have fretted where to place Rangoon, for one Sunday afternoon, a few weeks after the experimenting was begun, while Charles was cutting away the grass from between the brick steps, a white Jaguar drew up in the street below and through the trees he saw a girl bend from under the low, sleek top and stretch her leg to the road. Turning to his cutting again, he heard a girl's heels on the bricks below him, and gazing around to her and prepared to tell her where this neighbor or that lived, he saw her paused below, her face lifted. "I'm looking for Charles Corbett," she told him, "or his wife."

At once he recalled the Jaguar of the girl who had roomed in Martha's house, and he smiled a sweet quirk of a smile, replying, "You flatter us. It's Rangoon you're looking for."

They laughed together, and he put his clippers aside and led the way up to the house, not in any hurry, moving with an erect ease in his long body to convey to her that they had her kind of visitor every day. Under the fuchsia bushes by the front door, one of the Siamese brothers was sitting drowsily. The girl bent to stroke it, but it sprang away from her and bellied out of sight, setting the little red flowers aquiver. "One has to introduce oneself, of course," the girl said.

Charles chuckled ruminatively, opened the door and called Mayda. Fortunately, she had just freshened herself after a day in the garden and was in a crisp yellow frock and Japanese sandals.

"Mayda, this is Rangoon's mistress," he said, and they all laughed because the cat was given more importance than the girl.

Charles went in search of Rangoon, returned in a minute, when Mayda was asking the girl what drink she preferred, with the cat riding backwards in his arms, paws upon his shoulder, muzzle delicately examining his ear. He placed the cat in the girl's lap, and Rangoon stood for a moment startled, balancing on spindly legs. The girl cupped the cat's narrow face, cooed its name, and asked if it had missed her.

"They thought I'd forsaken it, can you believe it?" she cried to Mayda. "When I left I was so upset, I was mad at everybody, even Rangoon, and I said I didn't know when I'd be back." She had, Charles thought, the languidly clutching manner of the University Beauty, and he wondered if she'd left the cat with a certain design, a studied carelessness. "Believe me," she said, "I couldn't have gone back any sooner because I couldn't bear it. The town, I mean. Emotionally, you know. But yesterday I drove up, and there were absolute strangers in the house. The woman said there was no cat around like I described. She told me her landlady was in a hospital, and the kids were staying with friends down the street. She pointed the house out to me, and I went over and knocked on the door, and there were about six kids swarming to answer it, and I thought, Oh, my God, they've skinned it! And I recognized the boy and shook him and screamed at him, What have you done with my cat? Well, he told me you'd taken it, but he didn't know your address, so I had to put in a call to the hospital and get his mother on the line, and she told me where you live."

"And how is she?" Mayda asked, alarmed, and happening at that moment to be seating herself with drink in hand, she hoped that the activity of her body—the flouncing skirt, the crossing of legs—obscured her voice so that the girl would neither hear nor answer.

"She didn't say, she just said to give you her love and that she hoped Charles was better. She said she was awfully sorry to hear about Charles' breakdown . . ." The girl looked him over, and Mayda hastened to explain that it wasn't a breakdown, really. "It's only that the cats bring on his asthma," Mayda said. "He went through several awful spells of it and had to take a vacation from his work. We're so attached to the creatures that we really can't bring ourselves to part with them. You can't do it at the drop of a hat, you know," she said. "So we're in the midst of experimenting now, we're forbidding them to come into the bedroom, and I brush their fur ritually. If that doesn't work we'll simply have to give them away."

"Oh, for God's sake, Mayda," Charles protested, as if she were praising him, for the girl was gazing at him with glittering sympathy.

"But how selfless of you!" the girl cried at him. "Rangoon couldn't have asked for nicer folks to live with. He won't want to come home with me now. But things were so upset," she explained, and, bowing her head and stroking the cat alongside her hip, she was pouring out the story of the assemblyman and herself: that she had followed him to the capital and met him in an East Indian restaurant she'd discovered for them and that he had his opposition to her all jotted down on a card, like notes for a speech, and that she had prevailed against him. She was discreet enough to withhold his name and the part of the state she was from, but that was her only discretion in the rambling story.

With misgivings, Rangoon went along with the girl, cradled in her arms. Going down the brick steps, she felt her way with the pointy toes of her high-heeled pumps, for she had to bend her head to soothe him so he wouldn't bolt, and Mayda and Charles, following after her, were poised to catch him if he ran back up the steps. In the car Rangoon inhaled the odor of the red leather upholstery, and, standing on his hind legs, redis-covered the familiarity of the top of the seat. Leaping up there and stretching out, the cat gazed with mollified yellow eyes at Mayda and Charles who had bent their heads under the top to gaze at him.

"Thanks again, awfully," the girl said, and her white cotton dress slipped back from her young knee as she put her foot to the clutch. They waited in the middle of the road until the car reached the turn that went downhill, where the girl slowed and waved to them. They stood waving back with an appealing awkwardness, like two wise persons attempting to be less serious, until the car was hidden by the trees.

The Science of Life

At nine o'clock the wife came home alone. The babysitter was startled by the reckless sound of the tires and the scattering of gravel. She was a homely girl with such a consciousness of herself that she felt under scrutiny even when alone. She felt that people saw a homely girl as someone not to be trusted because there was so much that was wanting about her, so much that was unpardonable, as if she herself had chosen how she was to appear on earth, and chosen badly. Whenever she was hired to take care of children at night, she remained in one chair, reading her school books while they slept. So now, hearing the car and the woman's high heels on the porch, the girl sat still long enough for the woman to see that she had not been surprised in some tacitly forbidden part of the house. When the woman threw off her coat, the girl got up and reached for her own coat on the back of the chair.

"Did they wake up?" the woman asked.

"No," the girl said, pulling on her coat.

"Is there a boy waiting for you?" the woman asked, her voice climbing.

"No," the girl said, tossing her scarf around her throat.

"Then what's your hurry?"

The woman walked away, swinging her hips so that the skirt of her red strapless dress flared out. "Come on and have a little cognac. You can't say no to that. You can't go out there without a little cognac. It's cold, cold enough to snow. You ever seen snow?" she asked, confrontingly. "So many kids out here, they've never seen snow. It never ceases to surprise me. Where I come from it snows up to your eyebrows."

She jerked at an earring to remove it, then clapped her hand over her ear, weaving up and down in pain. "The brandy's there," she cried.

The girl slid open the doors of the dark, polished cabinet. She could not identify the cognac bottle among the three rows of bottles. "There!" the woman said, coming up behind her just long enough to point out the bottle. Then she flung herself down on the sofa and lay with one arm across her eyes. The girl found glasses and poured the cognac near the woman's hand that hung out over the coffee table. The hand was plump, the fingers long, and the nails were the same red as the dress.

"You can't drink it standing up," the woman said, her arm still across her face.

The girl sat down in the same chair, holding her glass in both hands. The woman sat up and leaned forward to lift her glass. "You picked the right glasses," she said.

The girl was confused by the remark. If she accepted it as praise, would she be a fool because it was intended as derision? She could not even begin to speculate why a woman in a dress so beautiful, a woman with her dark hair in angelic curls, her slender legs in black nylons and her feet in delicate sandals with high heels, why a woman so perfect for the party would come home early and sit with a girl who was almost a stranger.

"You want me to call a taxi for you?" the woman asked.

"It's only a few blocks," the girl said. "It's early."

"Besides, you're a big girl," the woman said. "How tall are you?"

The girl was tallest in her class. She was big-boned and her long legs were large, but though they were awkward indoors, they ran fast and unerringly and never tired.

"What're you going to do when you graduate?" the woman asked, not waiting for an answer to her other question. "What is your ambition?" she asked with mock solemnity.

The girl stared at her bare knees. "I think I'll be a biology teacher, or something in biology."

"Oh, biology!" the woman cried. "You're just the person I want to ask. What is the difference between a man and a woman?" She gave a short, sharp laugh.

The girl wondered if she was being told that she would have a difficult time coming to any knowledge of man outside a textbook. She stared over her brandy glass at her knees, wanting to escape this assault that was not only an assault but also a plea to attend the woman's misery.

"So you're going to be a biologist," the woman said. "Isn't that what you'd call a fundamental thing? I mean, here you are studying about plants and animals, life on earth. I remember something about it, things like assimilation and excretion, and what is the name of that—what is it called, phenomenon—where the plant turns toward the sun? That's always seemed remarkable to me. You can turn the plant upside down, and it makes a U-turn and starts to grow upward again, or sideways, wherever the sun is. Do you think it's remarkable or are you used to it?"

The girl had never been asked a question like that. If she were to say, yes, it was remarkable, would the woman think she was a simpleton?

"Oh well, don't answer," the woman said. "You professional peole, you don't let us laymen in on your deep secrets. You think that when I say, 'Oh, isn't that remarkable?' that I'm only asking a silly question. Only you people way down under the sea or way up there in the stratosphere know how really remarkable it is. Isn't that right? No, never mind," she said, waving her hand. "Don't tell me. I'd never feel your kind of remarkable even if you spent the whole night explaining it to me."

Outside, a car came to a stop on the gravel and a car door slammed. The woman bent her head toward her knees and waited in that contrite position.

The husband came into the room, averting his eyes from his wife. "I didn't know you were still here," he said to the girl. "I would have had the taxi wait. I'll take you home now."

The woman got up and with the same agitated swing in her hips began to walk around the room. "She's not just any old baby sitter," she said. "I asked her to stay with me. She's got something fundamental. I knew it when I first saw her. You really ought to sit and listen to her."

The girl caught the man's glance at her and found in it a puzzlement, an attempt to comprehend the joke. The wife, apparently relieved that he had followed her home but afraid of his anger, went on walking around, twisting her rings, slapping at cushions. "You can't say that about anybody at that party," she said, her voice trembling. "Nobody there was what you could call fundamental. They were all trivial. What's it called when a plant turns toward the sun? I felt myself turning homeward because I knew she was here."

The overcoat made his anger more perilous—he could turn around and never come back. "You call them trivial," he shouted, "because you can't stand my interest in them."

"All of them are, and you and me," she cried. "And whatever it was you were saying to her for so long while everybody was looking at me to see how I was taking it, that was the most trivial of everything ever said on earth. I wanted to come home because I knew there's a girl here who's got nothing to be trivial about." The woman covered her face and wept. "She thinks I'm making fun of her, but I wish I were her so I could forget all the trivia she doesn't know about and never will. When she suffers it won't be like this—something you know isn't suffering but there's no other name to call it."

One of the children began to call and the woman ran down the hallway, her weeping converted by the calling into an act of concern for the child. The girl picked up her textbooks. The woman's prophecy about her was the worst of the night's ridicule. It was impossible to imagine how her suffering was to be in any way enviable. If there was suffering here, between this man and the woman, it was a kind reserved for those fortunate enough to know the pleasures, also. She drew her scarf up over her head, pulling it in against her cheeks to conceal her face from their mistaken sight of her.

"Come on, I'll drive you home," the man said, hurrying to open the door. Before he put his hand on the knob he took three dollar bills from his wallet and handed them to her. She pushed them into her coat pocket. "I hope you'll be warm enough," he said, smiling at her to make up for everything his wife had said, but her eyes avoided his smile that was more attentive to the charm of the apology than to her.

Anna Lisa's Nose

It was a family of three sons and four daughters, every one of whom had a great arched nose. Since both the mother and father had a nose of that kind and before their marriage were often mistaken for brother and sister, there was hardly room for variation among the children. The family had other features in common. They had black hair, thick and smooth, fair skin highly suffused with rose, and large, dark eyes with heavy lids. They were tall and strong, and the women were voluptuous. These characteristics were, however, overshadowed by their great bony noses whose arch began to jut out directly between the thick brows without waiting, without discipline from any natural accord of features.

The family, except for one child, accepted this nose without complaint and some were proud of it, the father and mother especially, as they would be of a son who had become a general. But the next-to-the-youngest daughter contended with it as with an arrogant parasite. At the age of eighteen, a few days after her birthday, she underwent surgery for its removal, or the removal of more than half of it. The surgeon's fee was taken care of by her father who, although not a prosperous man, a vine grower with a small vineyard and winery, was so affected by her threats to drown herself that he had come to feel a personal blame for not only his children's noses but his own, as if in his mother's womb he had asked the Creator for just that kind of nose. The night that he gave in was the most alarming night the family had ever known. When their sister threw herself down before their father, tearing at her long hair and beating her fists on the floor, the younger children jumped from their beds in terror and, clasping one another, howled, and the older ones sprang up trembling above their homework and their sewing. Her mother fell down beside her child, holding the writhing body to her bosom, wailing *Anna Leesa, Anna Leeesa,* while the father, exhausted from nights and months of defending the shape of his family's nose, stood above them, his strong legs shaking, unbuckling his belt, at last defeated and on his way to bed.

The night before she left home, Anna Lisa stood for an hour before the mirror above the basin, transfixed by the nose that was so beautiful it was like a gift direct from heaven. No surgeon, no fee figured in the transformation. It seemed to her that her future was like tremendous angel wings urging her body to rise.

With the money she had earned at a poultry farm, candling eggs every day after school, she bought a bus ticket to New York. She wore a tan, belted raincoat that before the transformation had been no more than a raincoat on a girl with a large nose. It was now a raincoat on a girl with a beautiful figure whose face, glanced at in the depot by curious men coming from behind her, did not fail them. On that bus ride she received two proposals of marriage: one from a Texan, a radio singer in a cowboy hat, and the other from a Missourian, a bulldozer operator, and for the first time in her life was kissed by a man. In that dark bus roaring across the country, as the clustered lights of towns and the sole lights far afield were left behind a hundred times over, she put her lips to a cigarette that, in the same moment, had been on a stranger's lips, and then felt the stranger's mouth itself on hers, and this was her initiation into the world of the normal, the unobsessed, the indefective. When the Texan got off, the Missourian got on.

She found a job modeling coats in a department store. She was a bit too large to model dresses and, although she was pleased to model anything because to model meant that she was an ideal, and, although the big fur ruffs framed her face like a reward for her years of shame and suffering, she felt that to lose a few pounds was a challenge. She felt that she must answer any challenge now because of a sense of betrayal that underlay her exhilaration. To do her exercises and to diet was not of minor consequence, for from that more tasks would follow, more challenges and more successes that would prove to those at home that the alteration of her nose was not a frivolous act, was not a derogation of them but a rite that had conditioned her to take life by the horns. When her hips were less she felt perfect enough to apply for a job with the famous couturiere, Natasha.

In time she was invited to parties at the home of the couturiere. The woman was rather overbearing, crackling with energy and with commands that she thought were the most subtle of hints, as she often said of herself that her one virtue was diplomacy. Anna Lisa was grateful for the woman's friendship and did not in the least mind the woman's large, curved nose. She felt that the couturiere's obliviousness to her nose was to be commended, for that unconcern made all other noses a matter of no significance. It made the alteration of Anna Lisa's nose so minor an act that she felt she ought to forget about it and not be troubled by it and always believe that she had been born with the present one. The significance of Natasha's nose was recalled for her one night after a party at the couturiere's, when a young man she had met there, an attorney, was fondling her in his Lincoln. In the first recess, while they smoked cigarettes, he began to criticize their hostess.

"She presides," he said. "She's got a presiding nose. That's how she got where she is. The most casual conversation, not to say trivial, she's got to preside over it. And that's why she never got married and never will, she'd preside over the lovemaking. With a nose like that she can't do anything but preside."

The young man, aware that Anna Lisa was no longer burgeoning against him, embraced her again at once. She wanted to dispute his theory but she had no words to begin; neither had she a leg to stand on, for hadn't she herself fallen for that theory, convinced that people had mistaken her nose for the shape of her entire being, and mistaking it herself? Yet, after all, didn't she feel that her true self was the girl in this man's arms, in the arms of this tall and well-to-do young man who was satisfied with nothing less than the best in everything, and not the girl who had been forced by nature to present a false front? At this point she lost patience with the couturiere. If Natasha allowed her nose to misguide, then she must suffer the consequences. Anna Lisa's flesh began again to swell, and at that moment the young man underwent the premonition that the astounding girl in his arms was to be his wife.

In the month preceding the marriage, Anna Lisa could not bear the couturiere. It was as if Natasha had become a member of her family and might disgrace her, and since Anna Lisa did not tell her family of the marriage until after the ceremony, fearing that someone might show up a day or two before, she felt that Natasha ought not to know about it, either. Anybody else, anywhere, on a bus or in a restaurant or in an elevator, who resembled her family was avoided in her mounting fear of her family and its power to ruin her life. Natasha, who had brought Anna Lisa and Richard together, was avoided as if she had attempted to keep them apart.

Anna Lisa left the establishment after her marriage. She became a model for fashion photographers and because of her large eyes and square face and heavy black hair and because she was angular and rounded at the angles and could, at will, assume a coercive stare, and because she appeared to possess the moody material of experience such as that of a mistress of a man in high places, she was among their favorites. After several years among the anonymously famous, those women whose faces and bodies are famous and whose names are unknown, she began to weary of her career. She had seen herself so often in the magazines, she had seen herself in so many poses, lying and leaning and curled up into a ball, and against so many foreign palms and rocks and urchins, deserts and seas, ancestral stairs and arches, that she was quite convinced of her fame. She was quite convinced that the alteration of her nose had been entirely justified by the fame that followed, that, indeed, it had been a kind of public service. She was now nearing thirty and felt the need to retire into her marriage, to give of herself to her husband who had become a partner in a law firm whose counsel was sought by great corporations and the Federal Government. They left the apartment in the city for a remodeled farmhouse and garden in the country.

Richard had often mused on the images of four children resembling himself and Anna Lisa in four combinations, but because he was proud of her career and preferred not to disrupt it at its peak, he had never brought up the subject except in jest. Among his friends there were many who, at his age, were already fathers of three and four children, and one, whose wife had died after bearing two, had married a woman with three of her own. Now that Anna Lisa had quit her career, he wanted very much to be caught up by the waves of the generations, to be swept off his feet by that cognizance of his own mortality and the endurance of the race. She said that she was not yet in the mood to devote herself to a child. She had given so many years to her career and felt that she deserved a period of rest in which, of course, she intended to study all the things she had neglected. She took up the piano again—at the age of twelve and again at fifteen she had had some lessons, and she began the study of botany in order to become a wizard of a gardener, and she did become that and grew the most beautiful garden in the county. She also developed a genius for exotic meals, Japanese and Samoan and North Chinese and Balinese, and so her time was taken up with music and botany and gardening and the preparation of rare suppers, and all these talents enhanced her in the eyes of her husband and dissuaded him from insisting on a child. She hinted that she was afraid of childbirth, but this was not her real fear. She was afraid that the child, boy or girl, would bear a great, arched nose—strangely, because both she and her husband had small noses. Then he would suspect that she was unfaithful to him or, worse, suspect that she was not the woman he had chosen to be the mother of his children.

It was while she was in the midst of these several gratifying pursuits that she received a letter from her brother in the army. He wrote that he was coming up to New York for a few days, on leave from his base in the South. The prospect of her brother's visit terrified her. One minute she resolved to write to him, telling him she would be out of town; the next minute, conscience-stricken about her previous decision, she made up her mind to meet him at a designated place in the city; the minute after that, she vowed to bring him home and the vow brought on an awful contraction in her stomach that forced her to walk around hunched over. She changed her mind and sat at her desk, imploring him to forgive her for having to depart for Europe the day before his arrival, but unable to lift the pen and write it down. She walked through the house and garden for an entire day, wringing her hands, feeling a five-pound loss, unable to eat or to sit.

She met him at a restaurant that no one she knew patronized. He was her youngest brother, now nineteen, and with his great, arched nose in a face saddened by army life, he was someone she was glad she was not taking home. He was tall and thin and shy, slow-moving and awkward, conscious of his dull uniform and of her beauty that seemed unrelated to him. She told him that her husband was sick with the flu. Since he had not expected to be invited to her home, he took this information for a warning that she could not remain with him long. Under harassment by the aborted time, he lost whatever voice and color he had, and ate with his eyes always down. Anna Lisa, desiring silence so that the meal would be over sooner and yet anticipating that once she was home again she would collapse and curse herself for a traitor and a coward, plied him with sisterly questions about mother, father, sisters, brothers. Then, to her surprise, she heard herself confessing an unhappy marriage. She said that her husband was running around with other women. She lied so that he could tell their family that the deed to make her different from them had not brought her happiness. Sullenly, he insisted on paying his own check. On the sidewalk they parted, shaking hands. At the last minute she kissed him on the cheek, and as she felt his poor, sunken chest against her she reexperienced the agony of her adolescence. He lacked the vigor and breadth of the other men in her family and she felt responsible for his lagging condition. Had she stirred up in him a shame about himself, back on that night when he was a child watching her beat the floor?

From that time on she complained to her husband that he was ignorant of her inner life, and yet felt that if he knew it he would be as intolerant of it as he would have been of her sad and great-nosed brother. And she began to suspect and investigate others' dissatisfactions. They were very friendly with a couple so smugly similar she sometimes, in her thoughts, almost confused one with the other; they were both painters, neither having more recognition than the other nor more talent, and they were both not much over five feet tall, the wife reaching that height, however, only in very high heels; they were both of delicate frame, both with moon faces, both with cultured drawls that expressed the same opinions. Anna Lisa, at the edge of her round bathing pool in the garden, questioned the wife just before the couple left after a Sunday visit. The husband was still inside the house with Richard.

"Do you feel that your husband really loves you?" Anna Lisa asked. "I mean," she said, "do you feel that he is forced to love you because you are just his size? I mean, do you think that he wonders at times what kind of woman he would have spent his life with if he were, say, six feet tall? Do you think he resents you because he was forced to love you because of his height?"

"You're out of your mind," her friend said. "What I think he thinks is that there are tall people and medium-sized people and short people and all the nor-nor'east and sou-sou'west in-between people and that he happens to fall in the short group along with a woman who seems to have been made just for him."

"You don't feel he's dissatisfied then?"

"With what?"

"Well, with you. With himself."

"Well, one night he said to me, 'Thank God for small women,' but I didn't take it as synonymous with small favors. I felt that it was praise unto me. But God, maybe I was wrong."

"Nooo, no," Anna Lisa cried. "I think that he's the kind of man who, if he'd fallen in love with a woman six feet tall, would have wooed her and married her."

"You make him sound like a courageous midget," said the

wife who by this time had swiftly pinned up some loose strands of hair, thrust her yarn and needles into her bag, dug her feet into her high-heeled sandals, and stood up.

Anna Lisa was secretly glad when this couple did not come by anymore and word came back to her, through a friend, that they thought Anna Lisa unbearable. They had always disturbed her; she had suffered for them for the very reason that they appeared to be unconscious of any need to suffer for themselves. They had reminded her of the unconcern of her brothers and sisters who accepted their noses with no despair and went about the business of living.

One day she received a telegram that her mother was dying. When she was packing, after having made reservations on an evening plane to the Coast, another telegram informed her that her mother was dead. She ran to her closest neighbor and threw herself into the woman's arms, weeping with grief and with guilt for not returning to see her mother in the almost ten years since she had left home. The memory of her mother as she had been when Anna Lisa was a child, the memory of her drudgery and of her pleasures, of her cascading Italian, and of her consoling wail that she had hoped would take the place of Anna Lisa's operation—these memories put a wild sound into her weeping. When her husband came home, Anna Lisa hid herself in his arms from a decision about the funeral. She told him that there was no point in her attending it since she had not gone back to see her mother alive; it was a sanctimonious practice, the return of the child to the body of the parent. And what comfort could she bring her father and her brothers and her sisters, since she was like a stranger? She wept and wandered and, fatigued by her day of grief and guilt, fell onto her bed.

She felt compelled now to deny her husband the love she had denied her family; she felt compelled to criticize him as she had criticized her family with her years of keeping her distance. Baffled by this cruel change, he made love to her by force. He tumbled her down, his years of bag-punching and rope-skipping at the athletic club put to an ultimate use; yet, once down, her sudden lassitude spurned him as much as her fighting. She took revenge on him for his ignorance of her secret, she took her revenge on him for surely turning away from her if he had met her with her other nose, for refusing her as his bride, for not even entertaining a thought of her as his bride, and for refusing her family as his family-in-law. And when their marriage became intolerable and he developed an ulcer, on that night he was first stricken with a terrible pain in the pit of his stomach, a pain so fierce that he ran his car into a fence and had to be driven home in somebody else's car, sweating and incoherent, on that night she became more solicitous, more tender than she had ever been before.

She saw to the strict observance of his diet, of his hours of rest, of his abstention from liquor, saw to it all with a concentration born of remorse and abiding love. And when he was calm again and had put on twenty pounds from his diet of milk and starch and his disinclination to exercise, and their discord was a thing of the past, she told him that she was going to invite her eldest sister, who was a widow, to stay with them for a time. As a result of his own suffering, he might, she thought, be able to comprehend, at her sister's arrival, what she, Anna Lisa, was suffering.

Anna Lisa did not invite her sister outright, however. She wrote that she hoped the time might come when her sister could see her way clear to visit, and even that inert invitation kept her in a state of agitation until the reply. The sister declined, and she was both relieved and miserable that her courage had come to nothing. The sister wrote that she did not, for the present, wish to leave her home, because her daughter was expecting a baby and, besides, a job was promised her by their eldest brother who ran a small variety store and whose wife, who had assisted him for years, was failing in health. *She is very heavy now,* the sister wrote. *It's a sad sight, she is so heavy. The doctor says it's a glandular disease, and it's better that it is a disease than a willful act because she has an excuse. But, believe me, he got more woman than he bargained for.*

It was not long after the letter that Anna Lisa began to put on weight. Complaining that she found it a nuisance to prepare

two kinds of meals, she ate the cream and potatoes that his diet
called for and swelled out until her clothes were obscenely
tight and began to split at the seams. She bought loose garments where before she had preferred those garments that fit
like a glove; she wore muumuus, kimonos, Roman togas, and
gave up high heels because they wavered under her weight.
Her husband suggested that what was good for his health was
not necessarily good for hers, but she smiled a surfeited smile.
The once famous angular face was blurred by the Rubens'
flesh. Her long black hair was not glossy anymore, since she
seldom felt the energy to go to a hairdresser, and she wore it
dragged up to the top of her head. Her husband gave up sug-
gesting. Since *he* was not in his former condition, he felt that it
was unfair of him to demand that she be as attractive as before.

In that time of her fleshy indolence, as she lay one day on her
chaise longue in her weedy and overgrown garden, a woman
rode up on a bicycle to her gate.

"Oh, just a bit of water," the woman called through with a
reedy voice and an English accent. "It's such a beastly hot day
I've drunk all the water in my thermos jug, drunk it all up."

Even from where she lay, and in spite of the obscuring mesh
of the gate, Anna Lisa saw that the woman was burdened with
a nose so large, so curved, that she resembled a supplicant bird.
Her age, which was rather advanced, her size, which was
small, the fact that her short, skinny legs were bare below the
knees and encased in black Bermuda shorts above, and that a
blazing blue handkerchief was tied on her head and hung in a
triangle at the back, all contributed to the effect of that beaklike
nose.

"If you please," the woman's imperiously servile voice rose
over the garden. "Can you spare a bit of water for my thermos
jug?"

It seemed to Anna Lisa that the woman was a member of an
accursed race to which she, Anna Lisa, also belonged but whose
membership she had been able to conceal with artifice and with
the energy of the best years of her life, and, trembling in her
large legs with penitential fear, she rose to admit the woman.

"Oh, my dear, and herbs!" the woman cried, breaking off tiny leaves to rub between her fingers and raise to her nostrils that were like the flying buttresses of a cathedral. Water was brought by Anna Lisa in a capacious pitcher. She forgot a glass, forgot also that the woman had her own thermos cup, and ran back into the kitchen, and since Anna Lisa had gone to the trouble of running twice to the kitchen, the supplicant felt called upon to be congenial beyond the degree expected of someone given water from only one run. She sat down in an elaborate wicker chair and said that she was a housekeeper for a family that just a fortnight ago had returned to England; he was with the United Nations, she said, but had got a liver affliction and given up the diplomatic service. She had some nice offers, but she was taking a bit of a vacation. She loved to bicycle, she said, and if Anna Lisa had a bicycle or could borrow one she would show her some delightful roads. Anna Lisa offered her the position of housekeeper and the woman accepted. She had never felt the need of a housekeeper, but a stubborn coveting of this woman rose in her breast.

One afternoon, a few days after the woman came to live with them, Anna Lisa, returning on the train from the city, thought she saw reflected in the glass next to her face, as the train passed through shade, a great, arched nose that appeared to be on her own reflected profile. She clapped her hand to her nose and was assured that its size had not increased.

"God bless you," said the voice of a confident man who knew his far-flung influence. "Go on and sneeze, don't be shy. Don't hold back what is part of nature."

She turned her head and saw that the reflected nose was his. A large man with white plump skin that gave off an antiseptic perfume, he had a bald head fuzzed over with gold and a small beard of darker gold. When he told her that he was a dentist, she told him that she found her own dentist rather indifferent, taking her for granted as the years went by, and he nodded reluctantly, knowingly, a man pained to admit the malpractice of others in his profession. Not only did she promise to make an appointment with his nurse, she also promised that she and her husband would come by the following Sunday to see the doctor's collection of music boxes. This sudden confidence in his skill, and the sudden sociability, were demanded of her by the same fear that had gripped her when she had risen to admit the woman with the bicycle.

Not long after the encounter on the train with Dr. Braun, Anna Lisa and Richard attended the opening of a gallery exhibit by a young artist by the name of Hagopian, also from California. There was a crowd around him, and as her husband, taking her hand, drew her through the crowd to meet the artist, she again underwent that panicky yet not unpleasant sensation of retribution. The artist's nose was so large that the dark hair that rose in a high wave, arching from ear to ear like a lion's mane, seemed to frame the nose rather than the face. They purchased a painting, and Anna Lisa, in what appeared to be a mood of near-infatuation, asked the artist to visit them.

On the drive home her husband expressed some jealousy. "I bet he has a difficult time of it, using his brushes," he said. "His nose gets in the way."

"That's why he's an abstract expressionist," she said. "He stands off from his canvas and thrashes it on. And he gets more on it than those artists with nothing in their way."

It was unexplainable, the number of persons she met with large noses. She had never run into so many before. A harpsichordist moved in a few doors north, a buxom woman with flaxen and gray hair that hung in one huge braid down her broad back, and a nose like one half of a castle door. Anna Lisa called on her with bulbs. Shortly after, a friend who was an interior decorator brought over a woman he had taken into partnership, a young French woman with a nose so large that, observed from the front, it divided her very thin smile in two. These persons, lately met, were more of the material of friends than any persons she had ever met, and they were frequent guests in her home. A frenzied, obsequious desire to please them caused her to lose most of the weight she had gained, but not quite aware of the loss she still went about in muumuus and kimonos that were too loose and too large but also, because of that, more evocative of the body to be found somewhere in the folds and airy spaces, and in them resembled a servant who wears the castoffs of an obese and indiligent mistress.

One evening she gave a party for all of them and observed to herself, in the midst of them, that it was like a party for members of the same order or lodge for the purpose of interesting a few others in the rites and regimen that would grow them noses as large. She felt that she was in an hallucination, that she was among people whose souls perched on their faces. She was ecstatically terrified and drank too much, jabbering and sprawling and almost falling, singing, and hanging on the arms of her guests. The artist and the dentist attempted to kiss her, misinterpreting her behavior as erotic, but she could not bear to have the exalted meaning of their noses lost, and tore herself away from their embraces.

In the clutter and stale smoke after everyone had departed, her husband commented on the similarity among their guests. "They're all of a sameness," he said.

"Yes, they've all got souls," she cried.

"That's not what I meant," he said.

"Why don't you sit there and notice their souls?" she cried.

"I think they are extremely talented people, all of them," he said placatingly, "but it just so happens they've all got large—"

"They've all got enormously large souls," she cried, striking herself above her breasts, throwing her head back. "Oh, my God, I might have had as large a soul as any of them."

"Anna Lisa," he begged, following her over ashtrays strewn on the floor, "Anna Lisa, you have a soul as good as any of them. Just because they play the harpsichord or paint. That's not the soul, Anna Lisa. A talent isn't the soul."

"I know what the soul is," she cried. "You don't have to tell me what the soul is."

He went into his room, too weary to debate her soul with her.

It was not many weeks after the party that Anna Lisa ran off to Europe with Dr. Braun. After that night—indeed, before the night was over, Anna Lisa began to yearn for the embrace she had repulsed. She preferred the dentist to the artist because the artist had a meditative hand always hovering over his nose, whereas the dentist was not in the least discomfited by his nose. Her desire for the gold-bearded dentist began to consume her. It seemed to her that it was a desire that had lain dormant all her life and that her desire for her husband, back in the beginning, had been only a fraction of the desire that now ran rampant through her body. She had acted unrealistically the several times that night she had repulsed the doctor's embrace for the sake of her obsession with his soul. There was no way to revere his soul other than to throw herself into his arms.

She left a long letter on her bed, begging her husband to forgive her and thanking him for the nine years of love and kindness. She had not been, she wrote, an easy person to live with, this she realized. Then she kissed her housekeeper on both cheeks, and the women wept together. The dentist left his affairs in order, having taken the time to find a bright young dentist to replace him and to print up announcements of his leave. These were not mailed until the night before he left, and his wife and son, on the mailing list, did not learn of his departure any sooner than his patients.

Seven months later, Dr. Braun returned alone. It was obvious that he had been through an ordeal. For six months, he told his friends, they had enjoyed themselves, traveling from London to Paris to Rome. She had been devoted to him, almost idolatrous, anticipating his every want, no matter how small, and responding to his desire with equal desire. They had moved on to Greece and Turkey and Iran, and it was in Teheran that she changed toward him. She became infatuated, he said, with the proprietor of a cafe. In one day she developed an inordinate craving for coffee.

"The man was not what you would call irresistible," he said, "but for her he was. I have never seen a woman so infatuated. It was like watching her come down with a fatal fever. But the man," he repeated, rubbing his troubled white hands together as he sat bent forward, his head down, "the man was not what you would call attractive. That man was a public freak, let us say. He was known as the man with the largest nose in the city.

The British colony called him Muhammad because he was stuck with his mountain. They proposed to set him up as a ruler in case of civil strife. Muhammad returns, you know. It was their daily joke at his tables. He had, I understand, although it was hard to believe, a wife. He had a wife and six children, but that didn't bother Anna Lisa, not at all. She became his mistress." He lifted his eyes to his friends and the incredulity in them was not less than on that day when she had confessed her love for the other man.

Some friends who visited her in Teheran a year later found her still the mistress of the cafe owner. On their return they reported that she lay around all day in a room that he rented for her, reeking of sweet oil and jangling with cheap jewelry. They did not try to persuade her to return with them, they did not even bring up the subject, because her subjection to the man forbade it, because she was, they said, like a convert whose subjection makes it a profanation to question a belief with even one, small, timid question.

The Cove

Sometimes the realtor's listings book will fall open to the photographs of homes not within the means of the couple on the other side of the desk, and the wife will put out her hand, almost instinctively, to see what is beyond them. Of the several properties, the couple will pause longest over a particular house on the leeward side of the island. The woman will wish aloud that they could afford it, laughing, sighing, drooping, indecorous in a time that calls for reserve, while the husband will nod and agree robustly, even goddamning. They select, after the usual excursions with the realtor to several houses within the city and on its expanding edge, a house not much different from the one back home. The property that they coveted is shown only to those fortunate families for whom every hour is opportune. Persons who sometimes roam through houses they cannot afford in order to impress the realtor, or—though they have not met him before—vindictively waste his time, never venture onto the verdant grounds and across the threshold of that property. It is much too ideal to violate with one's lack of promise or even with that vindictiveness against the realtor that asks no reason for itself. Whoever might have in mind to dare an excursion is deterred by what might be suspicion on the part of the realtor: although everything is amiable and potential as they sit around his desk, elbows almost touching, knees almost touching, hands touching over maps and matches, a gulf suddenly divides him and them.

The realtor unlocked the wrought-iron gate, swung it open and stepped aside, waiting until all the members of the family had passed into the garden. Following at a discreet distance in order not to interfere with their breathtaking entry into a domain certain to be theirs and free of intruders such as himself, he bowed his head to choose the next key from the green leather case in the palm of his hand—both case and keys given him by the owner. The father went first along the path, his index finger held by the youngest of the four children, a girl of two who was walking clumsily on her toes. They were followed by the two boys, one twelve, the other nine, both lean, both wearing tan knee shorts and white pullovers edged thinly with red. The eldest, a girl of sixteen, strolled behind the boys, the wide pleats of her short white skirt parting and closing. The mother, young in spite of the number of her children, was the last of the procession except for the realtor who was, respectfully, not a part of it, following the mother by a yard, observing as if against his will how the flowers in the cloth of her dress vibrated with the movements of her body and with their own disputing colors. In the center of the emerald dusk of fern and bamboo and flowering shrubs, the father paused and so the rest paused. The garden was filled with a humming that seemed to emanate from its own exuberance until it became apparent that the sound was the sea's constant humming rising up through the density of mountain stone. Two myna birds flew up from a lichee tree in the garden, flapping over the road and settling in a breadfruit tree high on the upper slope.

The realtor unlocked the heavy teak door, found that it stuck, and pushed, his brow against it. The members of the family fanned out across the large room toward the wall of sliding glass that gave them an immense view of the sea. The realtor slid open one segment of the glass and they walked out across the terrace and over to the stone wall, and all, leaning there, gazed out on the masses of land to each side, tremendous green shoulders of earth that seemed to recede and swell in the hot light; gazed down on the vertical, winding stone stairs and, at its foot, far down, the cove. Black, volcanic rocks edged the cove, molding it into the shape of a three-quarter moon. The sea broke on the barricading reef and, after heaving and swelling on the inward side of the reef, swept almost languidly across the cove, breaking again.

The realtor took the liberty of leaning his elbows on the

wall, along with the rest of them. The soft, ascending wind pressed his shirt—so white it shone in the sun—against his chest. For a few moments the shirt beat against his chest as if stirred by the beat of his heart, then the wind continued up and his shirt hung loosely again, unstirring. He was neither tall nor short, neither fat nor lean, but this averageness was like a happy medium he had attained by his own efforts. The surface of his face was receptive of all reasonable requests; under the surface, as if it were a matter of modesty, lay a look of gratification for pleasures granted to past clients. In the eyes of the father, who was a shrewd man and who considered shrewdness a virtue, the realtor was a simple man, lacking shrewdness. The realtor was silent while they gazed down, musing and exclaiming, as if even one word might be an intrusion as intolerable as an uninvited guest down with them in that pricelessly private cove.

When they began to enter back into the house to inspect the rooms, the realtor walked by the side of the father, pointing out the stoutness of beams, the solidity of the teak floors, the lavish use of marble. Servants were no problem, he told them, although he would advise them not to inquire at the village. They might find someone there, but someone unreliable who would prefer to reside in the village and come to work in the morning, if that someone felt so inclined. In his office was a list of servants with references, and one couple—Japanese—he heartily recommended. The realtor did not accompany the father and older children down to the cove. He remained in the house, strolling from room to room with the mother and the little girl and waiting with them in the garden for the others to climb up.

The father returned carrying the coat of his dark mainland suit over his shoulder. His tie hung over the other shoulder, blown back by the warm wind down in the cove. The two boys refused to sit down, though they were panting from the climb. They stood shifting weight from one foot to the other, excited, tossing their hair from their brows. Their tennis shoes and white socks were wet and sand laced their bare legs. Although, with other clients, the realtor, by habit, strained to hear low conversations going on across a room from him or in the back of his station wagon, in order, later, to contradict spontaneously as if he had not heard the criticism or adverse speculating, and although he often used a contemptuous indifference to jolt the obsequious into action and the hostile into a recognition of the value of his time, with this family he was almost deaf, almost mute. While they were gathered again in the garden, the realtor thumbed through a black leather notebook, inquiring if they might care to see another house, closer to the city, with pool and an acre of garden, or a large apartment, a condominium, with a spectacular view. The father, still exhilarated from the descent and his exploration of the cove, suspected that this reminding of other places was a strategy to rouse the family to a desperate desire for this one. He smiled tolerantly, clapped his elder son around the shoulders, and moved toward the gate. The realtor followed the family, swinging the gate closed and locking it while they stood by the road, gazing up at the rest of the land above or gazing out to sea, familiarizing themselves with the spot.

By early June the family had moved in. Canvas chairs and chaise longues colored the terrace and in the cove a small rowboat rigged with a yellow sail resembled a floating flower. Children called to one another up and down the stairs, their voices always on the verge of echoing, and sometimes a brightly colored garment or towel lay for a night and part of the next day on the steps or on the sand and, seen from above, the fallen cloth claimed that region for the family. Lichee shells, like dry, brown, paper-thin cups, and their large, black, shiny pits lay scattered on the terrace, the soft, sweet, translucent fruit sucked from the pits with exaggerated smacking sounds by the two boys and the younger girl. The fragrance of plumeria and pikake drifted down to the cove and the scent of the sea rose, permeating the rooms of the house. At certain times of the day, early morning and late evening, the water in the cove was like a giant, dark, narcissist's mirror overhung by the mingled scents. Four cousins, ranging in age from seven to eleven, came over by plane from the mainland in July. They came all together, although from two families, the older ones in charge of the two younger. They were met at the island airport by the entire family. It was already early evening by the time the children got down into the cove. The sons and elder daughter of the host family ventured out farther toward the reef than their cousins who, adrift for the first time in the sea, were awed by the gradual loss of the others to the dusk and distance and by the eeriness of their containment in that large stone bowl that seemed to shrink when they dropped their heads back and gazed up at the great shoulders of earth and, far up yet only halfway up, the lighted house that hung in the green, darkening mass.

The realtor passed the house once, with him in his station wagon an executive of a hotel chain who was interested in acreage on the island. The client was talking incessantly, and the realtor did not glance out to find the foliage and the gate that marked the property until they had passed it by a mile.

On days that were oppressively warm, the damp heat, the metallic, lifeless shining of the waters, the steaming garden, and the land mass on which the house was perched, all seemed to comprise an initiation. They were more conscious than ever that they dwelled on an island. On more pleasant days it had begun to be as habitually under their feet as the continent they had been born to. Now the heat loosed the moorings of the island and of the memory, and the continent itself seemed to have been no more solidly in place than the island. The children swam in the morning and again in the afternoon, played cards and other games under the three large umbrellas on the sand, and indolently amused themselves in the house. The mother took her dips in the morning before anyone was up. The air was already warm and the sun bright, but a diffident presence was with her: a coolness that she was certan she would not have found had her family accompanied her. The father swam in the afternoon with the children. Each parent had a time that favored him.

After his swim, the father lay prone on the sand, his feet toward the land, his head toward the sea. He closed his eyes,

hearing the water, the barking of the small black poodle running back and forth in the shallows, and the voices of the smaller children under the umbrellas. He lifted his head from his
arms to face the other way, glancing out to the figures borne
high on the serene, incoming swell. Three were more or less in
a row, the fourth, his elder son, was at a farther distance, tread-
ing water. He laid his head down again and did not see the boy
tossed into the air. One of the younger boys on the sand saw
and laughed at what he thought was his cousin's amazing an-
tic. His son's scream came to the father in two ways: it came
over the water and it came through the sand, reverberating
against his body. The boy was in the same spot, his arms raised.
A few yards from the boy a dark fin detached itself from the
dark, swarming spots that plagued the father's vision in the
intense light, circled the boy, and disappeared. The boy disappeared with it, lost like the fin in the glittering air and water.

Their excitement in the water deafened the rest of the children to the terror in the cry. The father running into the water
was a common sight to them, and their abiding in the water for
so many more hours of the day gave them, as usual, a secret
sense of their superior adaptability. The great, dark body gliding past them and around and beneath them sent them to shore
as clumsily and eccentrically as if they had never learned to
swim. The children under the umbrellas huddled down on
their haunches, facing the sea or facing the cliffs, screaming the
name of the creature. The father felt the shark pass under him
and glimpsed it, and his own body seemed to dissolve, as if that
languidly, monstrously gliding creature destroyed him without touching him. Way above the cove a child was climbing the
steps, screaming up to the house the same word as the children
below, and stumbling on the dog that ran up before him and
stopped and ran up farther, barking all the way.

The daughter, with the help of the older boys, pushed the
small dinghy across the sand and out into the water. Alone, to
leave room in the boat for her father and brother, she rowed
out to the place where her father was diving and waited there,
the boat rocking and tugging away from her oars. She watched

for the fin and for the large, dark body again, sighting neither within the great bowl of water, luminous, clear, except for the spreading and separating patch of blood a yard from the boat. The father rose and dove again, rose and clung to the side of the boat, and the sound of his breath was the sound of their terror as they drifted, rocked by the water and by the boat's own rocking. When he had rested for a few minutes he dove again and when he rose he lifted up to her the body of the boy. Her thin arms straining, she held to the body against the tug and drag of the water while her father swung himself up into the boat. Then together they drew the body up.

The realtor unlocked the gate and stepped aside to permit the family to precede him. The family crossed the garden, the children, a small boy and a girl, maneuvering around and between their parents in order to lead the way. Not all of the family were present. Two of the older children were in boarding school and a third child was in college. Rain had fallen only a few minutes before; steam was rising along the roof and a glittering was going on in the shade of the garden. A few doves were stirring in the trees. When the realtor moved toward the house the parents followed without lingering. The realtor spoke very little as he led the way out onto the terrace and back through the rooms, as if words were unnecessary since it was obvious that the property was to belong to this family. The mother was confused by the certainty. Before marriage she had been a hungry actress, and the years of her marriage— only the two younger children were hers—had not overcome her mistrust of certainty. She felt the need to catch the eye of the realtor and, even if her glance appeared to be flirtatious, convey to him her desire to comply. He did not meet her eyes but, his head bowed as if in solemn understanding, he moved away to lead the family farther.

(*Esquire*, 1969)

Lonesome Road

Up on the sidewalk, glancing down through the high wire fence at the mothers on the benches, he recognized her by the way her head bowed over her knitting as it used to bow over her left-wing periodicals—meekly and thoughtfully and eager to lift and do somebody some good with what was in the print. He went down the concrete ramp and across the tanbark and spoke to her over the children in the sandbox.

She lifted her basket from the bench to the ground, hastily, to forestall, he knew, any humiliation there might be for him in the stares of the other women because he was a Negro approaching a white woman, and he went around the sandbox and sat down where the basket had been.

"You haven't changed much," he said.

"Don't tell me that!" she laughed.

"You got kids you're watching?" he asked, searching among the ones in the sand for one to resemble her. A little girl with light hair was watching them. She turned away with solemn shyness, when her mother introduced her, and resumed her digging.

"I have a boy, too," she said, looking out over the playground to the baseball formation. "He's older. He's eight."

The sight of the girl, the talk of the boy disturbed him. It was as if she had close allies now, allies she herself had created to reject him with, some other man's children. "That's a little army," he said. "I got a little army, too. I got three in mine, two girls and a boy. The other day the boy climbed up to the medicine cabinet and swallowed the iron tablets and had to go to the hospital to get pumped out. They're out of their minds," he said, laughing with her.

As the laughing waned she pushed back her bangs, a gesture he remembered that hid her face for a second in the pretense of clearing away interference. Her hair had darkened, and her eyes, glancing at him from under her hand with a flash of painful shyness, seemed less blue, faded to the color of a dim sky. He knew that she saw him as better-looking than he'd been twelve years ago. Then he'd had a skinny, agitated look; now, at least, he was a little fatter, a little calmer, his light gray, expensive suit the reward and requisite of a publicity man for a big insurance company. If one of them was at a disadvantage it was she. She was nobody to be intimidated by, anymore, to be saved by, to beg from. Up on the sidewalk he had seen that she was less than she had been and it was this lessening that had enabled him to approach her.

"That's what they'll do, scare the wits out of you," she said, and sighed, laughing. "I guess every joy brings a burden along with it. You don't realze that so much until you've got kids."

"That's true, that's true," he said, disparaging with a smile her ready wisdom. In the past she had given out her left-wing maxims but this had the sound of religion or some level of acceptance that was lower than that level of past maxims. "You can reverse it, too," he said, "Like, every burden brings its joy."

"That's so," she agreed, taking him seriously. "A burden can make you more humane, and there's a gratification, isn't there, in being humane?"—her voice fading out as it used to do when she had tried to help him with her aspirin kind of radical remedy for a disease that had got him by the throat.

"I can't hear you," he said, bending his head toward her.

"I was just agreeing with you," she said.

"If they don't kill you."

"Who?" she asked irritably.

"The burdens, the burdens. Weren't you telling me about burdens?" he said, keeping up his gibing smile to make a joke of their conversation, yet feeling again that misery that used to come of their attempt to be honest with each other. Everything they had said in honesty, in revelation of themselves, had had the sound of melodrama. Nothing had had the ring of honesty, perhaps because he had expected honesty to sound like an understatement, to sound modest. No matter how honest you were, he used to think, it all should sound like an understatement because you never knew the whole story. Instead, their honesty had always sounded like the shout of someone sure he knew the whole thing. "You never used to talk that way," he said, smiling. "When you were always deploring burdens there wasn't any compensation that went along with them."

"But I still deplore them," she said.

"That's good," he said drolly, wanting to ridicule her for past certainties because her rejection of him had come from some personal certainty that was unexplainable to him and more wounding because it could not be explained. There had been about her a certainty that she herself had not sensed but that he had sensed—everything in her life, he had felt, would be as she wanted it to be because she had that certainty from which all acceptance and rejection sprang, and it was that certainty that had infuriated him and that now, after twelve years, he still wanted to attack. "That's good," he repeated. "And are you still on the right track?"—smiling at her, "about how to get rid of everybody's burden? Though, the way I heard it, everything fell apart after the Khrushchev revelations. Is that right?"

She was not embarrassed, he saw. She was, instead, reflective, as if she herself had never been in the midst of whatever fell apart. "What we learned from that," she said, "is that there are more answers than one."

"Ah yes, ah yes," he said, nodding, engaged, clasping his crossed knees and rocking a little, seeing that he could be relentless about this certainty, too. "And what are you doing with all the answers?"

She glanced at him to see his purpose. "There isn't much you can do," she said. "I mean, you take the integration struggle . . ." She glanced at him again, smiling. "I still use the same old cliché words, don't I?"

"It *is* a struggle," he said.

"I mean, they're doing it on their own," she explained, flushing. "There were those three boys who were murdered down there. I mean, two were white, and people from the North are working down there, but up here there isn't much you can do. They're doing it on their own. They're mostly on their own."

She's all melted down to a spoonful of owlshit, he thought. He had refused her remedy in that year he had known her, he had argued with her for hours, but now he found himself contemptuous of her for getting melted down in the heat of old, lost battles. The men she had introduced him to, those men who had cornered him with their barrage of knowledge until he felt like a criminal in his ignorance—were they all melted down? Though he had opposed them, he felt now that they had deserted him.

"Yeh, they're on their own," he agreed. "They were always on their own," reminding himself, with that retaliation, of the accusation he had, to himself, leveled against her at the end: *You're leaving me on my own.* And he remembered what the end had done to him, how he had gone to hell for a year after. He remembered the last meeting in a flea-infested hotel room on the embarcadero. He had called her up, he had cried, he had threatened to kill her and himself. She had come up with a hamburger in a paper bag, trying to make it seem that all he required was food in his stomach so no more could be asked of her. He had been drinking for three days and he was sick, vomit was on his shirt and sour whiskey on his breath. He had wanted to be obnoxious, to reveal himself to her in all his possible obnoxious suffering, and he had wanted her to love him in spite of all and because of all. He had taken her face in his hands and covered it with kisses from the mouth that had cursed her, telling himself it was what she had come for. She had let him take the pins from her hair and lock the door, and she had stayed with him from noon to midnight, but it was the end. She had left him on his own. "Yeh, they're on their way," he said, musingly agreeable.

A boy was coming across the tanbark, gazing at them, a kid

with a wondering, bored look. He stood up and shook hands with the boy, who found a sandwich in the basket and walked away, eating.

"Do you want a sandwich?" she asked the little girl, who was watching, and the girl hung her head. "Come on," said the mother, and he heard again that sweetness in her voice, that light sweetness he remembered from the beginning when he had telephoned her every evening and talked with her for hours, always with his radio turned up loud with a symphony so that she could hear in that background music the possibilities between them, the young social worker with her unmistaken politics and the young reporter with his unmistakable intelligence.

"She shy?" he asked. "Mine is shy, too. The littlest girl. Always hanging out behind her mama."

"They grow out of it," she said.

"Oh hell yes,"—laughing indulgently.

She looked around for her knitting and found it beside her.

"You got thin," he said.

"Oh, maybe," she shrugged.

"You well?" he asked her kindly, and kindliness actually possessed him. He felt that his face had suffered its way to kindliness for her and he wished that she would look up and see before it was too late. Her hands were working the needles, her head bowed again. In among the darkening hairs were gray ones; there was no polish on her nails; socks instead of nylons; and old tennis shoes. He looked at her closely and thought: Frail, frail, frail. Was it just the way some women age fast? Or was it that her substance was gone, that certainty gone, and she was now simply a woman faded and darkened by a sky that belonged to each day and not, anymore, to some great future for everybody?

"Aside from the usual winter colds," she said. "I haven't been sick a day. And you?"

"Not sick a minute," he said, laughing.

From the sandbox rose a chorus of wailing and screaming. One child stood pouring sand over another's head, and a third tossed sand over both contestants. She got up to go for her child, who had covered her face with her hands and was crying, and something about the way she moved that was no longer the way she had moved up the stairs ahead of him on the way to his rooms, with his hands on her hips to feel their movement, something about the change, the lessening, brought on the memory that he had held off since the moment he sat down beside her on the bench. With the ending notes of his laughter unheard by her, with her moment's leaving him, he remembered the time before the end, before the hotel, when, lying in his bed, she had covered herself with the blankets because she had a question to ask and she wanted to disappear before she asked it. They had got honest with each other again, maybe because he had begged her again to marry him. I have to ask you, she had said, *because how can we know each other if I don't ask you?* and she had asked him if he loved her because she was white, and her eyes were afraid of him in his humiliation. Simpering up his face to imitate her, he had hurled newspapers and clothes around the room until she got out of bed and got dressed, too frightened to weep at his tormenting mimicry of her question and at his answer—that if there had to be truth to cement the damn thing together, then the truth was that he hated her, she was too goddamn much trouble. He watched her now, taking the child by the hand, leading her away from the melee and with the hem of her skirt wiping away wet sand from the crying mouth, and knew, watching her, that more was in that question she had asked him that time, more than the desire to be rid of him, to be finally rid of the burden they were to each other, more than to come at last to the core of their love and find no core.

"Never a dull moment," she said, sitting down on the bench, laughing, her short hair falling across her cheek as she bent to the basket to find something to appease the child, who sat on the other side of her.

"Oh, God, never," he agreed.

For a few more minutes he sat with her, leaning forward to say a few coddling words to the child and leaning back to laugh with the mother. When he stood up, she lifted her hand to shade her face from the sun, smiling up at him. She was relieved, he knew, to see him go. He walked briskly, with the step of good health, up the concrete ramp, and on the sidewalk again, as he leaned against the fence to pick a scratchy piece of tanbark off his sock, he saw that she was lifting the girl's hand and waving it at him, but he pretended not to see them anymore. He could not bring himself to wave back at them because his pity for her, the pity that he had failed to experience in the time of his love, forbade him small and amiable signals.

Sublime Child

Joseph Carmody was conspicuously absent from the funeral of his dear friend and mistress of five years, Alice Lawson. The ladies in black, climbing into their cars in the misty cemetery, liked him less and with a definite sense of relief, for they had admired him only for her sake. But when, on the long drive back to the city, Alice's daughter Ruth asked querulously, "Where was Joe? I wanted to hold his hand," those in the car with her glimpsed reluctantly all that he had meant to the girl and her mother.

He came that evening to visit Ruth, said his good evening to the other visitors—Alice's sister and cousin, two small, wealthy women—somberly settled his hefty body at the other end of the sofa from Ruth, who was lying under a comforter, and with weary grace accepted his coffee. While he was stirring his sugar in, more visitors came—the two tall, gray-haired women from the next apartment, who smoked cigarettes and wept, recalling their maternal love for Alice and hers for them, and then, to change the subject for Ruth's sake, told of the ups and downs of their dress shop to the shrewdly curious relatives. But the neighbors left soon enough, realizing that it was a family gathering, and after a moment the cousin went into the kitchen to rinse out the cups, and the tap water ran on and on in a forlorn pitch.

Vera, the sister, piled her big tweedy coat over her black jersey dress and sat on a chair's arm, swinging her foot and chatting with Joe. "She talks about living in a guest house. I agree it's good experience living with strangers, but it's only good if you've got a family to come home to. If you've got nobody then it's lonely, it's a substitute and you know it. You think so?" She strongly resembled Alice—the light curly hair, the angular face, the tiny, almost skinny body—but her mannerisms were of a different nature; she talked fast, she fussed. "I told her to come and live with Gordon and me. The girls adore her, they think she's so grown-up, being seventeen and all. Then in another year if she wants to move, that's fine. It'll be a healthier thing to do then because she'll have a family, she'll have us."

Joe looked down at his coffee cup, gazed up at Ruth, saying appealingly with his large brown eyes that he was in no condition to give an opinion now.

"She doesn't know enough about life, don't leave it up to her," Vera protested. "God knows she's been through enough this year, but at her age you don't learn from your experiences, you repudiate them. She'll think it's tragic and interesting living among strangers, but all the time she'll belong to nobody and pretty soon she'll take up with some kid who'll be mama and papa to her. She'll think he knows all the answers because he recites Eliot, when he won't even know how to blow his nose."

The cousin returned from the kitchen, picked up her furs, and threw the strap of her alligator purse over her shoulder. The two women bent to Ruth, kissing her on the mouth, sadly, emphatically.

The carpet in the hallway silenced them the instant they left the apartment. That sudden silence always aroused in Ruth the suspicion that visitors stood for a few minutes listening to what was being said about them. Was Aunt Vera laying an anxious ear against the door, afraid that her niece actually would accept the invitation? In that carpeted after-quiet, Ruth recalled her mother's complaints about Vera's lack of sisterly love, recalled the whisperings of the two little girls on their one and only visit to their Aunt Alice, a few weeks ago.

"Shall I heat that cocoa?" Joe asked. "Don't you want it? What did you have for supper?"

"Some toast and an orange."

"What do you want to do, starve?" He stood up, took the

cup from her. "It must be an old superstition still in our blood. We've got to atone for all our sins against the departed one, so we fast. Well, you're going to eat something. You think she wants you to starve yourself?"

While whatever he had found in the kitchen was heating on the stove, he returned to her and penitently squatted down on his heels beside the sofa. "You want to know why I didn't show up today?" he asked. "Because I didn't want to remember it. I didn't want to superimpose it on the things I wanted to remember." He covered his eyes with his hand. "Sometimes I wonder at myself," he said. "In order to make her sufferings bearable—to myself, I mean—I likened her to Camille. Not that the illnesses were the same. Your mother's was much harder to bear and less adaptable to any romantic story. But that was the only way I could bear the human, the ugly part of things, by likening her to a romantic figure."

She was frightened, called upon to listen with her mother's alertness and comprehension, called upon to reply in Alice's sweet, analytical voice. Why wasn't her mother here, somewhere in the empty apartment, to consider his apology and reply to it? She, the daughter, had no ability to ease him. As long ago as she could recall, she had been honored by her mother with listening privileges; she had been allowed to listen to conversations. Now she was expected to act as an adult and all she could do was complain for herself. "Joe, I don't feel well."

"It's no wonder," he said. "No food."

He tucked in her feet, felt her forehead and discovered a slight fever. He brought her a cup of hot bouillon, a rye and ham sandwich, and a heart of celery, and sat on the sofa by her feet, smiling over the paradox of her eating well and dropping tears into her food. And she felt that she had clumsily, yet deftly, helped him.

"If you don't want to live with your Aunt Vera, don't then," he told her. "What's her husband, a wholesale auto dealer? Sounds stimulating."

"I don't want to leave yet," she said.

"No, I imagine not," he agreed. "Anyway, a guest house might turn out to be rather disappointing. Sometimes, you know, the test of maturity isn't how well we mingle but how we handle solitude. If you get lonesome here, you can ask a friend to come and stay with you."

"And will you keep an eye on us, Joe?"

"Honey, honey," he said, squeezing her blanketed foot. "Do you need to ask me that?"

A month went by before she asked a friend to stay with her. She preferred in that time to return alone to the still air of the little apartment, to live alone among the articles made by her mother's nimble fingers—the needlepoint cushions, the hooked rugs. On Friday evenings Joe took her to supper and to a concert or an exhibit after, and he was all the company she could handle, for her attempt to be the comforting companion that her mother would have urged her to be proved exhausting; and ineffectual. He had sunk into a bitter mood, recalling in detail the times that he might have been more considerate of Alice. When, early in the fifth week, he came by to tell her he could not keep their appointment, she invited Carol to supper for that Friday and during the evening, listening to records, it was always on the tip of her tongue to ask this neat, this dark-eyed girl to live with her; but to invite her was to betray Alice and Joe. The following Monday, sitting by Carol in their French class, she extended the invitation out of the clear sky, and on Saturday Carol moved her things in a taxi from the small room she rented in a family house, and Ruth transferred her belongings to her mother's small, sacred bedroom, giving the larger, airier room to her friend.

That evening Joe brought up a delicatessen spread to honor the girl he was to meet, and he complimented Ruth on her choice of a roommate. Carol was reciprocally impressed with him. Her curiosity camouflaged by her wit, she learned that he was an attorney and a scholar, and she engaged him in an evaluation of some of the modern American poets.

Everything—the conversation, the spiced meats and black

pumpernickel, the bottle of vin rosé, and the two girls yearning toward him—reminded Ruth of the time when her mother
had been well. Yet somewhere in the midst of it Carol grew
quiet and began to watch her. The girl had leaned her elbows
on the kitchen table and cupped her flushed face in her hands in
order to watch her better, and Ruth was caught as by a camera
in an attitude of feverish animation, her thin arms widespread
in a fancy gesture, her silver bracelets jingling.

"Is he a relative?" Carol asked when he was gone.

"Of a sort," Ruth said.

"Oh?" said Carol, clearing away the plates and glasses.

"He wanted to marry my mother."

"Why didn't he?"

"He's already married." She felt pressured by Carol's silence. "His wife and he, they grew apart. I mean, she's a
shallow sort of person, likes clothes, likes to compete. But
she's dependent upon him, she says she loves him more than
life and that she'll kill herself if he leaves her." But she had
never met Joe's wife, and conjuring up an image of her from
Joe's complaints made her feel unfair. She had not felt unfair
just listening and accepting.

"Was your mother a scholar?"

"A scholar? Well, in a way. But she was sweet!" She had
never delineated, never evaluated her mother. Not only had
the task never been necessary, even the thought of it, now at
this prompting, seemed sacrilegious. She had nothing to begin
the task with, nothing but her love. "When she used to get
dressed up, there wasn't anybody who had more class. She
liked nice things . . ."

"But so does his wife!" Carol said, sparing of no one's feelings in her pursuit of logic.

"But my mother didn't *care* about things like that."

The elation was gone, it had departed with Joe. They tidied
the kitchen, and each went to her own room. Ruth was dismayed by the girl's bright blindness. When, in bed, she opened
the French grammar to recite the day's vocabulary, she could
not speak aloud. Her voice was gone and it seemed to have left
her that moment she had found Carol's inquiring face absorb-

ing and rejecting her. She wondered if she had erred in asking the girl to live with her. Had she brought someone into the house who was smugly, stubbornly ignorant of life? *La vie d'amour?*

Sunday evening Joe returned, and his anticipation of the girls' attentions softened his mouth, imparted a dancer's aplomb to his heavy body. He brought a bottle of Benedictine, and they carried their glasses to the living room and listened to him describe a day in court. Carol had lost yesterday's enamored air; she listened courteously for, having accepted the liqueur, she owed him in return an appreciation of his wit. When he left, Ruth accompanied him down in the elevator and walked the block to his car, hanging to his arm.

At the car he said, "Well, I guess you won't be so lonesome anymore."

"Carol's nice," she said. "Except a little stuffy."

"She'll grow up," he assured her, smiling a narrow, nostalgic smile. He patted her head, resting his hand in her pale curls so that the weight of his hand was the weight of their shared sorrow. After he got into his car, she walked along the sidewalk toward the apartment while he drove slowly along beside her. She could not see him very well in the dark of the big Buick, only his hand waving, and she shivered with wisdom, hugging her arms to her breast.

It was only for a few minutes following his visits that she felt under stress with Carol. After all, why should she expect Carol to be enlivened by his presence to the same degree that she was and her mother had been? At all other times the girls got along well together, and finally, one evening, when Carol commented just after Joe had left, "You know, Ruthie, you're like a century plant? You bloom only when Joe comes by, and then so extravagantly?" the loyalty that bound the girls together, compounded of experiences in which he did not figure, allowed them to laugh together.

In June she went with Carol to spend the summer at her friend's house, on a hill below Mount Tamalpais, not quite an hour's drive from the city. They wandered into the eucalyptus grove

where the warm air was saturated with the oily fragrance, and
they climbed into the dense woods where they picked miner's
lettuce and watched hawks soaring in the static sky. But lying
on her cot at night, lying in a house her mother had never
entered, under the same roof with a family her mother had
never met, she had to cough into her pillow to relieve the fear
of her separate existence. Not until now was the fact made
clear to her that she had been left to her own devices. And
sitting at the table with Carol's parents—the slight, gray-haired
father who was a postal clerk and the tall, dark-haired mother
who was a teacher; with the three young brothers, always fid-
geting as if from a tickling to the soles of their feet; and with
Carol, wearing her oldest brother's T-shirt, Ruth would remember her mother in the small apartment, and she would be
confused by the number of persons around her at the table.
They all had the same face, they all had the same name. If Carol
had to love so many, was it possible that the girl had never
loved anyone wholeheartedly? Joe and Alice and herself, they
knew what love was because they had only one another.

Yearning for him, she lost weight, and she would have returned to the city if he had been there, but he and his wife had
left several weeks earlier than the girls and intended to be away
until September. She told no one about her eighteenth birthday coming up, but the Sunday after her birthday, Vera and her
husband and the two little girls drove up to visit her, bringing
gifts. They sat on the veranda with Carol's parents, and someone said that there would be no holding her now that she was
eighteen, and she knew they were laughing because the wild
mare implication did not fit her at all, a thin, child-size girl in
shorts and bra and sneakers, sitting dutifully on a bench to
receive her guests, the tan on her skin put there forcibly like a
prison pallor.

When Joe came up to the apartment early in September, a few
days after the girls had returned to the city, she reached out her
hands to his in an attempt at that almost impersonal, casual
devotion with which fast friends greet each other after a long

separation, but before she reached him she broke into an awful weeping that at once made her bones ache. He walked her over to the sofa and sat beside her, stroking her arm and laughing a little with embarrassment, commenting to Carol, standing by, that this really wasn't the way he had expected a girl of eighteen to act.

He slipped her birthday gift onto her wrist—a heavy silver and turquoise bracelet from Taos—and he unwrapped the tissue paper from two pairs of beaded white moccasins, gave a pair to Carol and placed the other pair in Ruth's lap. She quieted after a time and was able to look at him. His navy blue suit and his tanned skin made him appear thinner; he was fragrant with some spicy lotion that was the distillation of all the languid, heady pleasures of his summer; and his shirt was white as snow. But her reception of him was dispelling the healthy, end-of-summer equilibrium that he had entered with. He said that in spite of the beauties of New Mexico, in spite of the good living on his friend's ranch, something was missing from his summer, and she saw that his hands were fussing with the tissue paper in his lap. Her upset was contagious.

She glanced at Carol, who was leaning back in her chair with the moccasins on her feet, and their eyes met in spontaneous shame. This reception she was giving Joe, this deluge, was a disparagement, Ruth realized, of Carol's family, of the whole summer spent in the house among the eucalyptus trees. No one, nothing, had taken the edge off her longing to see Joe.

On Friday Joe took her to dinner, as before. Over the veal scallopini he said that his wife had bought herself a "parlor organ" and that he thought it was the silliest cure she had ever tried and entirely at odds with her character. "A piano, she could have taken up piano," he said. "But something has been nagging at her for an organ. Maybe she's getting pious in her forties, maybe she's atoning for the sin of flimsiness." He gazed at Ruth.

It seemed to Ruth an admirable thing, learning to play an instrument; she remembered that when she was nine her mother had persuaded her to take up the violin, but after a few lessons she had to give up because she couldn't remember anything, her fingers gripped the instrument with a kind of paralysis. "Isn't it all right, an organ? If she wants one?"

"Yes, of course," he said, and she saw that he was irritated by her inability to perceive his wife's motives. Any motives.

They ate in silence, his satisfaction with the food and his dissatisfaction with her answer mingling in his face.

"Carol doesn't like me, does she?" he asked.

"She likes you, Joe."

He snorted softly. Lifting his eyes, portentously large and dark, he said, "Ruthie, you're just like your mother. She was so loyal it broke your heart. If you think I'm hanging around too much, tell me to stay away. If I'm boring you girls by trying to extend the past, please don't coddle me." Then soothingly he was saying, "All right, no more. I always get self-pitying after a good meal. It keeps my weight down." And she knew that her eyes were the color of hysteria. He began to talk of the decorations in the restaurant, of the girl cashier. And the rest of the evening, spent wandering about the Museum of Modern Art, he commented on everything, persuading her with his chatter and his constant cupping of her elbow that he was entirely reassured, that he knew she was glad to be with him because he was so lively and so erudite and so dear.

He began visiting, after that, as frequently as he had visited her mother, and she felt that in this effort of his to make amends for the hurt he had dealt her that evening, he was finding release from his mocking self that even her mother had been unable to exorcise.

One evening late in October, he paused in the lobby with her as she was seeing him to his car. "All set for the holidays?" he asked.

Aunt Vera, she said, had invited her and Carol to Thanksgiving Day dinner, and at Christmas she thought she would go up to Carol's family and make her apologies for being such an unhappy guest in the summer.

"That's fine," he said. "You don't feel neglected, I bet."

And they flashed smiles at each other. But he paused again out in the entrance where the slick, heavy leaves of the potted plants were bobbing in the moving mist. "Well, that's it," he said resignedly. "Sigrid's going to New York to spend Christmas with her sister, who's just returned from Europe. I'd been thinking . . . well, this is the first Christmas since Alice left and she'd probably like us to carry on in the old way just once more. We could ask her friends in the next apartment to help decorate the tree and I'd make eggnog for everybody, and then on Christmas Day I'd roast a duckling for us and bake a mince pie. You remember? The only reason I'm thinking this way is that I've made a New Year's resolution already. After the first of the year you won't be seeing so much of me anymore. It's time I snapped out of it, it's time I left. I think that you and Carol ought to move to a sorority house or a dormitory. You need to get away from the place, too."

But how could he make a cut-and-dried resolution, right in the midst of her wisdom? The thought that she had failed, after all, and he was leaving because she was obtuse was so humiliating that she overrode it by embracing his arm, begging him to please roast the duckling, to please make the eggnog.

They walked to the car with their arms about each other. "Now don't cry," he said. "Everything comes to an end." He laughed a bit when, standing by the car, she did not want to release him, and then was silent for a long minute, listening to her crying under his arm.

After Carol left, a week before Christmas, Ruth spent the days in museums, saw a play, and mingled with the shopping crowds, for the apartment with only herself in it was an expectant place. She shifted her friend's little antique alabaster clock from the mantel to the dresser in Carol's room, for it was an intruding note. Only she, Ruth, lived there. Joe came by only once; it was in the middle of the week, and he brought the tree and left for a board of trustees meeting. They spent the day before Christmas together. She met him in the lobby of his office building early in the afternoon, and they bought everything for their dinner the next day, and in an import shop where all the clerks knew him, they chose exquisite tree decorations. They carried the things up in the elevator before they went on to dinner, and the two women who owned the dress shop, hearing them laughing and complaining in the hallway, helped them to carry in some of the packages and stayed on for an hour, drinking sherry and unwrapping the decorations they all were to hang later in the evening. When finally they sat down across from each other at the restaurant table, they were weary of chatting.

Later, when they stood alone in the tiny elevator, Joe took her hand, and when she unlocked the door of the apartment he still held her hand. She entered first, raising her arms to remove her red beret, and Joe, following, clasped her shoulders. When she tried to turn toward him she did not know whether it was to cling to him or to struggle to be free, but, as though complyingly, he lifted her, and there she was, carried like her mother in his arms, and he was saying, "Sweet, sweet," his voice tangled. "Oh God, how sweet you are!"

She closed her eyes, and was carried to his chair and down into his lap, and felt his legs trembling under her. The past year was bearing fruit, they were at last, she thought, easing Alice's concern for them both. But opening her eyes to see his face, wanting frantically to find his face familiar to her, familiar as it had been when it was more dear to Alice than to her—for only that earlier face could reassure her that everything was right— she saw only his dark head cradled on her breasts. The sight of herself lying like a babe-in-arms in the midst of his consuming figure shocked her into imagining that Carol was coming from the kitchen and saw her enfolded there, her thin legs dangling down. *No, no, don't make me be my mother,* she begged him, but it was only whimpering, and frightened by her inability to speak she struck him with her fists.

For several minutes after her attack he wandered falteringly around the room, trying to find something to say but able only to cough from some arid place in his chest. He leaned forward on the table, knuckles on the edge, in the pose of a sagacious attorney preparing to speak, but whatever it was he intended to say he apparently decided that it was not to the point, picked up his overcoat, shrugged himself into it, and picked up his hat. And in that time, until he closed the door after him, she stood by the chair, watching.

When the hallway carpet absorbed him in silence, she went rocking about the room almost in his footsteps. "Mother, forgive me for hurting him! Mother, Mother, forgive me!" she cried, and appalled by the dryness of her eyes she rained her fists upon her own face.

Nocturne

So the old woman got herself a yellow apple today. Val, entering quietly by the front door, saw, sprawled in the rocker, Eulalia, the visitor who came every day, her pink felt hat over her gray curls lest the family think she was making herself at home; her skinny legs stretched out, her eyes closed, she rocked forward and back, atwitter with a thousand comments on the delight of eating an apple given to her as a gift.

Beyond the rocking figure in the living room, Mrs. Rand, Val's mother-in-law, was squatting down before the hot water tank in the kitchen, turning up the flame, grasping the back of a chair so she could rise again; she was too big to rise without help.

Val slipped down the hallway to her bedroom; there she leaned over her baby, sleeping in a laundry basket on the bed, and kicked off her high-heeled shoes.

"Val?" called Mrs. Rand. "Did I hear her come home?" she asked Eulalia.

"I'm here!" called Val.

"We're going to Monterey!"

"For fish dinner!" cried Eulalia, who wasn't going at all.

"John and me and Mr. Bellucci," Mrs. Rand shouted on. "Bellucci's brother got a fish boat down there, got a nice little house, and we're all going to visit him, Bellucci and John and me. If we leave before Bessie gets home from work, you tell her where we took her son, and tell her we'll be back tomorra, Saturday." Her voice changed to a cooing: "John's going to take a bath, ain't you, John?" And Val heard the boy flying around the living room, snuggling up against walls. "You go to Eulalia," Mrs. Rand coaxed him. "Here, Eulalia, is his picture book, it'll calm him. What kind of animals you got there, Eulalia?"

Val heard the old woman sing out the names of the animals, heard John repeating the song, and suddenly Mrs. Rand was behind Val, a soft body bungling against her.

"She'll probably stay on after we leave so she can beg something more to eat." Mrs. Rand's whispering voice was like something frying in a pan. "But don't you give her nothing, please, honey."

Val nodded, unbuttoning her jacket. Up to now she had paid little or no attention to Mrs. Rand's cautioning, but now she realized she had walked backwards to a point of least resistance. It wasn't, she reflected, a matter of her mother-in-law's selfishness wearing down her, Val's, generosity. In the first place, she wasn't generous with Eulalia, she was simply uncomfortable in the presence of a hunger that buzzed like a huge bee. If she gave the old woman a slice of cheese, a bunch of grapes, an orange, it was only to stop, for a few minutes, that constant sound. And, in the second place, Mrs. Rand wasn't selfish, she was simply afraid that Eulalia, given more, might begin to take with her own hands rather than receive, and already the grown-ups and children crowding the apartment— her daughter Bessie and grandson John, son Ralph (whenever he came home) and son's wife Val and their two children, the baby and four-year-old Greg—all opened their mouths for food like baby birds whose gaping beaks make the nest appear smaller.

"You always slip her something," Mrs. Rand complained. "She never had it so good before you came. I bet she's put on five pounds in the month you been here. The food around here is yours as much as mine, you help pay for it. But it's the principle of the thing, honey. She'll be crawling into your bed . . ."

All right, Val said to herself, nodding. Today I'll slap Eulalia's wrist. Beggars soon learn not to pity each other. It didn't matter that one came posturing for food and the other, herself, hung around for a different kind of sustenance, for the sour wine of familial sympathy, poured almost as generously by Mrs. Rand as Val's own mother would have poured it. They were both beggars, Eulalia and she, and it was time to elbow Eulalia aside.

"Besides, she gets her old age check. It ain't much, but they don't let them starve," Mrs. Rand went on. "She just likes to eat with us. I can see how she feels, not having a family or anybody, but that's kind of selfish of her, ain't it?"

"All right, all right," Val chanted, nodding and nodding. "Not anymore." An answer that sent Mrs. Rand back to the kitchen on conspiratorial feet.

Val lifted the baby high, smudging his white gown with the day's office ink on her fingers. If we leave here, she said to him, if we leave your father, who never comes home anyway, if we leave Anna Rand's embrace, who will take care of you while I work? Will the woman who materializes from the classified ad, *Board and Room for working mother with children,* drop cigarette ashes into your bawling mouth when I'm away? She felt no inclination to kiss the baby's face, hanging above hers. It would be a Judas kiss, a kiss of false promise, for she was a weak sort of person, lacking the courage to end the marriage and to go out into the city with her children. Returning the smiling, uncritical baby to his basket, she went on bare feet to the kitchen to prepare the formula.

Mrs. Rand was sitting by the kitchen table, peeling John's clothes off. In his underclothes he leaned against her knee, his shoulders twitching. "Naked John, naked John," crooned Mrs. Rand. "Shall we go and take a bath, little naked John?" With both hands she stroked his pale head, trying to impart to it, as one imparts liniment to the ailing chest, the concept of reality that every nine-year-old ought to have and that this poor one lacked. Lumberingly, she arose, nudged him along into the bathroom, and shut herself in with him and the steam and the rushing water.

Eulalia moved herself into the chair vacated by Mrs. Rand and set her elbows modishly, languidly upon the red oilcloth. "Monterey, dear, has nothing to compare with a fish dinner you used to get down on the wharf, right here in San Francisco, oh, twenty years ago. You didn't have to go all of fifty miles to that Portuguese town just to get a fish cooked right. One night I remember we had scallops, fried scallops, each one like a man's gold watch . . ." But senility whisked her meal away, like a proprietor who has just learned from behind someone's hand that this patron was unable to pay, and she sat blinking with her moment's loss of memory, an old woman whose clothes were so seldom changed and faded to so neutral a color that they seemed to be a part of her by nature, and whose years sucked like a scavenger snail in the cavities of her face.

Ah, God, will I look like that? asked Val. An old woman, she thought, is more piteous than an old man because she is less pitied, for there is something like a betrayal about a woman's growing old, she seems to be betraying her own nature. You didn't quite know what she was when she got old . . . Val poured the formula into the row of bottles on the sink, set the empty pan on the stove, then picked up a loaf of bread that sat so tantalizingly under Eulalia's nose and slipped the loaf into the tin breadbox on the refrigerator. In the moment her back was turned to Eulalia, Val saw herself with the old woman's eyes, saw something shrewish in her girl's body, in her straggly, bleached hair.

Bellucci knocked with dignity and dispatch, and entered at Val's bidding, wearing a trim suit and a Panama hat, carrying an overnight case of simulated alligator. He was, this heavy, rich-eyed old man, who carried his chest as carefully as if it were a leaking wine barrel, a friend of hers the moment he met her, bringing small gifts of candy to her because she was a hard worker, but repaying himself by teasing her. Val poured coffee for him and for Eulalia while he waited at the kitchen table, his eyes restless for Mrs. Rand, his Annie-Aniseed.

"Did you ever eat fish roe?" cried Eulalia, drunk on the afternoon's second cup of coffee, granted her because of Bellucci. He spread his hand over his heart with the pain her foolish question gave him.

Anna Rand was ready to go, her short, gray hair combed

with water, her nurse's shoes white as chalk. She carried John's tweed coat in one hand and a twine shopping bag, stuffed with oranges, her purse, and a box of crackers in the other hand. John at her side wore a tan gabardine suit, cut and sewn for him by his grandmother from a discarded suit of Bessie's. He was a little spider caught in a jar, unable to conceive of the jar's destination. Belluci rose, picked up her round, red overnight bag, picked up his own.

"There's corn chowder on the stove for everybody, and potatoes, and there's chops in the icebox," Mrs. Rand said. "And if that son of mine comes home tonight, there's a couple chops extra for him," she called from the doorway.

Bellucci, halfway down the long, outdoor flight of stairs, shouted up: "Hey you, Val? Whatsa matter with you your husband don't stay home? You don't kiss him enough, maybe?"

They descended the stairs stompingly, and it seemed to Val, waving from the doorway, that their bodies were already fatigued by the journey. It was the step of return and they were setting out with it.

Eulalia cried goodbye from where she sat by her cup, airily swinging her crossed-over leg. This is what you'll come to, Val thought, sitting down across from Eulalia to drink a cup of coffee and pursue her dread. Only you'll have no fluttering gestures to cover your senility, as this woman has. You'll be the bulky kind and you'll wear men's shoes on your swollen feet, the leather slit to accommodate the pain. Your legs will be flumpy with veins, little curling carrot-tops of whiskers will sprout from your chin, and your white hair will be cut straight across your neck to oblige the executioner.

"After Harry Rand died of a heart attack, the family almost starved," Eulalia began without preliminaries, for Val's sitting across the table from her in an empty house called for great revelations. "She couldn't make any money with her sewing, so my husband and me, we took in Ralph, we took in Ralph when he was a little fellow and made him our son. My husband had a position in the post office, worked right through the depression, and you should of seen that boy eat. That first dinner he scared us, he ate so much. He stayed with us for six months, put on a little flesh. But he's still got a mean, hungry look in his eyes. No matter how much he eats, he's never going to be able to get rid of that look. It's there until he dies. What did you see in him, honey? What you hang around him for?"

See in him? It wasn't anymore what she saw in him, Val mused, it was just that she couldn't see the future. The first year they were sufficient unto themselves and there was no need to see a future, and, during the worsening years when Ralph couldn't get up before noon, (*the goddamn day rises with its back to me,* he used to say, *and I don't have the strength to make it turn around*) and she had worked, and Greg had pottered around the one-room apartment in wet diapers heavy as a stone, she was able, somehow, to imagine a rosy future. But then she got pregnant again, and when the baby was two months old, Ralph quit his clerking job and disappeared, and she had moved Greg and the baby and herself to Mrs. Rand's. After she'd been a couple of days at her mother-in-law's, Ralph showed up again, and when he lay down beside her that night they both had cried, they had cried from love and weariness of spirit. But while they kissed each other's eyes, she felt the certain loss of the future. It was as if someone told her in words, bending over the bed, and she had felt as bereft as when they had told her about her mother.

"Paupers, paupers," Eulalia said. "His clothes stank. My husband and I had to buy him new clothes so I could wash the old ones. And that tall daughter of hers, that Bessie with the big head and the long legs, built strong enough to give birth to twelve children, what does she have but an idiot? A boy with a cup of water where his brain should be. Maybe it isn't Bessie's fault, maybe it isn't in the blood like you think. Maybe it's her husband's fault, but she should of known better than to marry a steward on a ship, the way they carry on with all the women on board. Don't ever come around to see what he brought on himself, does he?"

Val sat huddling her cigarette, her bare heels caught on the rung of the chair. Eulalia, she knew, was telling her these things

to shame the Rand family for drawing Val at last into the conspiracy against an old woman; she was exonerating Val for
snatching the bread away, telling her that she was a hapless
victim, like Oliver Twist in Fagin's gang. But Val declined the
pardon. What she had done was done by herself. Eulalia had
become, all in a tired moment at the end of the day, an intolerable image, the end result of Val herself. Val, too, would grow
old, and who would care that in her youth her face had been
dimpled and her fingertips pointed, and who would care that
she had read a thing or two and carried bits of wisdom like a
bouquet of tiny flowers other minds had given her because
they loved her. Whatever flowers Eulalia had carried were lost
now, and the possession she prized the most was the ingratiat-
ing manner that got her a yellow apple, and there was no one
who cared enough for her to speculate about who she had been
in her youth.

Val dropped her cigarette into her coffee cup, unknotted
herself and went into the bedroom for the baby, calling to Eulalia that she was going to the nursery school to bring Greg
home. Eulalia, forbidden by Mrs. Rand to remain alone in the
apartment, ran around the living room, searching for her purse,
and followed Val down the stairs, her flat heels clacking. At the
corner by the gray stucco high school in whose basement the
public nursery school was housed, Eulalia parted from her,
scooting down the street, hugging her elbows, her step still
imitating Val's, the busy, determined step of a young mother
setting out to find her child.

Giant red apples were pasted above the blackboard, blanch-
ing by contrast the faces of the children who sat at the long, low
table, awaiting their mothers. Greg sat knee-by-knee with a
girl older than he, who was reading to him from a picture
book. When he saw his mother, he knocked his chair backwards and ran to clutch her legs. Val pinched his face, and he
laughed up at her in a silly, gasping way from the folds of her
corduroy skirt. By the door hung a large cardboard sheet with
rows of paper pockets on it, and she paused to see if there was a
note in Greg's pocket. The folded paper stuck up like the tip of

a trim white handkerchief, startling her. It was the first note since she had enrolled him a month ago, the day after they moved in with Mrs. Rand. Had he stolen something? Or did he sit with mouth agape, wanting spectacles? Val released his hand and reached for the note, aware that the young teacher in a blue denim smock was only a few yards away, talking with another mother. *Seems to like his music class very much,* said the black, upright handwriting. *Listens to the records and tells us whenever he hears a violin. Does someone in your family play the violin?*

They climbed the concrete stairs, and the wind of evening met them on the street, blew her skirt between her thighs, blew Greg's straw hair into a peak. *So he listens to music, this bit of a creature!* she thought. Was he born with it, this taste, like some human beings are born with vestigial fish gills, something that didn't belong in the atmosphere they were born into? Was it left over from the years of her dreaming, before she had ever met Ralph? To his small hand in hers, to his hand with the thin thread of its own will, she said, *Kid, you'll only make it tough for yourself. Don't listen anymore to the sounds of the violin, or the flute, or any of the other instruments that lead you up and away from the ground that ought to be under your feet.* The wind was strapping her forehead with a lock of hair, and, desiring to be neat in the eyes of her son, she reached up and wound it back among the others.

Up in the kitchen Greg hopped around her as she took the loaf from the box and spread butter on a slice. The baby began to complain from the couch in the living room where she had laid him down, and Greg, afraid that she would leave her task undone, stepped between her feet and stretched up his arms stiffly as high as they would go.

She gave him his bread, and the mealy laughter down in his satisfied throat did not dispel the man he was to become. And if, she wondered, she came holding Greg's hand, could she enter Eulalia's room without flinching and ask her to come to supper? She had entered it once before, when Eulalia was sick and Mrs. Rand had asked her to take over a jar of chicken soup.

An old woman is so public in her aging that her room becomes her only refuge, more intimate than the room of a girl waiting for her lover. But if, this time, Val came holding her son's hand, she would have no fear of the old woman and of her possessions, of the curved amber comb and the webbed china cup on the dresser, and of the thin bed with the putty-colored crocheted spread. It was a matter of braving the lions' den, holding the hand of Daniel.

"You want to come with me to Eulalia's?" she asked him.

"No," he said. He did not like Eulalia.

"You'll come along anyway," she told him.

Greg bent his knees and did a shuffling dance into the living room, eating his bread, a small figure in a blue sweater and with no inkling at all that it was he who led.

God and the Article Writer

One night toward the end of his marriage, James G. Burley, an article writer, was wakened by someone's heavy breathing. He switched on the bedside lamp but when the scene was lit he was confused over how to respond, whether to make a joke of it or to be alarmed. His son, sixteen years old, was confronting him with a shotgun in his hands. While Burley debated with himself, his wife leaped out of bed and tore the gun from the boy's shaking grip.

After a confinement of two months in a psychiatric ward, the boy went to live with a foster family and enrolled in another school. At the end of the semester, the region's gas and electric company awarded the boy a bronze paperweight in the shape of a bolt of lightning, first prize for the most interesting scientific experiment by a high school student. The boy's marvelous recovery failed, however, to recover his parents' marriage.

Burley's wife, a nurse, moved into an apartment close to the convalescent home where she was employed. She took with her all the furniture and he did not object. He loved her and wanted not to deprive her. His dearest wish was for their reconciliation. If only that wish were granted he would be eternally grateful to Whoever took care of wishes. His wife refused to see him or to speak with him on the phone. Often, now, living alone in a residence hotel, the article writer wondered if the end of the marriage had come about not with his son's attempt on his life but way back on the wedding day. The dictum he had come across years ago in a manual on how to write for a living, that the end of the story was inherent in the beginning—did it apply as well to life?

So, alone, without wife or son, pained by his wife's absolute rejection of him and by the greater mystery of how his life had come to this stage, he went on with his writing. Always a hard worker, now he worked even harder because the meager income from his articles, an income he and his wife called chickenfeed, was enough for his son's support but barely enough, after that subtraction, for his own needs. On his hotplate he cooked rice and bony stews, and his breakfast was coffee. He ate on the same table where he typed his articles. At times the thought of suicide snaked over the page, a glittering viper. Then his nimble fingers at the keys would curl into helpless fists and his tired head go down to the typewriter's cold metal.

One day he got into his 1969 Chevrolet, bought in a used car lot after his wife claimed their later model, and drove the sixty miles from San Francisco to Saratoga to interview the renowned physicist, Ancel Wittengardt. The physicist was now a controversial figure, plunged into disrepute by some of his colleagues and apotheosized by the rest. The assignment was Burley's first from a national weekly, *Instant,* devoted to articles pertinent to the very moment. He was instructed to be brief.

At the time agreed upon he was seated in the physicist's kitchen, accepting gingersnaps from a carton and nodding his thanks for milk, poured by his host into a plastic cup. Had he been given a choice he would have chosen to conduct the interview in the study. Here in the kitchen he felt that he was treated lightly, expecting at any moment to be treated rudely. It was his experience that no matter how warmly he was greeted by celebrities, sooner or later they granted him a reason for disliking them.

When he set his pen to his tablet he saw that the pen was out of ink. Lint clung to the nib of the second pen and he wiped it away, staining his thumb and index finger. Lately, he was without protection against contempt, real or imagined. His shirts now were seldom laundered and his two suits reeked with the stale and bitter tobacco odor that permeated his hotel room and caused him to gag when he first set foot in that room. Some persons of the punk rock world whom he had interviewed were far from clean, but their failings had reflected on him as contempt.

"Sir, you are a Nobel Prize recipient. What year was that?" he began, smiling his congratulations as brightly as though the award was announced that very day.

With the edge of his hand Wittengardt brushed crumbs from the table, catching them in the palm of the other hand, then dropping them to the floor. The physicist's smile appeared to be over something that lay farther back than the year of the award.

A news item, three weeks ago, about the death of the physicist's wife had prepared the article writer for a man in mourning. Instead, all curtains were parted, sunlight streamed into every room, a canary warbled on and on, inanely ecstatic, and the man himself wore an old sport shirt figured gaudily with tropical fruits. The sun, the physicist's smile, the song of the bird—all were puzzling. Anything contrary to Burley's expectations seemed a deliberate attempt to humiliate him.

"Well, sir," he began once more, "I understand you've come up with a whole new theory about the universe. Some big bang in the mind, eh? If you like, you can begin with the equation and go on to explain it in terms for the average Joe." A year ago he had quit smoking, but a suspect granule remained in his throat. He coughed briefly.

Wittengardt sat up very erect, like the smartest student in first grade, who is always bursting with answers. "Ah, but the equation has slipped my mind." The lapse appeared to delight him. "Something so apparent requires no equation. So I let it go. For over fifty years I worked it out by logical progression, and then—whoosh! In an instant I realized I had known it all before I began. I had known it so well it must have scared me out of my wits. And a scientist scared out of his wits, what's to become of him?"

Just below Burley's heart, anger bit. He kept his attention from it by patting his breast pocket for cigarettes no longer there, by fingering around in his larger pockets for the indigestion mints that had disappeared days ago from the twisted foil.

"Sir," he began again. "You scientists have always waged your internecine wars. If that equation of yours is heavy ammunition, our readers will want to see it with their own eyes.

It's bound to become as familiar as Einstein's E=mc². So let's get on with it."

Obligingly, Wittengardt rose and paced the room, raptly attentive to what Burley hoped was his memory. Then, raising his head, tossing back from his brow a lock of gray hair, and settling one hand on his hip, he began. "There is no existence except God. He is and there is with Him no before or after, nor above nor below, nor far nor near, nor union nor division, nor how nor where nor place. He is now as He was, He is the one without oneness and the single without singleness. He is the very existence of the first and the very existence of the last, and the very existence of the outward and the very existence of the inward. So that there is no first nor last nor outward nor inward except Him, without those becoming Him or His becoming them. He whom you think to be other than God, he is not other than God."

Wittengardt clapped his hands together once, a gesture of surprise beyond all other surprises of his life. "An Arab fellow, a poet. He beat me to my theory by seven hundred years. You can say that I took the hard way and got there a bit late. Or you can say there is no late and no early. That way I won't look like a slowpoke."

The shorthand scrawled over several pages was not to be of any help to him, Burley knew. He was lagging, though every word the physicist had uttered was there in the tablet.

Wittengardt sat down again, but only to draw on a pair of black rubber overshoes, and Burley wondered if the man had received a signal from somewhere that rain was to fall the very next moment. "Come," he said, "and have a look at my garden."

With tablet and pen in hand, Burley followed him into the garden, noting for his own secret use the ravages of time on the man's head and neck. The man was so fragile that death in the guise of anything, in the guise of air, could whisk him away from his anchorage in rubber overshoes. Unspeaking, he followed, feeling more slighted with every step, dismissed by

Wittengardt's agility and by his absorption in the unwinding of hoses. And the garden itself troubled Burley. The flowers were so profuse, their fragrance and colors so varied and so mingled, the entire garden so lush and so involved with its own growing and blooming, that he felt himself under attack. The beloved persons of his life who had brought him pain had assaulted him in just this way.

"Sir," he said, when at last they came around to the gate. "I must tell you the fact of the matter. We have not yet begun."

"You are so right!" the physicist agreed, grasping Burley's hand and shaking it heartily.

Under the gate's arch of jasmine Wittengardt waved good-bye, and Burley saluted with two fingers to his temple as he drove away. At the first stop sign he tore off his coat and loosened his tie, but an entanglement other than his clothes was at work upon him. As evening came on, passing motorists signaled to him by blinking their headlights, and after many miles he realized at last that he had neglected to turn on his own lights.

Weary past relief, he lay down on his bed. A day ago the presence of his dead grandfather came to reside with him. Although the room in which that old man had lived was in another hotel in another city, this room had become that other. When he was a boy in his teens, agonizingly ambitious, knowing his faults more than they who pointed out his faults to him, always in a turmoil over his desires and the premonition of their defeat, Burley had visited his grandfather almost every day. By impressing the old man with life's wonders, he developed his powers of persuasion over his own future. The old man never bathed or changed his clothes and hardly ever spoke, but the boy sat by him faithfully, attempting to engage him in conversation about politics, great discoveries in medicine, and historic battles. The old man had been an electrician, and one night he did away with himself in that hotel room. Not much knowledge of electricity was required to accomplish that deed, but, for the boy, the act was a prodigious one. Almost twenty-five years later, Burley, lying on his bed, was urged on to his own end by the suspicion that this was his last chance.

Carrying his hotplate, he went down the hall to the bathroom shared by the tenants on that floor. There he turned on the faucets in the gray, claw-foot tub, and the water rose. Then he plugged the hotplate into the wall outlet, and, by the time he removed his clothes, the round little burner was beaming away on the toilet seat. A pellet of rice, stuck to the coils, began to stir. With the hotplate in both hands he lifted his foot to the rim of the tub. At that moment he began to consider the possibility that suicide was not what it used to be. An authority figure, bearing an evanescent resemblance to Wittengardt, was denying him a way out. Without bothering to dress, carrying his clothes and his hotplate, he stepped out into the hallway that had become, easefully, surprisingly, like one in his own home, and passing down that hallway he nodded on his way to an elderly woman returning from a late night television show down in the lobby.

The hotel manager, a young man in derelict jeans and T-shirt, his long hair in nervous strings, appeared at Burley's door the next morning. The other tenants, he said, were disturbed by Burley's unsociability, and he asked that the room be vacated.

Burley found a hotel in a neighborhood less littered. The lobby was as drab as the other lobby but considerably larger, and its mottled ruby carpet was vacuumed twice a week. The monthly rate for his room was only six dollars more, and although the room was not larger than the one from which he was evicted, it had two windows, side by side, and the other had but one. The genial woman clerk brought up from the basement, with his help, an extra table for his typewriter and papers, and he set to work again. In his letter to the editor of *Instant,* he explained his failure to turn in the Wittengardt interview by calling the physicist obstinately taciturn.

Almost every night, now, he was wakened by the night itself and whatever were its particulars. If rain was pouring down the panes of his windows, he fixed his gaze on the street lamp's shimmer between the grimy strips of the venetian blinds. And, with morning, he was always surprised by the everyday sight of his naked feet setting themselves down on the threadbare rug. He desired nothing, neither the return of his wife nor his son's love. He was in a state of astonishment but he did not yet know over what.

Works of the Imagination

The silent train ascended through forest and alongside a torrent so cold and so swift the water was white, and small white birds flew up like spray. On a bridge undergoing repairs the train came to a halt. Just outside Thomas Lang's window, a workman in a black knit cap was hammering at a railing, and the silence all around isolated each ring of the hammer.

Lang arrived in Grindelwald in the evening, coming from Bern where, contrary to his intention to call on a friend from the States and tell him about the insoluble task his memoirs had become, he had stayed only half-a-day and called on no one. In the early night he wandered along a path on the outskirts of the town. The day was a national holiday, and fireworks opened in languid sprays all around in the dusk, and the boom of fireworks echoed against the mountains. Someone approached him on the path, a figure twice as tall as himself. Closer, he saw it was a little girl, half as tall as himself, carrying a long stick covered with tallow, the torch at its tip casting around her a high, black figure of shadows. Up on the dark mountains small lights burned here and there, far, far apart—fires perched on the night itself. In the morning, a snowy mountain stood just outside his hotel window, brought closer by the sun almost to within reach of his hand.

On a small, quiet train he went higher, up to Kleine Scheidegg, up to an old hotel where twelve years ago he had stayed a few days in winter, and not alone. The mountains had impressed him then as a phenomenon on display, but now he was shocked by their immensity, hypnotized by their beauty and crystal silence. Cowbells and voices rang in the silence with an entrancingly pure pitch, and the density of the stone was silence in another guise.

The elderly, elegant manager registered him at the desk in the small lobby. A very tall, strong man, also elderly, in a dark green apron, whom Lang had observed carrying up four suitcases at a time, carried up his two, while another assistant, also in a green apron, a slight, dark man, surely Spanish, graciously shy, stepped in a lively way to the foot of the wide, curving staircase and gestured for him to go up. Lang climbed the stairs with his hand on the rail. He had not often assisted himself that way and had no need to now. He was an erect, lean, and healthy sixty, and why, then, was his hand on the banister?

The silence in the room was like an invasion, a possession by the great silent mountains. The cloth on the walls, a print of pastoral scenes with amorous couples, flute players, and lambs, roused a memory of another room, somewhere else in this hotel, where he had lain in an embrace with a woman who, at the time, was very dear. All that he remembered of the previous visit were the three persons he had been traveling with—the woman, a close friend, and the friend's wife—all now no longer in touch with him and perhaps not with one another. They had come to watch a movie being made of a novel of his. In the novel there had been only a brief mention of the Alps, but the movie director and the script writer had worked out a counterfeit scene from that remark, and he had watched, amused and apart.

Once in the night he was wakened by his heart's terror. His heart always wakened him in time for him to witness his own dying, and he waited now with his hand over his heart. When the terror subsided he took his notebook from the bedside table and fumbled to uncap his pen. Through the translucent curtains the sky and the white mountains gave him enough light to write by, but his hand was given no reason to write. Was this another place he would leave, his notebook empty? Traveling all spring and into the summer, he had found no place where he could begin his memoirs. If one place had been so full of the

sound of the ocean—not just the waves, whose monotonous
beat often went unheard, but the threat in the depths—another
place was too full of the sounds of the city—insane noises. And
in quiet places he heard, in memory, the voices of his healers
back in the States, men who had never truly known just what it
was he had lost, and gave the loss such facile names—confidence, faith, whatever—and the names of several persons who
had been dear to him and were lost to him. These healers had
promised him his completed memoirs, and other novels in the
future, if only he would begin, because, they said, work itself
wrought miracles and brought the spirit back from the grave.
But there was a loss beyond their probing, a loss they were
unwilling to accept as the finality he knew it was, a loss, a
failing, that might even be commonplace and yet was a terrible
sacrilege. It was indifference, like a deep, drugged sleep, to
everyone else on earth. Ah, how could that change have come
about in himself when his very reason for being had been the
belief that each human life was sacred?

He got up and drew aside the mist-like curtains. The train
station was dimly lit, the awning rippling a little in the night
wind. Out on the dark hills a few hazy lights burned through
the night, miles apart. And beyond and all around, the luminous mountains. When he was inside the hotel their unseen
presence warned him of his breath's impending abeyance, but
now, gazing out at them, he felt his chest deepen to take in their
cold breath across the distance, a vast breath as necessary to
him as his own.

The day brought hikers up from the cities, way below. They
came up in the small, silent trains, and wore big boots, thick
socks, and knapsacks, as if bound for a climb of several days.
But they roamed over the grassy hills for an hour or so and
converged at the tables below the hotel's lower windows.
They sat under colored umbrellas and under the windows'
reflections of the mountains, and ate what appeared to be sa-
vory food. He kept a distance from them. There was room
enough.

The only guests in the spacious parlor were far off, a family group playing cards at a table covered with green felt. On the parquetry floors lay rich, red Persian rugs, and the many couches and chairs of antique beauty took up only small space in the large room. A long and narrow glassed-in sunporch with an abundance of wicker chairs adjoined the parlor, and he paced along its length, remembering the hotel in winter, the parlor's black-and-white marble fireplace ablaze, the pleasurable jostling and agitation of the many guests, and the hieroglyphs of distant, dark figures against the snow. He settled himself at a large table in a corner of the parlor, but all he could do was trace the glow and grain of the wood around his empty notebook.

On his way down the hall, restless, wondering if he would move on the next day, he paused before the first of several framed photographs along the wall, an early one of four climbers assembled in the photographer's studio against a backdrop of a painted mountain, all in hats and ties and heavy boots, with pots, picks, a goat. Few attempted the scaling of mountains in those years; now climbers were swarming up every mountain on earth. Farther along, he stopped before a photograph of *Der Eiger,* the mountain looming up over this hotel and over the town, miles below, a sheer, vertical face of stone. White lines were painted on the photograph, marking the ascents to the top, and at the base were the names of the fallen, preceded by white crosses. He passed along before the faces of the triumphant ones, a row of them, all young, and spent a longer time before a couple from Germany, a man and a woman, she a strongly smiling blond and he a curly-haired handsome fellow, the kind who would take a woman along.

Then he went out, keeping apart from the many hikers who walked in a line toward Eiger as if on a pilgrimage. He strode over the lush grass, over the rise and fall of the hills, and on the crest of a hill he halted to take a look at the great stone's face. Two figures were slowly, slowly, climbing. His vision lost them in an instant and it took him some time to locate them again, so small were they and at the mercy of the atmosphere, appearing and disappearing. He sat down on the grass to watch them, his hand above his eyes to prevent the sun from playing tricks on him. The roar of an avalanche shocked him, convincing him that a mountain was collapsing, and then he saw the source of the thunder—a small fall of snow, far, far away. Somewhere he had read that the Alps had moved one hundred miles from their original location in Italy, and he wondered if the move had been centuries long, or cataclysmic, in a time when there were no human beings around to be terrified and obliterated. When his eyes began to ache from the searching, from the finding and losing of the specks that were his climbers, he returned to his room and lay down, his hand over his stone-struck eyes.

Toward twilight, when no one sat under the mountains' reflections, when they had all gone down on the trains, he went out again, strolling to higher ground over patches of tiny wildflowers that were like luminous rugs on the grass. Up near the entrance to the train tunnel that cut through stone to the top of the Jungfrau, he came to a large, heavy-wire pen where several restless dogs roved. The dogs resembled wolves, tawny with black markings, and their wild intelligent Mongol faces reminded him of the faces of nineteenth century Russian writers. It was a comparison against his will, yet he was amused by it and felt lightheaded over it. They paused to look into his face and into his eyes, slipped by along the fence, then returned, curious about him as he was about them. Soon in the darkening air he felt he was gazing at Gogol, at Tolstoy, at Chekhov, their faces intent on each human soul.

Stumbling a time or two, he made his way back down to the hotel that stood in a nimbus of its own lights. Before he went in he took a last look at the great stone. No fire burned anywhere on its enormous expanse. The climbers had made a bivouac for the night on a ledge and were already asleep.

Once in the night he was wakened by a deep wondering about the couple on the ledge. The fact of their lying on a ledge somewhere on that great stone stirred in him a concern for all persons he had ever loved. Then he slept again, and the couple was lying somewhere on the cold vastness of the night, on no ledge.

In the morning he went out under an overcast sky, before any hikers appeared. The stone was monstrous. Each sight of it failed to diminish, by repetition, the shock of it. So steep was the north side, the mountain must have been split down the very center, and the other half was a hundred miles away. The climbers were not yet halfway up the wall. Often, as before, he lost sight of them, found one again and not the other, and then found the other after losing the first. After a time he covered his eyes to rest them. If they fell, would the silence and the distance deny to him their terror? He lowered his hand, searched again, and found one dark figure on a snowy ledge. The figure fell the instant he found it. It fell so fast he was unable to trace its fall and unable to find it on a lower ledge or at the base. Nowhere, now, was the other climber. Then both had fallen, and their terror entered into his heart without his expecting it. It was the same terror that wakened him in the night at the last moment so that he might witness his own dying. It was the same kind of moment now, under the sun. With his hand over his heart he went back over the hills to the hotel.

No one was at the desk in the lobby, neither the manager nor one or the other of his assistants in their green aprons. One of them would confirm the tragedy. Somewhere, back in an office, there must be a radio voice informing everyone of the climbers' fate. Outside, the murmur of the crowd under the umbrellas and the fitful, labored music of an accordion were like the sounds the deaf make, that are unheard by them. In the parlor he found the shy assistant passing through, the one he was convinced had been a child refugee from the Spanish Civil War.

"El hombre y la mujer en la montaña, ellos se cayeron?"

The man smiled sadly, graciously, implying with his smile that if he did not understand Spanish at least he understood the importance of the question for the one who asked it.

With faltering German he tried to repeat the question, but a strong resistance, following disappointment, whisked away his small vocabulary. He went back to the lobby.

The manager, wearing a fine suit the same gray as his hair, was now standing at the desk, glancing through some papers. A fire wavered in the small fireplace.

"The couple on Eiger, they fell?"

The manager's brow, high, smooth for a man his age, underwent a brief overcast. "May I ask who?"

"The couple on Eiger."

"Ah, yes, the photographs in the corridor? Only those who succeeded. Only those."

"The couple up there now," he said.

"There is no one climbing now."

"Then they fell?"

"No one is climbing and no one is falling."

Lang went up the stairs, hand on the rail, a weakness in his legs from the terror of the lives lost, no matter if they were specks, motes, undulations of the atmosphere. Up in his room he sat down at the desk, opened his notebook, and wrote the first word on the first of the faint lines that he likened now to infinitely fine, blue veins.

The Light at Birth

The immensity of light—the glare from the winter sky and the reflected glare from the ocean—shocked her asleep at noon, at two o'clock, at any hour of the day. She had always resisted sleep in the day except when she was sick and when, after loving, she had fallen asleep with a lover; but this sleep was an edict as from a healer more powerful than her own self, the self that had lost for a time the sense of how to heal itself in its own way.

The house where she lay, upstairs, on a rug, on a couch, on the bed, was a brown-shingled, two-story house trusted to pilings sunk deep into the sand. At high tide the water came sweeping in under the house, exposing more length of the upright logs, and the constant sound of the waves worked along with the light to make her sleep. The small noises, the low voices from downstairs where the owner of the house lived—a German woman, with her ninety-six-year-old mother—did not disturb her sleep; only the sharp sounds woke her, the barking of the three little dogs whenever a visitor stepped onto the porch or they fussed among themselves over a preferred place.

The ocean had been her first sight of the vastness of the earth when she was a child in a beachtown down near the border, and she had come to the ocean again, to this town north of San Francisco, to find again that vastness, that anticipation of great probabilities, now when she was in dire need of release from constrictions on the mind—such easy prey to all things that kept it small and afraid. The sleep was like basking in light, and after three days of it she came awake.

Out on her small, high porch, she threw bits of bread into

the air, and the sea gulls came swooping in. Close, hovering, their spread wings and tails pure white and translucent in the light, they were unfamiliar, nameless creatures. When there was no more bread and they returned to the sand, they became again familiar.

The old mother, wrapped in a large, richly blue woolen shawl, sat on a sofa in the front room, and her blue, long-lidded eyes appeared unseeing. A storm, rising up over the horizon at noon, was sweeping tatters of fog before it, and the room was dark one moment and bright again the next. The old woman seemed unaware of this play of light and shadow over her. She spoke only in German and only to her daughter. Once, when the dogs were dozing, she spoke a few words to the room, and Marie, on the other old sofa, facing the mother, a low table between them, called to the daughter who was in the little kitchen, "Is she speaking to me?"

"She spoke to Paulie. He's her favorite."

The darts of light disappeared again from the glasses and bottles in the room, and the colors in the stained glass window facing the ocean, colors that only a minute before were cast on the old woman's face, went dark. The old mother's face was from antiquity, and though her body was small and she could be half-carried to the sofa, her being was formidable with the past. And when Leni, the tall, robust, sixty-year-old daughter, sat down beside her mother—the daughter's smooth white hair drawn back from the brow, the mother's gray hair drawn back from the brow, both women's eyes the blue of an ideal sky—the visitor felt the same confusion in her heart, the same confrontation as on that night in Cologne, last summer. The night she and her lover came into their first city in Europe. They had boarded a bus at the airport in Luxembourg because the bus was sleek and empty and they were exhilarated and uncaring about which direction they took, and the bus went along a placid highway through forests to Cologne. Then, in the restaurant of the railway depot at midnight—so few patrons, so many empty tables, and a sad, pale, limping waiter in a shabby black jacket with a black satin stripe down the sleeves—she had felt past terrors lurking, as if what had happened in that country was happening still or was about to happen always. *You see our waiter,* he had said, his face steamed up by the food on his plate, *our limping waiter? He mistook strangers for the enemy, just like you're doing now.* But she was listening not to him but to her heart, to hear if it was willing to come along with her into that country.

Leni saw that the shawl was slipping and tucked it around her mother again. The mother wore quilted, padded long underwear of soft wool, fawn color. "They belonged to my brother, he hasn't worn them since his university days," Leni said, her voice a young girl's. "When he came to visit us he looked at them with longing in his eyes." The brother, a retired physician, older than Leni, had returned to Europe and was living now in Switzerland, and his bones were feeling the cold, she said, no matter how much he danced with young women.

"Where did you go in Germany? Did you go to Heidelberg?" Leni asked. "We were born there, my brother and me. Up above the river is the Philosophers' Path, and there you walk and look down at the river and the old bridge, and below you on the slopes are the hill gardens. We lived up there. Up there are almond trees, they're the first to bloom. And wild peach trees, the wild ones have bigger blossoms than the cultivated ones. The seed falls into the earth and it grows. And old cherry trees, the one in our yard was two-stories high. So many in bloom people streamed up there to walk under them."

The storm was on them, the house went dark in the heavy rain. She ran back up the stairs and into her rooms and watched the waves flinging ashore timbers and branches that had been rushed down the rivers weeks ago, in a storm all along the coast. South across the water she could see the silver shine of the city under rain, only the tip of it where the channel opened into the sea. And back in the classroom in the city, the rain pouring down the windows and voices barely heard, was any student wondering what had become of her, the lost professor? So many gentle sermons she had delivered on the necessity to rid the mind of cramps, duperies, and deathtraps. *Let in some light,* she had told them. *Let in some light,* she had pleaded with herself, alone.

She was kept awake all night by the rain striking the windows and the waves pounding all along the beach, up against every house's flimsy barricade of rocks and dunes, and by the wild brilliance of the buoy lights tossed into the air by the black waters, and by the white shimmer that was the city, a net of lights afloat. Downstairs it must be dark, the only light that of the white waves reflected on the window panes. They were asleep, she was sure, familiar with storms on the edge of the ocean, after twelve years in this rugged old house that had been their beachhouse in the years before, when they had lived in the city with Leni's brother. The old mother in her tiny bedroom on the safer side of the house, the daughter in her slightly larger room, and the three little dogs in their chosen places.

When it was light, the sky was revealed as clear. A flock of blackbirds pecked along the wet sand and flew up to the wires, preening themselves in a row. At noon she knocked again at the screen door. The dogs barked, Leni called out, and she went in.

The old woman was not on the sofa. The white dog with matted fur lay there; another dog was stirring somewhere, and the third was out on the sand nosing the debris. Marie sat down in her usual place, and Leni came out from the mother's room, sat down on the other sofa, and took up her knitting.

"When I was a girl," Marie began, and the listener must tell by the tremble in her voice that she had gone over this in the night, "we had a garden, too. My mother had orange trees and lemon trees and lots of rosebushes. One was as tall as the trees and its boughs hung down to the ground like a tent covered with roses. They were Jewish, my father and mother, refugees from Germany. They went to Cuba first and my father worked in a cigar factory where they handrolled the tobacco leaves, and then they came to California."

It left her with an anguish in her chest, this confession, this chronicle of two souls, told in one minute, the anguish of begging for release from somebody else's false image of you and of those dear to you.

No change in the woman's face, no pause of the knitting needles over the white sweater. "The earth is like a refugee camp," the woman said. "So many are refugees. They don't save their lives, maybe, but they save their souls. My mother and me, we were on the last voyage of the Bremen. My brother was already over here. They were suspicious of my mother. We had birth records, church records, city hall records, but it didn't matter. When she was an infant she wasn't well, and her parents took her to her grandmother in the country, and when she came back to her parents, the neighbors thought she was not their child. That strange child, who was she and where did she come from? Isn't it terrible how things are remembered about a child, years after, after a lifetime goes by? On that last voyage there were one-hundred, maybe one-hundred-and-fifty passengers, and the ship could hold, I think two-thousand. Young men weren't allowed to leave Germany, so that was one reason it was empty. The few Jewish people never came down to meals, they ate in their cabins. They were told to stay in there, I guess. So many empty tables in the dining salon, when always there were three serving times, and in the lounge—is it called?—many huge empty easy chairs. An English minister who was a passenger, he gave sermons, and I went to hear every one. Sorrow," she said. "He felt sorrow for the world. We felt sorrow for the world on that empty big ship."

The contours of the beach had changed; it was unfamiliar overnight. She went along over the wide strip of wet sand and broken shells as far as the lagoon, a long way. Higher up on the sand lay a number of dead shore birds. The sea was dazzling, and the air so clear the little islands, miles away, were visible. She came back while the sun was forming into an oblong blazing jewel at the horizon.

The old mother still lay in her room, the next day at noon. Marie had never looked into that room, but from her usual place on the sofa she could see that it was darker than the other rooms and hardly more than an alcove.

"She dreams of garden parties," Leni said. "I think it's one that keeps going on because the light is so beautiful, she says.

She told me they had a banquet and I could have the leftovers. Last night I asked her, Shall I turn off the light? She said, If it's all right with them. She calls them Herrschaften, nobility. They're strangers. She asks me who this one is and who that one is, and I tell her I never met them. This morning she told me she saw the Kaiser in splendid clothes. No, it was the Lord, on second thought. Come and take a little look at her. She told me you were her girl friend in Freiburg, where she was born, and I didn't tell her you only got as far as Cologne."

The little mother lay turned toward the wall, and the blankets over her were the color of her gray hair and pale skin. She took up no more space in the bed than a child. That was how her own mother had looked, though never as old as this one. No breath visible, the breath making not the slightest move under the covers. She had to back away from the sight, step back and cover her face to hide her grimace of sorrow over the old mother, over the memory of her own mother, dying.

She was wakened in the night by the strangers at the old mother's garden party. Visions of light and of luminous strangers in that light—that was what the dying saw. She knew who they were, those strangers. They were the first of all the many strangers in your life, the ones there when you come out of the dark womb into the amazing light of earth, and never to be seen again in just that way until your last hours. She got up and walked about the room, barefoot, careful to make no sound that would intrude on the congregation of strangers in the room below.